Paul B. Du Chaillu

The Country of the Dwarfs

Paul B. Du Chaillu

The Country of the Dwarfs

ISBN/EAN: 9783337234874

Printed in Europe, USA, Canada, Australia, Japan

Cover: Foto ©Andreas Hilbeck / pixelio.de

More available books at **www.hansebooks.com**

THE
COUNTRY OF THE DWARFS.

THE

COUNTRY OF THE DWARFS

A NEW WORK OF

STIRRING ADVENTURE.

BY

PAUL DU CHAILLU,

AUTHOR OF "WILD LIFE UNDER THE EQUATOR," "MY APINGI KINGDOM,"
"STORIES OF THE GORILLA COUNTRY," ETC.

LONDON:

JOHN CAMDEN HOTTEN, 74 & 75, PICCADILLY.

CONTENTS.

CHAPTER VII.

CHAPTER VIII.

CHAPTER IX.

CHAPTER X.

CHAPTER XI.

CHAPTER XII.

CHAPTER XIII.

CHAPTER XIV.

CHAPTER XXIII.

CHAPTER XXIV.

CHAPTER XXV.

CHAPTER XXVI.

CHAPTER XXVII.

CHAPTER XXVIII.

CHAPTER XXIX.

CHAPTER XXX.

THE

COUNTRY OF THE DWARFS.

CHAPTER I.

How Paul set out for the Country of the Dwarfs, and what he took with him.

IN the month of July, 1863, if you had been in London, you might have seen, in St. Katherine's Dock, a schooner called the *Mentor*, a little vessel of less than 100 tons measurement; and if you had gone on board you would have encountered your old friend Paul du Chaillu busily superintending the taking of the cargo, and getting all things in readiness for the voyage upon which he is now going to take you.

Captain Vardon, the commander of the vessel, was generally by his side, and I am sure you would have been happy to make his acquaintance, for he was a very pleasant man.

Everybody was busy on board, either on deck or below deck, storing away the goods. Boxes upon boxes came alongside the *Mentor* from morning till evening. These contained my outfit and the equipment necessary for the expedition.

Paul du Chaillu had an anxious look, and you need not wonder at it, for he was about to undertake a journey of explorations of about five years' duration, and had to think of many things. It was, indeed, no small undertaking. What an outfit it was! I will give you some idea of it.

Clothing for five years was to be provided; the very

B

smallest article must not be forgotten, even to needles, thread and scissors.

It would never do again to be left without shoes, as I was in Apingi Land, so I had 72 pairs of Balmoral lace-boots, made specially for journeying in the great forest, with soles flexible enough to allow me to bend my feet while jumping from rock to rock, or from the base of one tree to another. Besides these lace-boots I had 24 pairs of shoes, and 12 pairs of linen slippers. Twelve pairs of leggings were to protect my legs from thorns, briers, and the bite of snakes; so you see my feet and legs were to be well taken care of in that journey, and for my further comfort I laid in 12 dozen pairs of socks. I took so many because I do not know how to darn socks, and when a pair became full of holes they would have to be thrown away.

All my shirts were made of light-coloured flannel; these were more healthy than linen shirts, and, besides economizing soap, it saved me from the necessity of getting under-garments, and consequently allotted me space which could be devoted to other articles.

With an eye to the great wear and tear of pantaloons, I had ordered 6 dozen pairs made of the strongest twisted blue drill that could be got. Instead of coats I ordered 2 dozen blouses, made of durable linen stuff, of a colour not easily seen in the woods. The blouse was a very convenient garment, admitting of numerous pockets, in which I could keep many things while on the march. Everything was made for wear and not for show, and to go through the thickest and most thorny jungle.

Several dozen pocket-handkerchiefs completed my wearing outfit. Besides their ordinary use, these were to be worn, generally wet, inside the three fine soft Panama hats I had provided to protect my head from the rays of a burning sun. No collars, no neck-ties were necessary.

Clothes must be washed, so I took with me 100 pounds of the hardest Marseilles soap. That quantity was not much, but then I would probably be able some time to make my own soap with palm-oil.

Then came the drugs, and these gave me more embarrassment than anything else. If it had been only to take medicines for myself, the matter would have been simple enough. A compact little medicine-chest, with an extra quantity of quinine, laudanum, and a few other remedies used in tropical climates more frequently than in ours, would have sufficed; but I had to think of my followers and porters—a retinue that would sometimes number five and six hundred—and accordingly I purchased.

75 ounce bottles of quinine.
10 gallons of castor-oil.
50 pounds of Epsom salts.
2 quarts of laudanum.

These were the medicines which would be the most needed; but, besides these, I had pretty nearly all the drugs to be found at the apothecary's.

Of arsenic I took 100 pounds, to preserve the skins of animals and birds I expected to kill in my journeyings.

Most of these and my wearing apparel were packed in japanned tin boxes, which would be serviceable afterward for the preservation of my butterflies and stuffed birds. Tin boxes were safer than wooden ones; the white ants would not be able to pierce through them.

Though I did not set out to make war, I felt that I ought to be prepared for any emergency. Besides, I was to hunt, and I must have guns. After a great deal of thinking it over, I came to the conclusion that, for such a wild country, where I might get short of cartridges, the greater part of my guns should be muzzle-loaders, so I bought 4 splendid English muzzle-loaders, 4 long muzzle-loading rifles, 2 very short smooth-bore muzzle-loaders, and 2 very short muzzle-loading rifles.

Then I took a magnificent double-barrel breech-loading rifle which could throw steel-pointed bullets weighing more than two ounces. I had Dean and Adams's revolvers, magnificent arms that never got out of order, and several long, formidable hunting-knives.

These guns were for my own special use, and they were supplied with moulds for making bullets, &c. &c.

Besides these, I had ordered in Birmingham 250 cheap guns for my body-guard and the native king, to whom I might desire to give one. Most of them were flint-locks, and of the pattern called the Tower.

I had great trouble in knowing what quantity of ammunition to take, for lead is heavy; but, then, what would a man do in a savage country without powder and bullets?

The great difficulty with rifle muzzle-loaders is, that when the charge has been driven home the bullets cannot be easily withdrawn. So it is with the revolvers; and a great deal of ammunition would be lost on that account.

My ammunition consisted of 15,000 cartridges for my revolvers, in soldered tin boxes of fifties; 15,000 bullets for my guns and rifles, and lead for 20,000 more, for the practice of my men before starting into the desert; 1000 pounds of small shot of different sizes, for birds; 400 pounds of fine powder; 50,000 caps. I also took 200 10-pound barrels of coarse powder for my body-guard and to give away to my friends, or as presents.

So you see the warlike and hunting apparatus of the expedition was very heavy, but we were to depend in a great measure on our guns for food. Elephants, antelopes, hippopotami, gazelles, crocodiles, and monkeys would be our chief diet. Then came the scientific instruments:

4 strong, splendid hunting-case watches, by Brock, London.
1 watch made by Frodsham, London.
48 spare watch-keys and 24 spare glasses.
3 sextants, 8, 6, and 4 inches radius.
1 binocular yachting-glass.
1 telescope.
1 universal sun-dial (a magnificent instrument).
1 aneroid.
2 compasses, prismatic, with stand, shades, and reflector three inches in diameter, to take the bearings of land, &c. &c.
2 pocket compasses.

1 set drawing instruments (German silver).

2 dozen drawing-pens.

2 artificial horizons, folding roof, improved iron trough, and bottles containing quicksilver, in sling case.

1 hypsometrical apparatus.

2 bull's-eye lanterns, copper boiler, 3 reservoirs for spirits, oil, or candles.

3 thermometers for measuring heights and boiling water.

2 thermometers for the sun (to know its power).

2 thermometers graduated Fahrenheit and Centigrade.

1 thermometer graduated Centigrade and Reaumur.

1 powerful electro-magnetic machine, with 90 feet of conducting wire or cord.

2 large magnifying-glasses.

7 pounds of mercury, in a bottle, as a reserve supply.

Parallel rule (German silver).

Protractor, circular, with compass rectifier, in a mahogany box.

3 rain-gauges and spare glasses, to tell the amount of rain falling at a given time.

Scale, 18 inches, metal, graduated to inches, and subdivided to tenths and hundredths, in a box.

Tape, 100 feet, to measure trees.

75 sheets of skeleton maps, ruled in squares, to mark out in the rough my daily route as determined by compass.

4 Nautical Almanacs, 1863, '4, '5, '6, to be used in my astronomical observations; and several other scientific books.

12 blank books for keeping my daily journal.

10 memorandum books.

10 quires of paper.

Ink, pens, pencils, slates.

For illumination I provided 100 pounds of wax candles, 10 gallons of spirits (alcohol) for lamps, thermometers, &c. &c.; 12 gross of matches in boxes, each dozen boxes enclosed in a separate soldered tin box. Though I had fire-steel and flint, the matches could light a fire much quicker, and they were "big things" with the natives.

So you see I had a complete set of instruments, and in sufficient number, so that in case of accident I could replace the injured one ; and accidents I knew were sure to happen.

If I did not explain to you why I took 5 watches, I am sure you would say that I was foolish to spend so much money in watches. Then let me tell you that I bought so many because I was afraid that if I took only 1 or 2, they might stop running, and in this event it would have been impossible for me to know my longitude, that is to say, how far east or west I might be, and to ascertain the day and month, should illness have caused me to forget the calendar. No watch can be safely depended upon to run for 5 years in such a climate without cleaning. But as 4 of them had been made specially for the journey, I felt assured that at least 1 or 2 out of the 5 would run till my return.

But we have not yet done with my equipment. There were 18 boxes containing photographic apparatus, with tent, and chemicals for 10,000 photographs. The transportation of these alone would require 20 men.

All that I have enumerated to you constituted but a small proportion of the things that came on board, and were for my special use, with the exception of the 250 common guns and a great part of the ammunition.

There are yet to be mentioned the presents for my old friends, who had been so kind to me in my former journeys, and whom I hoped to see again. These were the chiefs whose hospitality I had enjoyed, and my dear hunters Aboko, Fasiko, Niamkala, Malaouen, Querlaouen, Gambo, dear old Quengueza, Ranpano, Rikimongani, and Obindji, the Bakalai chief. Presents, too, were indispensable for the people who were to take me from tribe to tribe, and the right of way I knew would often have to be bought. So more than two months had been spent by me in the London clothing, hardware, and dry-goods establishments, finding what I wanted.

I bought more than 5000 pounds of beads of different sizes and colours, several hundred pieces of cotton goods, some pieces of silks, coats, waistcoats, shirts, 2000 *red caps,* a few umbrellas, files, knives, bells, fire-steels, flints, look-ing-glasses, forks, spoons, some *stove-pipe* hats for the kings near the sea-shore, straw hats, &c. &c.

Then, to impress the wild people with what I could do, I bought several large Geneva musical boxes, one powerful electrical battery, several magnets, and 6 ship clocks, etc. etc.

The abundant results of the sale of my "Adventures in Equatorial Africa," and the proceeds arising from the disposal of my gorillas, and my collection of beasts, birds, insects, and shells, alone enabled me to undertake this new expedition, for not one dollar has ever been given by any scientific society to help me in any 'of my travels or explo-rations; but I was very happy in expending a part of my means in the interest of science and for the enlargement of our knowledge of unknown countries. I only wish now I could have done more, but really I think that I did the best I could.

Years had passed away since I had gone first to Africa, my parents were both dead, I was alone in the world, and the world was before me, and I thought I could do nothing better than make another exploration.

I had made up my mind, without confiding my purpose to any one, to cross the continent of Africa near the equator, from the west to the head waters of the Nile, and to set out from the Commi country. I knew my old negro friends would help me. That was the reason my outfit was on so large a scale.

The only thing that worried me before my departure was our civil war, but then I thought it was soon to end.

CHAPTER II.

On the African Coast—Meeting with old Friends—Changes in
four years—The Captain's Misgivings.

ON the 5th of August we sailed from London. I will
not weary you with a narrative of the voyage. The
days passed pleasantly on board the *Mentor*. By the end
of the month of August we were not far from the Tropic
of Cancer. September glided away calmly, and on the
7th of October Captain Vardon said that the following
day we should come in sight of land.

Accordingly, the next morning I heard from the main-
top the cry of " Land! land !" Two hours afterward from
the deck I could discern the low lands of the Commi
country. Nearer and nearer the coast we came, until we
could see the white surf breaking with terrific force on the
shore, and hear the booming sound of the angry waves as
they dashed against the breakers. The country was so
monotonous in its outlines that we could not make out
exactly where we were; we only knew that we were south
of Cape Lopez, and not very far from it. I thought it
strange that I could not recognise the mouth of the
Fernand Vaz or Commi River.

No canoes could ride through the surf, so no natives
could come on board. In the evening we stood off the
land and shortened sail, and afterward we cast anchor.

The next morning we sailed again in a southerly direction, and at last we saw a canoe pass through the
breakers; it came alongside, and the negroes in it shouted
in English, " Put down the anchor ! Plenty of ivory,
plenty of everything; load the ship in a fortnight."

We had passed the Fernand Vaz, having sailed too far

south. The mouth of the river itself is very difficult to discover. Perhaps you may recollect my having formerly described it as discernible only by the white surf combing over its bar, by large flocks of fish-eating birds hovering in the air above it, and by a long, white sandy point forming the extremity of the land on the left bank.*

As we approached the river, two canoes left the shore and made for the vessel. In the first, as it neared us, I recognised my friend Adjouatonga, a chief belonging to the clan Adjiéna, whose villages occupied the mouth of the river. He climbed up the vessel's side, and went to shake hands with the captain, and then advanced toward me to do the same. I had not said a word, but upon my raising my hat, which had been pulled down so as partly to conceal my face, and turning round upon him, he stepped back in astonishment, and, recognising me at once, cried out in his own language, "Are you Chally, or his spirit? Have you come from the dead? for we have heard you were dead. Tell me quickly, for I do not know whether I am to believe my own eyes. Perhaps I am getting a kendé" (an idiot, a fool). And I said, "Adjouatonga, I am Chally, your friend!" The good fellow embraced me in a transport of joy, but he hugged me so tight and so long that I wished his friendship had been less enthusiastic. Four years had nearly gone by since I had left the Commi country.

As the second canoe came nearer, I ordered Adjouatonga not to say a word. My heart leaped for joy, for in it were my own people from the dear, good old African Washington of mine. Sholomba, the nephew of King Ranpano, was there, and my boy Macondai; all my former canoe-men, Kombé, Ratenou, Oshimbo, were in that canoe. I longed for them to come on board. I could hardly restrain myself; but I felt that I must appear like as if I did not know them, and see whether they would recognise me.

In a moment they were on deck, and a wild shout of joy came from them. "Our white man has come back!

---

* "Explorations in Equatorial Africa."

Chally, Chally!" and they all rushed toward me. Good fellows! in their savage natures they loved me, and they remembered the friend who had never wronged them. I was seized and almost pulled to pieces, for they all wanted to hug me at the same time. Captain Vardon looked with perfect amazement at the scene of greeting. They seemed to be crazy with joy to see me again.

Then followed a long and confused account of what had taken place since my departure, all talking at the same time.

When we had come back to our senses, the next subject to be considered was how I was to get ashore. Of course I wished to go by the mouth of the river, but Sholomba assured me it could not be done. The mouth of the Fernand Vaz had changed much for the worse, and it would be less dangerous to run a canoe through the surf to the beach than to attempt to cross the bar of the river. It was now the beginning of the rainy season, when the winds are less violent than in the dry season, but the surf had not subsided from the agitation of the heavy south winds of the dry season.

The anchor was cast, and I left the *Mentor* in Adjouatonga's canoe, which was a better one than the other.

All was excitement in the canoe, and the men sang. Adjouatonga, looking more and more anxious as we approached the rollers, rested outside for a while, and then, at the proper moment, skilfully directed the frail canoe over the crest of a huge wave, which bore us with lightning speed to the beach, where I was caught up by the natives that were waiting for us, and carried safely to dry land. Tremendous huzzas were given.

Once more I stood on African soil.

The people recognised me, and I was hurried along, amidst a crowd of several hundred savages, all dancing and shouting with frantic joy, across the sandy tongue of land to the banks of the Commi, my own Commi River, where canoes were waiting to take us to Washington and to old King Ranpano.

Time had wrought great changes in the land of my former explorations. The mouth of the river had altered so much that I could hardly recognise it. The long, sandy, reed-covered pits, which projected three miles from the southern point of the river's mouth, and which had been the scene of many hunting adventures with ducks, cranes, and sea-gulls, had disappeared, and the sea had washed the sand away, and taken the greater part of it to the northern side of the village of Elinde, whose chief, Sangala, had given me so much trouble in former times. The spot where Sangala's village had stood had become untenanted, and the people had removed. Many a dear little island, where I used to hide to shoot birds, had also been submerged or washed away, and I no longer saw the flocks of seafowl which formerly frequented the locality.

I felt sad indeed; a pang of sorrow shot through me. It was like a dream; the scene of my former hunting had vanished, and nothing but the record of what I had written about the land was left. I cannot express to you the lonely feeling that came over me. Though everything was changed, the former picture of the landscape was before me. I remembered every island, every little outlet, the herd of hippopotami, the *Caroline* inside the bar quietly at anchor.

Oh! I would have given anything if I could have seen the country as it was when I left it! I had been so happy, I spent so many pleasant days there, I had so loved to roam on that sandy point, and to lie on its sand! Now it was nothing but a dream; it had been swept away.

The canoes in the river being ready, I embarked in one, followed by all the others, the people singing, "Our ntangani (white man) has come back. Oh, how we love our white man! Oh, how our white man loves us! for he has come back to us. Yes, we never stole from our white man; our white man remembers that, and he comes back to us, for he is not afraid of us."

Paddling up the stream, many, many sights I recognised; many mangrove-trees I remembered; the old banks of the river were familiar to me. I looked eagerly at everything around.

Halloo! what do I see yonder? a herd of hippopotami motionless in the water, and looking for all the world like

old logs stuck in the mud. Familiar species of cranes
stalked about here and there, the pelican swam majesti-
cally, the kingfishers were watching for their prey, with
white cranes and ducks not far from them.

Thus we glided along up the river. My heart was full;
I did not speak a word. Soon we came in front of my old
settlement of Washington, of which I gave you a picture
in my Apingi Kingdom.

Oh! what do I see? Nothing but ruins! The houses
had all tumbled down; a few bamboos and rotting poles
alone remained to show me where my big house stood.
The four trees between which my house had been built
were still there; the gum copal tree was in front. The
little village for my men was not to be seen; desolation
had taken possession of the place. One single house was
still standing. The men stopped their singing; their
faces became sad. A feeling that some misfortune had
happened seized me.

I got up and shouted, looking the men steadily in the
face, "Where is Rikimongani, my friend, he whom I in-
trusted with the settlement of Washington?" "Dead,
dead," said they. "The people were jealous that you
loved him so well, and they did not want him to see you
again, and they bewitched him; he fell ill, and died."

"Rikimongani dead!" I exclaimed. I took off my hat
as we passed the place, and said, "Oh, how sorry I am,
Rikimongani! What shall I do with the fine old coat I
have for you? what shall I do with the nice cane and the
fine hat I have brought for you? Oh, dear Rikimongani,
I have many presents for you. Rikimongani, did you
know how much I loved you?"

"See," shouted the men, "how much he loved Rikimongani!"

"Oh yes!" said the canoe-men, "he always talked of
you, and said he was sure you would come back, though
we all said that you would not, and that you would forget
us. Rikimongani used to say, 'One day we shall see a
white sail, and Chally will be on board, and he will land
and come to see us again.' In the evenings he would talk
of you to us boys."

Tears filled my eyes. Then Sholomba whispered to me, " When the wizards who were accused of having bewitched Rikimongani were about to drink the mboundou, they said, ' Chally has killed Rikimongani, for he will never come back here, and he loves Rikimongani so much that he has killed him, so that he might have his spirit always with him.' And," said Sholomba, " many believed them, but many did not."

" We must not land here," said Sholomba. " Chally, you must never build here ; the people are afraid of the place ; nobody will dare to come here, for people die always in this place. Several times villages had been built, and the people had to leave this spot. Witchcraft is here."

I felt that I had come back to a wild life, full of superstitions and legends.

We paddled till we came two miles above my place of Washington, which had brought back so many reminiscences to me. Though I would have liked to build again there, I could not think of it on account of the superstitious dread of the natives for the spot.

When we stopped, Sholomba and Djombouai had reached their little village. Ranpano was away from home, on the Ogobai River. So I resolved to build a new settlement close to their village.

Messengers were sent to King Ranpano to tell him to come, and the news spread over the country that Chally had come back, and the people from all the villages and the country round came trooping by land and water to see their old friend, and to hear about the stores of good things he had brought with him. They came pouring in day after day, camping in the woods, on the prairie, everywhere. They would endure hunger rather than go home. Many, many an old face I saw ; many a kind-hearted woman came and told me how glad she was to see me ; many boys and girls who had grown up said they wanted to work for me ; many people brought me presents of food.

How pleased I was! Oh yes, I had tried to do right with these savages, and they knew it, and they loved me for it. I knew that not one of them thought unkindly of me.

The day after my landing I despatched Sholomba with a canoe filled with paddlers up the river. Those among you who have followed me in my former adventures must guess where I sent that canoe.

To the village of King Quengueza, that dear old chief. I wanted to see his face. I had brought great numbers of presents for him, to show him that in the white man's country I had thought of him. I had brought presents for many of his people, his nephews, sons, and nieces. His old faithful slaves were not forgotten—good old Etia among them; and his head slave Mombon.

So one canoe had gone for friend Ranpano, and another for good old Quengueza.

Canoes strong enough to go through the surf were coming from all the villages. Huts were given to me in which to store my goods, and now we had reached the point of bringing them ashore.

It was necessary for me to go on board the *Mentor*, and arrange the mode of disembarkation of my extensive outfit and stock of goods. As the mouth of the river had become unsafe on account of the breaking-up of the sandy spit, and was now an uninterrupted line of breakers, we resolved to land everything on the beach through the surf, and then carry them across to the river, and put them in other canoes, which were to carry them to my new settlement.

So on the 14th I went to the schooner, and slept on board that night. Captain Vardon was somewhat anxious; he had never been on this wild and unfrequented part of the coast, so far from any civilized settlements, and when he saw me he was delighted, and said that he began to think that the natives had murdered me. He had kept an armed guard on the watch all the time, for, said he, such a country looked exactly like one where the natives could pounce upon the unsuspecting vessel, murder the crew, and rob the ship. I assured him that there was no danger; that I could do what I wished with the Comm people, as he would be able to see for himself; and that, though many of the boxes would have to be opened, and the goods deposited loose in the canoes, not a single thing would be stolen.

Knowing the negroes of the Coast (for he had been a trader), he seemed somewhat incredulous at my statement.

CHAPTER III.

Landing Goods—Among the Breakers—King Ranpano—Loss of
Instruments—King Quengueza—A Palaver—Changing Names.

THE next morning, at daybreak, three canoes came
alongside to take off the cargo. The men brought
the news that King Ranpano had arrived, and was on the
beach.

My most precious things were lowered into the canoes,
and when everything was ready, the captain concluded to
go ashore with me.

The captain and I got into the canoe containing all my
scientific instruments, medicines, some of my best guns,
my watch chronometers, five Geneva musical boxes, &c. &c.
Before we left, the captain ordered the mate to keep a sharp
look-out, and fasten to the anchors seventy fathoms of
chain, for the sea was heavy. The crew came to say
good-bye to me, and as our canoes left the side of the
Mentor they gave three cheers for me. Then, as fast as
our paddles could propel us, we made for the beach.

As we approached the breakers, the faces of the canoe-
men looked anxious, for the swells were heavy, and I
could hear the roar of the surf. Nearer and nearer we
came. The two other canoes were ahead of us.

The men were watching the swells, resting on their
paddles. At last we hear their cheers; they plunge their
paddles into the water, and onward they go towards the
shore, rolling on the top of a heavy, long swell.

My men thought we were too late, as we were behind,
and had better wait for the next lull. In the meantime
we watched the two canoes; they seemed for awhile to
be buried in the foaming billows. " Surely," I said to

Captain Vardon, "those canoes will never reach the shore safely."

"I don't believe they will," was his answer.

We had reached a point just outside the breakers, where we watch; the two canoes appear again; they have not capsized; the men are covered with spray; they are paddling as hard as they can; they are over the breakers; they land safely; the people on the shore seize the canoes, and bring them up the beach.

Now our time has come, and the men are watching anxiously. I have the finest canoe-men of the Commi tribe in my canoe. Oshimbo holds the steering-paddle. Kombé, Ratenou, Ondonga, Gonwe, Sholomba, and the others, are not only splendid paddlers, but they all swim like fish—a very important thing for me if we capsize. My sixteen men are resting on their paddles; they are all looking outside, and watching the heavy rollers as they come in. Generally six of these come, and then there is a kind of lull. "Get ready! paddle hard!" shouted Oshimbo. The men gave a terrific Commi hurrah, and down went their paddles, and with heavy strokes we got on what we thought a gentle swell. We had hardly got on it when the swell became higher and higher, carrying us almost with lightning speed; then it began to crest itself; we were caught, and finally were dashed upon a white foaming wave with fearful force. "Be careful!" shouted Oshimbo. "Have your eyes upon our white man!"

Though we did not upset, our canoe was partly filled with water, and the rush of the wave had prevented Oshimbo's paddle from acting as a rudder, and the canoe was now lying broadside at the mercy of the next wave that should come.

"Hurry!" shouted Oshimbo to the men; "let us bring back the canoe's head on to the waves!" and the men put forth all their might to rescue us from our perilous position. Just as we had succeeded in bringing the canoe round, a second immense roller, coming from far out at sea, and mounting higher and higher as it approached, threatened our destruction. We were in fearful suspense.

c

Perhaps we will be able to ride upon it; perhaps it will break ahead of us. It was a terrific one. My men cried again with one voice, "Let us look out for our white man!"

These words were hardly uttered when the huge wave broke over the stern of our canoe with appalling force, instantly upsetting it and hurling us into the sea, where we were deeply submerged in the spray.

I do not know how I ever got back on the surface of the water, but when I did I was some forty feet from the canoe, and all the men were scattered far and wide.

I was almost stunned. Breaker upon breaker succeeded each other with awful rapidity, sending us rolling about under them, and giving us hardly time to breathe. The sea all round became a mass of foaming billows. By this time all my faithful negroes were around me, shouting to each other, "To our ntangani—our ntangani (white man)!" It was indeed high time, for I felt myself sinking. A minute more, and I would have sunk helpless to the bottom of the sea, never to rise again. The Commi swam round me and held me up, till another wave would scatter us again, and then they came back to my succour.

In spite of all their efforts, I became weaker and weaker. They had succeeded in ridding me of the greater part of my clothing, but, notwithstanding this relief, my strength was fast failing me, and I had drank large quantities of salt water.

I cried, "Where is the captain? Go for him!" My cry was just in time, for he was in his last struggle for life. Once we had got hold of the canoe, but the waves had made us loose our grip. Loud shouts came from the shore; the people were almost frantic. Canoe after canoe was launched, but only to be swamped in the breakers the next instant.

At length the tumult of the waves subsided; there came a lull, and the rising tide had driven us toward the beach. We were not far from it, indeed, and now we rested a little, holding fast to our capsized canoe.

At last a canoe succeeded in leaving the shore, and

came to our rescue. As it reached us the crew jumped
into the sea to give us their places, and, in order not to
load it too heavily, they swam alongside, holding fast to it
to keep it steady.

As we neared the shore, the natives did not wait for me
to land, but ran into the water, and seizing me, carried
me off in their arms, in the midst of deafening cries and
cheers, the women wringing their hands and shouting,
" The sea wanted *to eat* our white man ; the sea wanted
to eat our white man."

The people led me into a thicket of trees, where a
bright fire was lighted, and whom should I see but King
Ranpano seated on the ground, his little idol before him,
his eyes shining with excitement, and his body trembling
all over. I drew myself up, trying to look haughty and
displeased.

" Ranpano," I said, " if any one had told me that you
did not care for me I would not have believed them.
What!" said I, " every one was on the shore to see what
they could do to save us from drowning ; even your wife,
the queen, was there, and went into the sea to catch me
as we landed, and I might have died and been drowned
for all that you cared. You were cold, and you sat by
the fire."

" Oh," said Ranpano, " my white man die in the water?
Never, while I am alive ! How could it be ? how could
it be ? Oh no, Chally, you could not be drowned—you
could not, my white man ; my Chally will never die in
our country. I have a fetich, and as long as I wear it
you cannot be drowned. I was talking to my idol ; I
was invoking before her the spirit of my father to protect
you in the sea. When the waves were around you I
begged the idol to send the sharks away from you. Oh,
Chally, I would not leave the idol for fear you might
perish. Oh!" exclaimed Ranpano, with a stentorian voice,
" there are people already jealous of me and of my village.
Some village has sent an aniemba to upset the canoe."

The wildest excitement prevailed around me. I was
partly stunned, and I had drunk a great deal of salt water.
Poor Captain Vardon had a narrow escape, and, as he

said, he was sinking when my boys—my good boys—clinched him. And once more I thanked silently the great God that had watched so mercifully over me.

After a while I realized the severe blow I had received when the great loss I had sustained presented itself to my mind. Scientific instruments, watch chronometers, medicines, guns, musical instruments, &c. &c., had gone to the bottom of the sea.

"Oh dear," said I to myself, "I must remain here on this barren and lonely coast, and wait for a vessel to come back and bring me new scientific instruments, for without them I cannot go across the continent toward the Nile. I wish to make a good map of the country, to take accurate astronomical observations, to determine the height of the mountains, and to be able to ascertain at any time the day and the month if I should forget their regular succession in the calendar, and, without my instruments, all this will be impossible."

I cannot tell you how sorry I felt. That evening I felt utterly heart-broken, and I could have cried. "But," said I to myself, "to bear my misfortune with fortitude is true manhood;" and, though it was hard to believe it, I knew that all that had happened was for the best.

Captain Vardon felt a sincere sympathy with me. The poor man was himself an object of commiseration, for he was so exhausted and had drunk so much water that he was quite ill.

My mind was made up, however, that very day as to what I should do. I must manage to have a letter reach the island of Fernando Po, and then that letter would be forwarded to London. That letter will be for Messrs. Baring Brothers, and I will ask them to send me a vessel with all I need.

The next night, as I lay on my hard bed pondering my wondrous escape from the deep sea, I could not help thinking bitterly of the heavy loss I had sustained. It was not so much for the large sum of money that had been sacrificed, but for the great waste of time this catastrophe had entailed upon me.

I could not sleep; these thoughts kept me awake. I

turned from side to side in the hope that an easier position would put me to sleep, but it was of no avail, when suddenly I heard the sound of the natives' bugles on the river. The people were blowing their bugles made of antelopes' horns, and then I heard the songs of a multitude of paddlers. The sound became more and more distinct as the canoes neared my cabin. Then I could hear distinctly, "Quengueza, our king, comes to see his great friend Chally—Chally, who has returned from the white man's country."

Soon after the singing stopped, and I knew that they had landed.

All my gloomy fancies were soon forgotten, and I got up and dressed myself as quickly as possible. As I opened my door whom should I see, as quiet as a statue in front of my hut, but King Quengueza, the venerable chief. He opened his arms to receive me, and we hugged each other without saying a word. The great and powerful African chief, the dread of the surrounding tribes and clans, the great warrior, held me in his arms, and after a while he said, "Chally, I would have stayed before your door all night if I had not seen you. I could not go to sleep without embracing you, for you do not know how much I love you. You do not know how many times I have thought of you, and many, many times I have said to my people, 'We shall not see Chally again.' And first, when Sholomba told me you had come, and had sent for me, I said, 'Sholomba, this is a lie; Chally has not come. Four rainy seasons and four dry seasons have passed away, and if he had intended coming he would have been here long ago. No, Sholomba, why do you come and make fun of me? It is a lie; Chally has not come—Chally has not come, and he will not come any more to the country of the black man.'"

"Here I am," I said, "friend Quengueza; your friend Chally is before you. He has thought of you many and many a time in the white man's country; he has not forgotten you;" and I whispered in his ears, "He has brought you a great many fine things which no black man has seen before, and which no black man will have but yourself."

Then the old chief ordered his attendants to retire, and when he had entered my little hut I lighted a torch, and he looked at me and I looked at him without our saying a word. Then I seated myself on the edge of my bed, and the king seated himself on the little stool close to me, and filled his pipe with native Ashira tobacco, and we had a long talk.

I said, " Quengueza, I have come. Since I saw you a great many things have happened. I have been in different countries of the white man. Many know you, many love you, for I have told the white man what great friends we were—how much we loved each other. I have told them how kind you were to your friend Chally ; that everything he wanted you gave to him, and that not one of your people ever took anything from Chally—if he had he would have had his head cut off or been sold into slavery. Many white men and white women, boys and girls, know you, and I have presents from them for you, which you shall see in a few days. I have told them what we did together, how we went into the woods together, and how we cut that big ebony-tree"—here I stopped a while, and presently said, " how I hope to go farther inland than I have ever been, and will come back again by the sea."

Then I remained silent, and the old chief rose up, the shadow of his stately form falling behind him. For a few moments he did not utter a word, and then he said :—

" Chally, my town is yours ; my forests, my slaves are yours ; all the girls and women of my village are yours : I will have no will of my own when you are with me. You shall be the chief, and whatever you say shall be obeyed. You shall never know hunger as long as there is a plantain-tree on our plantation, or a wild animal in the forests. And, Chally, when you shall say ' I must go—go far away, where nobody has been,' I will let you go ; I will help you to go, though my heart will be sad when you depart."

I found Quengueza still in mourning for his brother, whom he had succeeded, and that he had taken his brother's name, " Oganda," which is the name taken by every chief of the Abouya clan. What a queer custom they have!

The law of inheritance there is from brother to brother, and Quengueza's name had been Ratenou Kombé Quengueza, and now came the last, which he was to carry to his grave, OGANDA.

I said, " Friend Quengueza, it will be hard for me to call you Oganda, for the name by which I have learned to love you is Quengueza."

" Never mind, Chally, call me Quengueza," said he ; and, as he left my hut, he implored me once more in a whisper not to tell any one that I had brought him presents, " for," said he, " if the people knew that you had brought me many fine things, they would bewitch me, and I should die."

I saw that poor Quengueza was as superstitious as ever.

The old chief then went to the hut that had been prepared for him during his visit to me. By this time it was four o'clock in the morning, and the cock in the village had already begun to crow when I lay down to sleep.

CHAPTER IV.

Honest Africans—Distributing Presents—Quengueza's Diplomacy
—Another Palaver—A New Settlement—Rabolo's Monda—
Ranpano's Superstition.

THE day after the arrival of Quengueza, word was
sent to me by the canoe-men on the shore that the
surf was quiet, and that canoes could go to sea and return
in perfect safety.

During the day seven large canoes were carried over
the narrow tongue of land to the beach, and twenty-one
remained on the river-side to take to my new settlement
the goods that would be landed.

It was important to expedite as much as possible the
landing of the goods, for this would only be safe for a few
days, till the change of the moon.

The next morning, at daylight, seven canoes left for the
vessel, and each canoe made that day three trips, so that
twenty-one canoe-loads of goods were landed and carried
across to the canoes on the river. Then we got ready to
go home, but not before hauling high up on the beach our
seven sea-canoes.

After four days' hard work, seventy canoe-loads had been
landed, and the cargo was all ashore. I breathed freely
once more; not a load had been swamped. We had just
finished when the breakers became dangerous again, and
in a day or two more it would have been impossible to go
through them.

Not an article was missing. Captain Vardon was amazed.
I said to him, "Did I not tell you that my Commi men
would not steal?"

You would have laughed to see the miscellaneous

articles which formed part of the cargo. Many of them were specially manufactured for the African market, and the heavy goods were to be given to Quengueza, Ranpano, Olenga-Yombi, Obindji, and the chiefs living on the banks of the Rembo and Ovenga rivers.

The great trouble was to put all the goods under shelter. They had to be stored in several huts. There were no locks on the doors, but I was not afraid of the people, and my confidence was justified, for not an article was stolen. Captain Vardon wondered at it; he had been a trader for a good many years on the coast, and said it was marvellous. So it was; there is no city in any Christian country where these thousands of dollars' worth of goods could be as safe. I loved the Commi, and the Commi loved me.

After everything had been housed, I thought it was time to make a distribution of the presents I intended for my friends. Quengueza's presents will give you a fair idea of the articles I had brought into the country.

So one afternoon I went for friend Quengueza when everybody was taking their afternoon nap. He followed me, accompanied by several of his great men, nephews, and wives; for a great king like Quengueza could not walk alone: he must have a retinue, or escort. Quengueza was very fond of this sort of thing, but that day he did not like it a bit; he did not want his people to see what I was going to give him, but he did not dare to send them away, so he whispered into my ear, " Chally, send them away when you come to your house, for I do not want anybody inside."

So I dismissed Quengueza's people, and after Quengueza and I had entered the hut, he closed the door himself, to make sure, and peeped through the crevices to see that nobody was trying to look in. Then he seated himself and awaited developments.

I opened a chest filled with presents for him. The first thing I displayed before his wide-open eyes was a huge long coat, similar to those worn by the London beadles. This coat had been made specially for his majesty, and to fit his tall figure, for Quengueza was over

6 feet high. It was of the most glaring colours—blue, with yellow fringe, and lined with red. There was also a splendid plush waistcoat, with big brass buttons. His coat fell to his feet. I gave him no pantaloons, for Quengueza never liked to wear them.

After Quengueza's admiring eyes had looked with amazement on his splendid coat and bright yellow waistcoat, he must try them on; but, before doing so, he went again to see that no one was peeping in. I wondered why his majesty, who was a perfect despot, was so much afraid.

Having put on his robe or morning-gown, I gave him an enormous drum-major's cane, with a tremendous gilded head, to be used as a staff.* He stiffened himself at the sight, and asked for a looking-glass, in which he regarded himself with an air of supreme satisfaction. Then I took out of my trunk my opera hat, which of course was flat when shut up, and gave it a slight punch, when the springs immediately threw it out into the shape of a splendid *stove-pipe hat* to the utter astonishment and bewilderment of King Quengueza. Then I put the hat on his head, and his majesty walked to and fro, drawing himself to his full height. After some minutes he took off his imperial costume, putting the clothes back in the chest were they came from, and proceeded to inspect the other presents, among which were

6 pieces of silk, of different colours.
100 pieces of calico prints.
6 silver spoons, knives, and forks.
1 silver goblet.
1 magnificent red, blue, and yellow silk umbrella.
Among the larger articles were
1 common brass kettle.
100 iron bars, 6 feet long, $1\frac{3}{4}$ wide.
50 large copper plates 24 inches in diameter.
50 small brass kettles.
50 iron pots.
50 guns.

---

* See Frontispiece.

50 kegs of powder.

25 wash-basins.

12 dozen plates.

6 dozen glasses.

300 pounds of beads, of different colours and sizes.

50 pine chests.

200 pairs of ear-rings for his wives.

Several chests containing trinkets, mirrors, files, forks, knives, &c.

A chest filled with nice presents sent to him by some of my friends.

The chests were his delight, for the wealth of a king here is composed chiefly of chests, which, of course, are supposed to be filled with goods.

King Quengueza never thought that his friend Chally would have remembered him so profitably.

After showing him all these things, I made him a speech, and said, in a low tone, "Quengueza, Chally has a heart (oré ma); he has a heart that loves you. When he left you the last time he was poor, and had nothing to give you, but you loved him the same as if he had possessed a thousand chests filled with goods. Now he is rich, and has just come back from the white man's country, and he brings you all these fine presents, for Chally loves you;" and when I said "loves you" I looked at him steadily in the face. The sight of all this wealth had almost dumbfounded the old man, and for a while he could not speak. Finally he said—

"Do you love me, Chally? If you do, do not tell the people what you have given me, or they will bewitch me to have my property."

The fear of witchcraft was a great defect in the character of poor Quengueza. He was always in dread of being bewitched, and consequently of dying.

Then he knelt down and clasped my feet with his hands, and, with his face distorted by fear, begged me again not to tell anybody in the country what I had given him. This taking hold of a man's feet is the most imploring way of asking a favour; it was the first time in his life that Quengueza, the great chief of the Abouya clan, had done such a thing. I promised him, of course, never to tell anything to his people.

After a while he went away, and his subjects crowded round him, expecting fully to hear what fine things his friend Chally had brought him, when I heard him shout, with the loudest voice he could summon,

"My friend Chally knows nothing but talk, and has brought me nothing." Coming toward me, he repeated the statement just as loudly, and looked at me at the same time with an imploring sort of a look, as if to say, "Do not say anything." But Quengueza's people knew me better; they knew very well that Chally, the great friend of Quengueza, would not come back from the white man's country without bringing him something, and they were smiling all the while, for they were well acquainted with the ways of their beloved old chief, who was a miser, and never wanted his people to know what he possessed. I kept his presents till his departure.

I gave presents also to good old Ranpano, to the chiefs that had come to see me, to their wives, and to my old friends, and then the people returned to their different villages. Quengueza's people were busy every day collecting the long bamboo-like branches of palm-trees for my new settlement, which they were to build for me.

Before the departure of the chiefs, I assembled them, and we held a grand palaver, at which they agreed that the *Mentor* should not leave their country until they had laden her with their products—woods, india-rubber, ivory, wax, &c.

The night Quengueza took leave his confidential slaves were busy taking his presents from my hut to the large canoes they had with them, which having been safely accomplished, they departed before daylight. Quengueza threatened with death any one of his men who should say a word of what had passed.

Then, for the first time since my arrival, it looked as if I was going to have a quiet time. I was glad of it, for I had been ill with fever, and wanted rest and quiet in order to get well. Old Ranpano would stay for hours by my bedside, hardly ever uttering a word, but I could see by his face that the old man felt anxiety on my account. He would say sometimes "Chally, Chally, you must not be ill; none of my people want to see you ill. I love you; we all love you:" and when he went away he muttered words which no doubt were invocations to spirits, for Ranpano, like the rest of his people, was very superstitious.

The superstition of the natives being so great about the site of my old settlement of Washington, I found it was impossible to build there again. Not far from it there was a nice spot, just on the bank of the river, which I liked very much; but at that spot there was a little Commi village, whose chief was called Rabolo. The only thing to be done was to buy Rabolo out, and I succeeded in purchasing the whole village for several guns, some kegs of powder, a brass kettle, a few brass rings and iron bars, and two or three pieces of cloth. I allowed the people to take the houses away with them, and I set to work immediately to build my new settlement.

Quengueza's people went at it vigorously, and, with the help of Ranpano's people, we began building in earnest, Captain Vardon, myself, and a negro being the carpenters. The doors and windows we made with the bottoms of large canoes.

The smaller buildings were soon finished, and the people were hard at work on my large dwelling-house; but when we came to the verandah, and the posts had to be put in the ground, my men were suddenly seized with fear.

There was in the ground a formidable *monda*, or fetich, which my friend Rabolo had buried in his village before I purchased it, and which happened to be exactly upon the site of my house, and almost in front of my door.

Poor Rabolo had never dreamed that I would build my house just on that very spot.

Rabolo was not in town, and the builders did not dare to remove the monda, declaring that there would be a great palaver if they touched Rabolo's monda; "for," said they, "Rabolo's monda, which he has put in the ground, is a very good one; for, since his village has been established, twelve dry and twelve rainy seasons ago, no one has died there." This was no great monda after all, for Rabolo's village was only composed of his family, and there were fifteen inhabitants in all, not including the dogs, goats, fowls, and parrots.

Rabolo was sent for. He was loth to agree to have the monda removed; " for," said he, " not one of us has died since I made it. You cannot take it." " Then," said I, " Rabolo, give me back the goods I have given you; I must go somewhere else." But poor Rabolo had given away the goods—had bought two more wives—and could not give me back my money. I knew it, and was firm. I insisted that the whole place belonged to me; that I bought it, above the ground and under the ground, to the very water's edge. So at last Rabolo, with a sad face, consented to have the monda removed.

To enter Rabolo's settlement you had to go under a portal, which was made of two upright poles and a cross-bar. Round the poles grew a talismanic creeper, which had been planted immediately after the queer gate had been erected; but at the erection of the gate there were great ceremonies, for Rabolo's powerful monda was to be buried in the ground, and that monda was to protect the village, and Rabolo and his family, from aniemba (witch-craft) and death; so I did not wonder that it was with a frightened face poor Rabolo allowed me to take away what he considered the protector of himself and family.

Rabolo was a quiet man—a good man; not a blood-thirsty savage. His little village lived at peace with all the Commi villages around him.

Rabolo asked to be allowed to take the monda away himself. This I granted. Then he began to cut the bushes and the creeper, which was of the same kind that grew on the gate, that in the course of time had grown over his talisman, and, digging a hole in the ground, soon came to the spot where the wonderful monda lay. The first thing he turned up was the skull of a chimpanzee; then came the skull of a man, probably of one of the an-cestors of Rabolo. The people were looking in silence at the scene before them; they seemed to think that Rabolo was doing a wonderful thing, and some thought that he would have to pay with his life for his daring deed. Poor superstitious fellow! around the skulls were pieces of pottery and crockery of all sorts, which had been put there as an offering or to keep company with the skulls.

Then we went to the entrance, and he removed the upright posts of the gate, and cut away the creeper that twined itself around it. This creeper was a long-lived species, and the superstition was that as long as it kept alive the monda would retain its power. Rabolo dug in the sandy soil of the prairie near where the creeper grew, and turned up more skulls of chimpanzees and broken pieces of pottery. The two idols on either side of the gate were removed also.

A few days after, I heard the people say that it was Rabolo's monda that had made me come to that spot; for they believe, in that far-away country which is the land of the chimpanzee, that the chimpanzee and the white man have something to do with each other, the pale yellow face of the chimpanzee seeming somewhat to resemble ours, while the dark face of the gorilla leads them to believe that the gorilla sprung from the black man. Skulls of chimpanzees were just now in great demand, as mondas were to be made with them in many villages, for they were fully persuaded that if they had them people from the land of the white man would come and settle among them.

Four weeks after my arrival in the Commi country my new settlement was built, and was exactly like my old settlement of Washington, a picture of which I gave you in my Apingi Kingdom, and I gave to it the name of Plateau, on account of the country being flat.

After the completion of my house there was great excitement in the settlement. Ranpano had declared that he could not enter my house; a doctor had told him that some person who was an aniemba, a wizard, had made a monda, a charm, and had put it under the threshold of the door of my house, so that if he entered my hut the witch or aniemba would go into him, and he would die.

I got furious at Ranpano's superstition, and said to him

that, while he pretended to love me, he insulted me by
not coming to see me.   His answer was that he loved me.
His people felt badly about it.   Doctors were sent for;
they drank the mboundou, and declared that it was true
that some one wanted to bewitch him, and had put a
monda under my door to kill him.

Immediately ceremonies for driving away the witch
were begun.   For three days they danced almost incessantly, making a terrible noise near my premises, which
almost set me crazy; drums were beating day and night.
At the end of the third day I heard suddenly a tremendous noise made with the drums, and a gun was fired at
my door.   Ranpano entered muttering invocations, and
wild with excitement, and the people declared that the
aniemba under my door that was to kill the king had been
driven away.

CHAPTER V.

THE day of departure of the *Mentor* had come. My
heart was heavy; my good friend and companion,
Captain Vardon, was going to leave me. I was to be left
all alone in that wild country, when but a few months
before I had been in the big city of London. How
lonely I should feel! My old life was to come again.

It was the 18th of January, 1864. I remember well
the day, for I left the shore with Captain Vardon to go
on board the *Mentor*, which was to sail that day for
London.

Captain Vardon and I did not talk much—our hearts
were too full; but the good captain kept repeating to me,
"My dear good friend, I do not like to leave you in this
wild part of the world all alone; who will take care of you
when you are sick?"

"Captain," I said, "God will take care of me."

Soon after we reached the vessel the anchor was weighed,
the sails were shaken out, the jibs were set, and the
schooner began to make a little headway.

I was loth to part with the dear little schooner *Mentor*,
for I knew I should never see it again, and perhaps I
should never see good Captain Vardon again.

When the moment of parting arrived, my negroes
stood ready to receive me in their canoe alongside.
I took Captain Vardon by the hand for a little time; we
looked each other in the face without saying a word; our
eyes were big—a little more, and tears would have rolled

D

from them. I went over the vessel's side, Captain Vardon still holding my hand, and began to descend the stairs into the canoe, when the captain was obliged to let my hand go. In a minute I was in the canoe; the canoe and the vessel parted company, and the distance between them began rapidly to widen. My men gave three cheers for the *Mentor;* the sailors responded, all standing by the bulwarks looking at me.

Captain Vardon had on board with him as passengers two chimpanzees, Thomas, and his wife, Mrs. Thomas. Thomas was, I judge, about three years old, and Mrs. Thomas might have been a year old. Mr. Thomas was a tricky little rascal, and I had any amount of fun with him. He was very tame, like all the young chimpanzees.

Thomas's capture was attended with adventures. He was with his mother in the woods; the mother was killed, and Thomas was seized and brought to the village two days after. Before he was tamed he escaped into the forest. The dogs were sent after him, and he was speedily retaken, but not without his having bitten the dogs and been severely bitten by them in return. Several of his fingers were broken, and upon knitting together they left his hand in a distorted condition.

I was compelled to keep Master Tom tied, for after he was quite tame he became very troublesome, and would go into my hut and disturb everything. He would upset the plates, break the glasses, and when he saw the mischief he had done he would run off, and that was the last seen of him for the day. So I tied him by a cord to a pole under the verandah of my hut, and at the foot of the pole I built a little house, into which he could retire when he pleased. Every day it was filled with fresh straw from the prairie, and he enjoyed it very much, and loved to sleep on it.

Everything I ate Tom would eat; everything I drank Tom would drink; tea, coffee, lemonade were drinks he liked very much. He would eat fish, crocodile, turtle, elephant, hippopotamus, chicken, bananas, plantains, biscuit, &c. &c.

Among the pets I had with me was a cat. One day

the cat came near Tom's pole, when suddenly Master Tom, who had never seen a cat, flew in alarm to his pole, and clambered up it, the hair on his body becoming erect, and his eyes glaring with excitement. He really looked like a porcupine-chimpanzee, such as I had never seen before.

In a moment, recovering himself, he came down, and, rushing to the cat before pussy had time to run away, with one of his feet-like hands he seized the nap of the animal, and with the other pressed on its back, as if trying to break its neck or spine. He was jerking the poor cat as hard as he could when I came to the rescue—just in time, for I am sure, if the struggle had lasted two or three minutes more, the cat would have been killed. The poor cat could not turn its head and bite, nor use its paws for scratching, and was indeed, utterly helpless.

The big chimpanzees and the gorillas are said to fight the formidable leopard in that manner. It must be a grand sight to see such an encounter.

One day, while hunting, my dogs captured another young chimpanzee, which I gave to Master Tom for a wife. He seemed exceedingly fond of her, and would spend the greater part of his time in embracing her. Their married life appeared one of unalloyed happiness. Unfortunately, Mrs. Thomas was never very strong, and she died of consumption on the passage, to the great sorrow of Mr. Thomas, who felt very sad for a good many days after her death.

I am happy to say that Mr. Thomas reached London in very good health, in the beginning of the year 1864, and was presented in my name to the Crystal Palace at Sydenham, near London, by Captain Vardon.

There he received a complete education; a nice place was built for him in the conservatory, where the exotic plants grew well, and there, for the sum of sixpence, he would sell his photograph to any one who chose to buy it. His principle was, money first, *carte de visite* afterwards; and if, perchance, any visitor took off his *carte de visite* without paying for it, he would rush forward, screaming, to the length of his tether, to prevent this irregular transaction, and would not cease his noisy expressions till the money was paid down. Then he would give a low grunt in sign of satisfaction.

Thomas thrived well there, and there was a prospect of his living many years; but he met with an untimely end when the Crystal Palace burnt. The poor fellow met his death in the flames, but not before giving the most fearful screams of despair, which were unavailing, since no one could reach him.

The breeze was stiff, and carried the *Mentor* swiftly away from the shore as we paddled toward the breakers. I turned my head back now and then to have a look at the dear little schooner.

We passed safely through the breakers, and after landing I seated myself to look for the last time at the vessel as she glided away ; fainter and fainter became the sails, till finally I could see nothing but the horizon.

I tore myself from the shore. How sad I was that evening! "How long," thought I, "shall I have to wait for a vessel to come to me? Oh dear, I hope the Messrs. Baring will send me one, with scientific instruments ; then I shall start on that long journey to the Nile, from which, perhaps, I shall never come back. Never mind," said I, " friend Paul, try your best. If you do not succeed, it is no disgrace."

I lay down to sleep sad and dejected indeed. That night I dreamed of my departed mother and father. I dreamed of dear friends—of girls and boys, the companions of my school-days, that were no more—of days when I was happy and without a care. That dream was so pleasurable that it awoke me. As my eyes opened, the walls of bamboo, the queer bed, told me that I was in a wild country. I got up feeling feverish and sick at heart in my loneliness, to which I was not yet accustomed.

That day I said to myself, "Paul, several weary months will pass away before a vessel can come for you, so take courage, go hunting, visit the country round, and do the best you can to while away the time. Keep up your spirits ; faint heart has never yet succeeded ; " and toward evening I felt more cheerful, and chatted with my Commi

men, and afterward said to myself, "How grateful I
ought to be that I can feel so safe in such a wild country;
that I have so many friends among the natives; and that
there is not a man of them all who would dare to rob me!
Surely," I reflected, "there is not a civilized country
where I could be as safe; the robbers of civilization would
break through these thin walls, and steal everything I
have." The next day I put into practice the resolution I
had formed, and made preparations for a journey. I
wanted to visit many Commi villages.

My premises were filled with goods under the care of
the Commi. "Be without fear," said good old Ranpano;
everything will be safe when you come back. Malonga,
my brother, will take care of your premises as did Rikimongani." So I set out and advanced toward Cape St.
Catharine, for I intended to make a visit first to my old
friend King Olenga-Yombi, with whom you have become
acquainted in one of my preceding volumes.

It was a fine evening when we left Plateau. We were
now in the height of the rainy season, and it was so hot
in the day that I thought we might sail more comfortably
on the river at night. We were pretty sure to get a
ducking, but I thought it was better to get wet than to
have the rays of a tropical sun pouring down on our heads.
Malonga (Ranpano's brother) and my men had been busy
making mondas to keep the rain off, and as we left the
shore old Malonga said we should have clear weather. In
this country, unlike South Africa, the doctors are un-
makers, and not makers of rain.

The evening, indeed, was fine, and I began to think that
Malonga, after all, might be right; the moon shone in an
almost cloudless sky; but after the setting of the moon at
10 o'clock, a thick black cloud rose in the north-east, and
we began to feel not so sure about a dry night. I was
watching all the time anxiously in that north-eastern direction, for I was afraid a tornado was coming. We were in
the season of the tornadoes, and a constant look-out had to
be kept, for it would never have done to have been caught
napping. The flashes of lightning became more and more
vivid as we skirted the river bank, paddling as fast as we

could, and looking for a quiet little nook; and we were getting near one, when suddenly a white patch shone under the black mass in the heavens. In an instant that black mass overspread the sky; the part which a little before was blue had become black and lurid; the clouds drove from the north-east with fearful rapidity, and all above seemed to be in a blaze with lightning; the thunder pealed incessantly, and the rain poured down, as it were, by bucketsful. Our canoes were driven ashore by the force of the terrific wind, and we immediately hauled them out of water, although it was pitch dark, and we could only see each other by the glare of the lightning. Near by was a little village composed of a few huts, and we made for it, but found only a few women, and not wood enough for a fire, in consequence of which I had to remain all night wet to the skin.

The next morning the sky was clear and the sun rose beautifully, and soon after sunrise you could have heard the paddlers sing merry songs of the Commi. We ascended the river till we came to the island of Nengué Shika. Nengué, as you know, means an island; you may perhaps remember Nengué Ngozo. Shika means white, silver-like. After paddling along the shore of Nengué Shika, which was covered with palm-trees, we made for the main land, toward the banks of a little creek over which swallows were flying. It was a sweet spot, of prairie and luxuriant wood. There a shed had been built for me by our old friend King Olenga-Yombi, and many of his slaves were waiting for me with a goat, a few fowls, several bunches of bananas and plantains. The king had sent these provisions and his best wishes for good luck in my hunts, and a message that I must come and see him when I was tired of the woods.

Not far from our camp there were several "ivolos"— wooded bogs; there the vegetation was very rank, and these bogs were known to be the haunts of the gorilla. That day we rested in camp, and the next morning we started with two native dogs for the ivolos. It was very hard work; we had to struggle through the thorny and swampy thickets for a long time, and now and then we would sink knee-deep in the mud. My followers were slaves of King Olenga-Yombi. Hark! hark! I hear a noise as if some one was breaking the branches of trees. I gave a cluck; I looked at the men behind. This noise was made by gorillas. Silence. My gun is ready; I advance, but it is all I can do to keep the dogs in check. The creatures of the woods were tearing down branches to pick off the berries. Unfortunately, one of the dogs broke from us. I heard a shriek—a sharp cry; the gorillas fled; they were females, but the men assured me the males could not be far off. This was, beyond all doubt, the spot for gorillas. I could see many of their footmarks on the soft mud; their heels were well marked, but their toes were hardly seen. Where they had been on all-fours I could see the marks of their knuckles.

But that day I could not come in sight of gorillas. The following day I hunted near the sea-shore, from which I then concluded to go to Amembié to see Olenga-Yombi.

On our way we passed by an island of trees growing in the midst of the prairie. That island is called "Nengué Ncoma." The people are afraid of Nengué Ncoma, and at night nobody would dare to pass by it; and, though we were far away, my men looked at it with superstitious dread, and quickened their steps. "Oh," said one of my guides, "whoever enters this island is likely to die suddenly in it; if he does not die he becomes crazy, and roams about till he dies. There is a woman that we see now and then, crazy and wandering all over it. In this island of Nengué Ncoma lives a crocodile, whose scales are of brass, that never leaves the island; he lives in the centre of it; no gun can kill that crocodile."

"It is a lie!" I shouted; "how foolish you are, my boys, to believe such things! To show you that it is a lie, I will enter that island of Nengué Ncoma," and I rushed, gun in hand, toward the island. A wild shriek came from the men. They shouted, "Oh, Chally, do not go." They did not dare to follow me. A little while after I touched the branches of the trees of Nengué

Ncoma, but before I entered I turned back and looked toward the men, and as I looked at them I saw them mute with astonishment; and as I turned my back and entered the wood, terrific cries rent the air. They thought it was the last they should see of me. Surely the crocodile with brass scales would kill me, who dared to go into that island of which he was the king and sole inhabitant.

I walked on and explored every part of this small island of trees. I need not say that I did not meet with the crocodile When I came out a wild shout greeted me; it was from my men, who were still at the same place where I had left them. I came toward them smiling and saying, "Do you think I am crazy? I tell you I have not seen that crocodile with scales of brass. I looked everywhere, and I saw nothing but trees." They all shouted, "You are a mbuiti"—a spirit.

We continued our way till we came to Amembie. Poor King Olenga-Yombi was drunk as usual; he was so tipsy, indeed, that he could not stand on his legs. Nevertheless, he welcomed his friend Chally, and said all his country belonged to me, and in joy he ordered another calabash full of palm wine to be brought to him, and drank off about half a gallon of it at once. This finished him up for the day; he fell back in the arms of his wives, shouting many times over, "I am a big king! I am a big king! I am Olenga-Yombi!" and was soon asleep. Poor Olenga-Yombi, he is an inveterate drunkard; not a day passes by that he is not tipsy.

The next morning I started for a large plantation of the king's before he was awake. The name of that plantation was "Nkongon-Boumba." There I found a large number of the king's slaves, and among them were a great many good hunters. These slaves knew me; they knew that I was their master's great friend; they knew I was theirs also, and that I had a good stock of beads for them and their wives. The head slave of the king, an Ishogo man called Ayombo, welcomed me, and brought me food.

I said to them, "Friends, I have come to live with you."

They shouted "Yo! yo! yo!" "I want to hunt, and kill an ipi." "Yo! yo! yo! You shall kill an ipi," they shouted. "I want to kill gorillas and chimpanzees." "Yo! yo! yo! You shall kill gorillas and chimpanzees." "But, above all, I want to kill an ipi. My heart will go away sad if I do not kill an ipi." "Yo! yo! yo! You shall kill an ipi. We know where some are. Yo! yo! yo! You shall see an ipi."

You ask yourself what an ipi is. The ipi was an unknown animal. How did I come to know that such an animal existed? One day I saw a monda to which was suspended a large and thick yellow scale, such as I had never seen before. The pangolin had scales, but they were much smaller. There was no doubt that this scale belonged to the pangolin family, only I learned that the animal from which it was taken was of a larger variety.

The ipi, I was told, was very rare. Years had passed away, and no ipi had been seen by me; but some time ago King Olenga-Yombi had sent me word that an ipi had been near his plantation of Nkongon-Boumba, and I had come specially to hunt the ipi.

Many of the king's slaves had come from far-away tribes, and queer and ugly fellows they were, with lean legs, prominent abdomens, retreating foreheads, and projecting mouths.

The day of my arrival we rested. The good slaves and their kind wives brought fowls, plantains, pea-nuts, sugar-cane, some pine apples, little lemons, wild honey, dried fish—in fact, they brought to me the best things they had. I gave them nice beads, and to some of the leading slaves I gave red caps.

That night there was dancing. The idol or mbuiti was consulted as to the results of the chase, for these interior people are very superstitious. They sang songs welcoming me.

The next morning a few of the leading slaves and myself started for an ipi hunt.

CHAPTER VI.

Hunting for the Ipi—Camping out in the Woods—Capture of an Ipi—Description of the Animal—A new species of Ant-eater.

WE left the plantation at daybreak. Mayombo, the head slave, was the leader, and some of his children were with us. We all had guns; the boys carried, besides, two axes. In a little while we were in the forest. It was an awful day's hunt, and the first time since my return that I had to rough it in such a manner. We wandered over hills and dales, through the woods and the streams, now and then crossing a bog, leaving the hunting-paths, struggling for hours through the tangled maze and through patches of the wild pine-apple, which tore my clothes to rags, and covered my poor body with scratches. The thorns and cutting edges of sword-like grass which grew in many places, and the sharp points of the pine-apple leaves, were not very pleasant things to get among. It was like the good old time, but I did not fancy the good old time. I was not yet inured to such tramps; I had forgotten all about them, but I knew that it was nothing but child's play when compared with the hardships I had suffered in my former explorations, or with what I expected to undergo in the future. I knew that I was hardening myself for what was coming by and by, and that it was necessary that I should go through such a schooling before starting for that long Nile journey from which I knew not if I should ever come back. I must get accustomed to sickness, to hunger, to privations of all kinds, to forced marches; I must be afraid of nothing, and trust in God for the result.

The end of the day was approaching; the birds gave

forth their last songs, calling their mates, so that they might not be far apart for the night; the butterflies had ceased to fly, and were hiding themselves under the large leaves to keep away from the rains.

We had not been successful, but did not despair. We were to sleep in the woods, for the plantation was too far away. Oh, I was so tired. Mayombo immediately went off to cut some poles to support the large leaves, which were to protect us from the rains, while his two sons collected as fast as they could the leaves, and I looked after firewood. I soon came to a spot where the dead branches lay thick on the ground, and I shouted, " Come here, boys!" A little after sunset our camp was built and our fires were lighted; then the boys pulled from their bags several plantains and a little parcel of dried fish packed in leaves. Not far from our camp a little rivulet ran meandering toward the sea; its water was clear and cool, so we had chosen a nice spot for the bivouac; but fires were to be kept burning brightly all night, " for," said Mayombo, " leopards are very plentiful here; we cannot keep our goats; and two men have been missing within a month." After that exhortation, Mayombo, who was a great smoker, filled his pipe and lay down by the fire. In the meantime my supper had been cooked, but I was too tired to enjoy it, and I was too tired even to sleep.

The next evening we returned to the plantation, where all were glad to see us. After a day of rest we started again, for Mayombo swore that I should not rest till I had an ipi. We went in another direction, and Mayombo again took his two sons with him. Toward noon Mayombo gave a cluck, and pointed out to me a dead tree lying on the ground, and a strange-looking track leading up to it, and whispered into my ears the word " Ipi !"

That dead tree had been lying there, I suppose, for hundreds of years; nothing remained of it but the trunk, which was hollow throughout, and looked like a tube fifty or sixty feet long.

I examined the ground carefully at one end of the trunk,

and saw no footprint there, so the animal had not gone out; at the other end the tracks were fresh, and it was evident that the animal had hidden inside the night before. I said to Mayombo, "Perhaps the ipi has gone away." "Oh no," said he; "don't you see there is only one track? Besides, it could not turn on itself, and, in order to get out, it has to go straight on to the other end."

Immediately he took the axe and cut down some branches of a tree, of which he made a trap to catch the animal if it should come out. The branch was put firmly in the ground, and the top was bent over with a creeper attached to it, at the end of which was a ring, through which the animal would have to pass before he could get out; a little forked stick held the ring, which the animal would shake as it passed through; the limb would fly up instantly, and high in the air would the ipi dangle.

When all this had been done, Mayombo, who had collected wood at the other end, set fire to it, to smoke the animal out. He was not mistaken; the ipi was inside, and it made for the opposite extremity and was caught. There was a short struggle, but we ran up and ended it by knocking the ipi with all our might on the head.

I saw at once that the ipi belonged to the pangolin genus (*Manis* of the zoologists), which is a very singular kind of animal. They are ant-eaters, like the Myrmecophaga of South America; but while the South American ant-eater is covered with hair like other mammalia, the pangolins have an armour of large scales implanted in the skin of the upper surface of the body, from the head to the tip of the tail, each scale overlapping the other like the slates on the roof of a house.

Like the ant-eater of South America, the pangolins have no teeth, but they have a long extensile tongue, the extremity of which is covered with a glutinous secretion so sticky that their prey after having been touched, adheres to the tongue and cannot get away. The tongue of an ipi may be extended out several inches. The ipi feeds on ants.

During the day the ipi hides itself in its burrow in the

earth, or sometimes in the large hollows of colossal trunks of trees which have fallen to the ground, like the tree just described to you; but they generally prefer to burrow in the soil, and these burrows are usually found in light soil on the slope of a hill. By the singular structure of the ipi, it cannot turn to the right or to the left at once; in fact, it is quite incapable of bending its body sideways, so it cannot "right about face" in its burrow. Accordingly, there are two holes in each burrow, one for entrance and one for exit.

But if the ipi and the pangolin cannot bend their bodies sideways, they are very flexible vertically, their stomachs having no scales; so, if they are surprised or want to sleep, they roll themselves in a ball, the head being inside and forming the centre, and they coil and uncoil themselves in this manner very readily.

The only way you can find the ipi or the pangolin is by the trail they leave on the soil, and following them till you reach their burrows.

The great trouble in finding the ipi is not only that the animal is very scarce, but that it never comes out except at night, when the rattle it makes among the dead leaves is great. The strange creature must see well with its queer little eyes to be able to perceive the ants upon which it mostly feeds, and it must take time in satisfying its appe-petite, for a great many little ants must be required to fill its stomach. When the ipi has found a spot where the ants it wants to eat are plentiful, it stops by them, and with its long tongue, which protrudes several inches, catches them one by one. When an ant is caught the tongue goes in again. I wonder how many hundreds of times the tongue must come out and go in with an ant before the hunger of the ipi is satisfied!

I was not mistaken; this ipi was a new species, and the scientific name is Pholidotus Africanus. This large one was a female, and measured four feet six inches from the head to the tip of the tail. It was very stout and heavy, the tail very short in comparison with its body, and the scales very thick, and of a yellow or tawny colour. The males are said to be much larger, and, according to

what the negroes say, must reach the length of six feet.
They are very ugly to look at. Their tail being very
thick, makes a large trail on the ground as they move
about.

Though in some respects they may be thought to
resemble the lizard, the pangolins have warm blood, and
nourish their young like the rest of the mammalia.

I need not tell you that I was glad to discover this new
species. After securing the ipi we returned at once to the
plantation, and as soon as I arrived I went to work and
took off its skin, and hard work it was, I assure you; the
scales were so thick and big.

When we came into the village with the ipi there was
great excitement, for the animal is so rare that but two or
three persons there had ever seen a specimen.

I went to bed happy, feeling that I had had the good
fortune of discovering a new and most remarkable animal,
which God had long ago created, but which had never
before been seen by the white man.

Of course I had a curiosity to see how the ipi tasted,
and I had some for breakfast the next morning, and it
was good, but not fat, though the natives said that at
certain seasons they are very fat.

CHAPTER VII.

Life at Nkongon-Boumba—Gorillas and Plantains—Odanga scared
by a Gorilla—A captive Gorilla—Superstitions respecting the
Leopard.

THE dry season had now fairly begun. We were in
the month of June, and the nights and evenings
were quite pleasant. The days were generally cloudy, and
it was a good time of the year for hunting, as most of the
bog-land was drying fast.

Nkongon-Boumba was situated in a charming spot on
the summit of a gentle hill, at the foot of which ran a
little stream of clear water. The country which surrounded it was partly prairie and partly wooded; the soil
on the prairie was sandy, but where the woods grew the
soil was better. In many places the primitive growth
had been cut down, and there the fine plantation of
plantain-trees and bananas of King Olenga-Yombi were
flourishing well.

How beautiful the country looked in the morning just
before sunrise, when a veil of mist seemed to hang over
it, and when the dew was still thick on the blades of grass,
or was dropping fast from the plantain-leaves! I would
get up just at daylight, and would start with my gun on
my shoulder, in the hope that I might see a gazelle or an
antelope feeding.

Gorillas were very plentiful near Nkongon-Boumba,
and were committing great depredations among the
plantain and banana trees; the patches of sugar-cane were
also very much devastated. I heard one afternoon that
the day before gorillas were in the forest not far from the
village, and had already begun to play sad havoc with the
plantain-trees.

The morning after the news, if you had been in the

village, you would have seen me, just a little before daybreak, getting ready to go after the gorillas. I was painting
my face and hands with a mixture of powdered charcoal
and oil. After my toilet was done, I put on my old,
soiled Panama hat, took one of my best guns, called
Odanga, one of my boys, to accompany me, and started
off. There was just daylight enough for us to see our
way, and in a short time we came to a plantation, surrounded by virgin forest, covered with plantain and banana
trees, most of which were bearing fruit in different stages
of growth. This plantation had just been made on the
skirt of the forest.

It was a lovely morning; the sky was almost cloudless;
everything was still, and one could only hear the slight
rustling of the tree-tops moved by the gentle land breeze.
Before reaching the grove of plantain-trees I had to pick
my way through a maze of tree-stumps, half-burnt logs,
and dead, broken, and half-burnt limbs of trees, where the
land had been prepared for a new plantation. If gorillas
are to be seen in a plantation near a village they most
generally come in the early morning.

By the side of the plantain-trees was a field of cassada,
and just as I was going by it I heard suddenly in the
plantain-grove a great crashing noise like the breaking of
limbs. What could this be? I immediately hid myself
behind a bush, and then looked in the direction from which
the sound proceeded. What do I see? A gorilla, then a
second gorilla, and a third one, coming out of a thick bush;
then another one made his appearance—there were four
altogether. Then I discovered that one of the females had
a baby gorilla following her.

So do not be astonished when I tell you that my eyes
were wide open, and that I gazed on the scene before me
with intense excitement. These gorillas looked so droll,
walking in the most absurd way on all fours, and now and
then walking erect. How impish the creatures seemed!
how intensely black their faces were! how hideous their
features! They looked like men, but like wild men with
shaggy hides, and their big, protuberant abdomens did not
make them less ridiculous or repulsive.

The gorillas went immediately at their work of destruction. I did not stop them but merely looked on. Plantain-tree after plantain-tree came down; it seemed to me that they were trying to see which could bring down the greatest number of trees in the shortest space of time. They were amusing themselves, I suppose. In destroying a tree, they first grasped the base of the stem with one of their powerful hand-like feet, and then with their prodigious long arms pulled it down. This, of course, did not require much strength with so light a stem as that of the plantain. Then they would set their big mouths upon the juicy heart of the tree, and devour it with great avidity; at another time they would give one bite, or would simply demolish the tree without eating it.

How strange sounded the chuckle they gave as if to express their contentment! Now and then they would sit still and look around—and such a look! Two or three times they looked in the direction where I was; but I lay so quiet, and was so concealed, they could not see me, and, as the wind was blowing from them to me, they could not smell me. How fiendish their look was! A cold shiver ran through me several times, for, of all the malignant expressions I had ever seen, theirs were the most diabolical. Two or three times they seemed to be on the point of running away, and appeared alarmed, but recovered their composure, and began anew the work of destruction.

The little baby gorilla followed his mother wherever she went. Gradually, without my taking notice of it, they came to the edge of the dark forest, and all at once disappeared like a vision—like a dream. I went to look at the spot where they had made such havoc, and counted over one hundred plantain-trees down on the ground, which they had destroyed.

The next morning I went again with Odanga to the same spot, with no expectation of seeing gorillas again, for I did not think they would make another visit there with their roving propensities, but I thought I might see an antelope or two, attracted by the young leaves of the cassada-tree, of which they are very fond. I carried a

E

light double-barrelled shot-gun, while Odanga carried my heavy double-barrelled rifle, to use in case we should see an elephant.

The part of the plantation upon which we had come extended over two hills, with a deep hollow between planted with sugar-cane. I was taking the lead in the narrow path, and just as I was going down the hill to get over to the other side of the hollow, my eyes suddenly fell upon a monstrous grey-haired male gorilla standing erect and looking directly toward me. I really did not know if he was looking at me or at something else, or if he thought of crossing to my side, in which case he would have come toward me. Without turning my head (for I did not dare to lose sight of the gorilla), I beckoned Odanga to come toward me, so that I might get hold of my rifle and shoot down the huge monster. I beckoned in vain. I made a quicker motion with my hand for Odanga to come, but no Odanga was coming. The huge beast stared at me, or at least seemed to stare at me, for two minutes, and then, without uttering any roar, moved off into the great forest on all fours. Then I looked round to see what was the matter with my boy Odanga, but no Odanga was to be seen; I was all alone. The fellow had bolted, gun and all; the gorilla had frightened him, and he had fled. I was furiously angry, and promised myself to give friend Odanga such a punishment as he would not soon forget, that he might not play me such a trick a second time.

Odanga had fled to the plantation, and a little after what I have just related I heard a good many voices. They were the plantation people, all armed to the teeth, coming to my rescue; but Odanga had taken good care to remain out of the way, though he had sent the gun. The little scamp knew very well what was coming, but when I went back he was not to be seen, and the fellow hid himself for two days. When at last I got hold of him he made me the most solemn promise never to do such a thing again, and said, "Chally, Abamboo (the devil) must have made me leave you."

On my return from Nkongon-Boumba a great surprise

Monarch of the Woods.

awaited me—a *live* gorilla. An old chief, a friend of mine, named Akondogo, had just returned from the Ngobi country, situated south of Cape St. Catharine, and there, with some slaves of Olenga-Yombi, he had killed the mother, and captured the rascal before me. He was bigger than any gorilla I had captured, or that had ever been taken alive. Bigger he was than Fighting Joe, which many of you no doubt remember.

Like Joe, this fellow showed the most ungovernable temper, and to bite somebody seemed to be the object he was always aiming at. We had no chain with which to confine him, so that a long forked stick round his neck was the only means we could employ of keeping him at a safe distance.

In the evening, as Akondogo and I were seated together, the good fellow, smoking his huge pipe, said to me, " Chally, I have had a great deal of trouble since I have seen you. A leopard has killed two of my people, and I have had a great many palavers with their families on account of their death."

I said, " Akondogo, you could not help it; you are not chief over the leopards. But after the first man had been killed, why did you not make a trap to catch the leopard ?"

" The leopard I mean," said he, " is not one that can be trapped; it was a man who had changed himself into a leopard, and then, after he had been a leopard for some time, he changed himself into a man again."

I said, " Akondogo, why do you talk to me in that way ? You know I do not believe that men are turned into beasts, and afterward into men again. It is stupid for people to believe so, but I cannot shake that belief in you alombè (black men)."

Poor Akondogo said, " Chally, I assure you that there are men who change into leopards, and from leopards into men again."

Not wishing to argue the question, I said, " Never mind ; tell me the story of your trouble." Then Akondogo once more filled his pipe with tobacco, gave three or four big puffs of smoke, which rose high in the air, and thus begun :

"My people and myself had been in the woods several days collecting India-rubber. One day a man disappeared, and nothing could be found of him but a pool of blood. The next day another man disappeared, and in searching for him more blood was found. We all got alarmed, and I sent for a great doctor; he came and drank the mboundou, so that he might be able to say how these two deaths came about. After the ouganga (doctor) had drank the mboundou, and as all the people stood round him asking him what had killed these two men, and just as we were waiting with breathless silence for what he was going to say, he spoke to me and said, 'Akondogo, your own child [his nephew and heir] Akosho killed the two men.' Immediately Akosho was sent for and seized, and he answered that it was true that he had killed the two men, but that he could not help it; he remembered well that that day, as he was walking in the woods, he suddenly became a leopard; that his heart longed for blood, and that he had killed the two men, and then, after each murder, he became a man again.

"There was a great uproar in the village; the people shouted, 'Death to the aniemba Akosho!'"

"But," said Akondogo, "I loved my boy so much that I said to the people, 'Let us not believe Akosho; he must have become a kendé' (idiot, fool). But Akosho kept saying he had killed the men, and took us into the woods where lay the two bodies, one with the head cut off, and the other with the belly torn open.

"Upon this," said Akondogo, "I ordered Akosho to be bound with cords, and tied in a horizontal position to a post, and to have a fire lighted at his feet, and be burned slowly to death, all which was done, the people standing by until he expired."

The end of the story was so horrid that I shuddered. It was a case of monomania. Akosho believed that he had been turned into a leopard, and committed two murders, the penalty of which he paid with his life. Here, in our country, he would have been sent to the insane asylum.

CHAPTER VIII.

Wounded Gorilla and her young ones—Taking their Photographs—
Tom and Minnie—Arrival of my vessel—Hurra for Baring
Brothers—A smoking Ship—King Quengueza goes on board—
Preparations for Journey.

A FEW days after my return home, one evening a
strange sight presented itself in front of my house
—a sight which I firmly believe had never before been
witnessed since the world began. There was great commotion and tremendous excitement among the Commi
people.

There stood in front of my bamboo house a large
female gorilla, bound hand and foot, and alive, but frightfully wounded. A large gash might have been seen on
her scalp, and her body was covered with clotted blood.
One of her arms had been broken, and she bore wounds
upon the head and chest. Now and then the creature
would give a sharp scream of pain, which lent horror to
the darkness by which we were surrounded, the half dozen
lighted torches making the scene still more wild.

This adult female gorilla had been mortally wounded
in the morning, and lay on the ground senseless for a long
time. A bullet from one of my hunters had fractured
her skull, and in that state of insensibility she had been
securely tied to a stout stick, and in such an ingenious
manner that there was no chance of her escaping. Her
wrists and ankles had been tied strongly together, while
the stick had been adjusted between her mouth and feet
and hands in such a way that she could not reach out to
sever the cords with her teeth.

Hanging from her bosom was a baby gorilla (her child).
The little creature was a female but a few months old,

and now and then, after feeding from its mother's breast, it would give a plaintive wail. By the side of both stood a young live male gorilla, a fierce-looking fellow, which seemed afraid of nothing, and looked around with its deep greyish, fiendish eyes as if to say, "What does all this mean? I have not seen this sight in the woods before." Not far off lay the corpse of a large female gorilla, quiet in the embrace of death, her face yet distorted by the death-agony.

It was dark, as I have told you, and the scene was so strange and so wild that I will never forget it. The fiendish countenances of the living calibanish trio, one of them—the wounded one—with a face distorted by pain, were lit up by the ruddy glare of the natives' torches, and they seemed even more repulsive than their dead companion. "What a commotion this sight would create," I said to myself, "in a civilized land!"

There was no sleep for me that night; the terrific screams of the wounded mother kept me awake. Two or three times I got up and went out to see what was the matter, for I was in constant dread of the big gorilla's untying the cords.

The next morning I immediately prepared my photographic apparatus, and took an excellent photograph of the wounded mother with her child on her lap. As for Master Tom (I gave that name to the fierce-looking young male), I could not succeed in taking a very good likeness of him; he would not keep still long enough. I untied his hands and feet after putting a chain round his neck, and to show his gratitude he immediately made a rush at me to the length of his chain, screaming with all his might. Happily, the chain was too short for him to reach me, or I should have come off minus a little piece of the calf of my leg.

The night after I had taken the photograph of the mother her moanings were more frequent, and in the morning they gradually became weaker as her life ebbed out, and about ten o'clock she died. Her death was painfully like that of a human being, and her child clung to her to the last, and even tried to obtain milk after she was dead.

Photographing Gorillas.

How still was that fierce, scowling black face! There was something so vindictive in it, and at the same time so human, that I almost shrunk from the sight as I contemplated that wonderful creature which God has made almost in the image of man.

Now all I had to do was to take care of Tom and of Minnie. Tom gave me no trouble, for he was quite old enough to feed upon the nuts and the berries that were gathered for him; but with little Minnie it was a different thing, as she was too young to eat berries. Happily, I had a goat that gave milk, and I fed her on that milk, but I am sorry to say that she lived only three days after her mother's death. She died the fourth day toward noon, having taken an unconquerable dislike to the goat's milk. She died gently; her tiny legs and arms had become shrivelled, her ribs could all be seen, and her small hands had wasted almost to nothing. She died on the little bed of straw I made for her as if she went to sleep, without a struggle.

So no one was now left of my family of gorillas but Master Tom, and he was healthy and strong enough, and ate all the berries, nuts, and fruits we brought to him. For days I tried to take the little demon's photograph, but all in vain. The pointing of the camera toward him threw him into a perfect rage, and I was several times on the point of giving him a severe thrashing. At last I succeeded in taking two views, not very perfect; but this was better than nothing.

The place where these gorillas had been captured was about thirty miles above my settlement, up the river; at this point a low, narrow promontory projects into the stream. This spot was my favourite hunting-ground for gorillas, which came there to eat the wild pine-apple, and it was there I intended to take my good friend Captain Burton, the great African traveller, the man who made the pilgrimage to Mecca, for he was now at Fernando Po, and had promised to make me a visit.

The gorillas were discovered in this way: A woman passing through that region came to her village and said she had seen two squads of female gorillas, some of them followed by *their children*; they were going, she thought, to her plantain field. My hunters were on the spot where I had left them the day before, and with the villagers, who armed themselves with guns, axes, and spears, at once sallied forth in pursuit. The situation was very favourable for the hunters, who formed a line across the narrow strip of land, and pressed forward, shouting and driving the animals to the edge of the water, their terrific noise bewildering the gorillas, which were shot and beaten down in their endeavours to escape. There were eight adult females together, but not a single male.

Time now began to weigh heavily upon me, and a weary interval passed by. I did not know how long it might be before a vessel would come to me. Had my letter to Messrs. Baring reached them? If it had not, what should I do?

I begun to feel very lonely despite hunting excursions and the gorilla scene I have just described to you. I would go almost every day on the sea-shore and watch for a sail; now and then I would see one, but it was the sail of a whaler or of a trader, who took good care not to come to anchor near this wild part of the western coast.

On the 30th of June, as I came down the River Commi from a hunting excursion, having bade adieu to Olenga-Yombi, and was returning to my own settlement, expecting to remain there and wait for the coming vessel, I saw a canoe with sail set coming up the river and making for us. I immediately ordered my paddlers to go toward the canoe. Soon we met, when Kombé shouted, "Chally, your vessel has come!" I jumped from my seat and cried back, "What do you say, Kombé?" He repeated, "Your vessel has arrived." I was wild; I was crazy with joy; no news could have been more welcome. I shouted (I could not help it), "Good for you, Baring Brothers! You have acted like true friends. Three cheers," I called to the boys, "three cheers for Baring Brothers, who have sent the ship to me. Let us paddle with all our might," said I; "let us not stop; I must reach Plateau before morning."

On my arrival at that place, Ranpano handed me two letters which the captain of the ship had sent for me. One was from the captain himself, announcing his arrival; the other was from Baring Brothers. Yes, they had sent me all the goods I wanted—a second supply of scientific instruments. These great bankers and merchants had taken the trouble to send to Paul Du Chaillu all he had asked for, and they did not know when they would be paid. I assure you I was so overjoyed that for a few minutes I did not know what I was doing.

I ordered at once all the sea-canoes to be ready. I must go on board; no time must be lost. The next morning it was hardly daylight when I had left for the mouth of the river. Soon after our canoes were put over to the sea-side, we passed the surf smoothly, and I was on board the vessel shaking hands with Captain Berridge, the commander.

Oh, what an enjoyment I had! how many letters from friends told me that I was not forgotten! Then newspapers came, and my heart became sad when I saw that the civil war was still raging in America; "but," said the captain, "there is a prospect that it will soon be over."

My vessel had only arrived two days when a native entered my hut in great consternation, and said that a smoking vessel with ten guns was in the river, and they thought it had come to make war. After a while, a flat-bottomed steamer, forty feet in length, put out her anchor in front of my settlement, and fired off a gun to salute me.

I need not tell you that there was tremendous excitement among the natives now that an ouatanga otouton (smoking ship) had entered their river. The name of this little vessel was the *Leviathan*.

A few days after I was on board of the *Leviathan* steaming for Goumbi, for I wanted Quengueza to see what a steamer was. The appearance of this little boat, which did not draw more than two feet of water, created the most intense excitement. The *Leviathan* was a screw steamer. "Oh," exclaimed the people, "look! look! the vessel goes by itself, without sails, without paddles! Oh! oh! oh! what does that mean?" They would spy

us far off, and then would crowd the banks of the river.
Many were stupefied at the sight, and could not make out
what it meant, especially when they recognised me, while
others would deny that it was me, and others exclaimed,
" Chally, is that you ?   Do not our eyes belie us?   Tell
us—shout back to us!" and then I would say, " It is I—
Chally."   Then they would recognise me, put out in
their canoes, and paddle with all their might in order to
catch us.

As we approached Goumbi, where the river, in descending from the interior, bends in its westerly course,
the banks were high and wooded, and the river very tor-
tuous.   Here the steamer puffed its way right up to the
villages before it could be seen, and the alarmed natives,
who heard the strange noise of the steam-pipe and ma-
chinery, were much frightened, and, as we came in sight,
peeped cautiously from behind the trees, and then ran
away.

At last we came in sight of Goumbi.   The excitement
was intense.   From Goumbi the people could see well
down the river.   The drums began to beat, and the people
were greatly frightened.   Then we cast anchor, and
as I landed the people shouted, " It is Chally; so let us
not be afraid, for no one will harm us when Chally is with
them."

Captain Labigot and Dr. Touchard, who had landed
with me, received an ovation ; guns were fired, and in a
short time we found ourselves in the presence of the great
King Quengueza.   He did not know what all this meant,
but he felt big.   Hundreds of Bakalai and Ashira were
around him ; he looked at them, and said, " Do you see ?
do you see ?   I am Quengueza; my fame is great, and
the white man comes to see me," and he turned away
without saying another word.

My great desire was to persuade Quengueza to come on
board, and I was afraid I would not be able to effect this.
I said, " Quengueza, I have brought you white people
who want to see your river, and I want you to come on
board with us ; they want to see the Niembouai and the
Bakalai."   The old chief said he would go ; " for," said

he, " Chally, I know that no one will hurt me when I am with you." Good Quengueza knew me quite well; he had perfect faith in me; he knew that I loved him as he loved me. I said, " Quengueza, you are right."

Early the next morning the steam was up, and, in despite of the protestations of his people, the old king came on board, and was received with a royal salute from the two small guns. The excitement on the shore was intense; the booming of the guns re-echoed from hill to hill, and lost itself in the immense forest. Many a wild beast must have been astonished; gorillas must have roared, and thought that it was strange that there was anything besides thunder that could make a noise louder than their own roars. The old African chieftain accompanied us unattended, and as the anchor was raised and we began to steam up the river, he looked backward toward his people, who were dumb with astonishment, as if to say, " Do you see? your old chief is afraid of nothing." I had induced good Quengueza to wear a coat, though he was in deep mourning.

You would have liked to see King Quengueza seated on a chair on deck. As we passed village after village, he looked at the Bakalai with silent contempt, and they could hardly believe their own eyes. The crafty old king took care to let the people see him, for it was to give him great fame: the people would say, " We saw Quengueza on a vessel of fire and smoke, going up the river without sails or paddles."

After two days we came back to Goumbi, and I said to the people, " I bring your old chief back to you." A feast was given us by Quengueza, and we steamed once more down the river. Then I ordered everything to be got ready, for I was soon to set out upon my long journey.

CHAPTER IX.

Down the River in a Canoe—A Strange Passenger—Talk with a Gorilla—Landing through the Breakers—Preparing to Cross the Continent—The Departure.

ON the 18th of August, 1864, I sent back the vessel to England to the Messrs. Baring, and early that morning we left my settlement and sailed down the river in my largest canoe. We had a strange lot of passengers with us. The most remarkable of them was Master Tom Gorilla; not far from him, at the bottom of the canoe, alive and kicking, was a yellow wild boar, which I had raised from a little bit of a fellow; and near the boar were two splendid fishing eagles. Another canoe contained the skins and skeletons of several gorillas, the skins of chimpanzees and other animals, besides a great many insects, butterflies, and shells.

Tom had managed to get on top of the little house I had made for him, and there he sat screaming. It was a good thing that the chain around his neck kept him at a safe distance from us. This morning, as we came down the river, he was fiercer than I had ever before seen him. Tom was much stronger than Fighting Joe, with whom you became acquainted in one of my preceding volumes, and consequently a more formidable fellow to deal with. Happily, he could not come down upon us and bite any of us. I could not help laughing when I saw him so angry. He could not understand why he had been disturbed; he did not like the looks of things around him, and his fierce and treacherous eyes did not bode us any good.

I said to him, "Tom, you are going to the white man's country; I wish you health. You are an ugly little rascal; all my kindness to you has not made you grateful. The day that I am to bid you good-bye sees you as intractable as ever. You always snatch from my hands the food I give you, and then bolt with it to the farthest corner of your abode, or as far as the length of your chain will allow. I have to be very careful with you, for fear of your biting me. Tom, you have a very bad temper. When you are angry you beat the ground with your hands and feet, just like a big, grown-up gorilla. I suppose, if you were a full-grown gorilla, you would beat your chest. Tom," said I, " many times you have woke me in the night by your sudden screams; often you have tried to take your own life—I suppose it was because you could not bear captivity. I have rescued you several times from death in your attempts to strangle yourself with your chain, through rage at being kept a prisoner. Oh, Tom, how often you have twisted that chain around and around the post to which you were attached, until it became quite short, and then pressed with your feet the lower part of the post, till you almost succeeded in committing suicide by strangulation, and would have succeeded if I had not come to your rescue. Tom, I have been patient with you; I have taken care of you, and you have my best wishes for a prosperous voyage, and I hope you will reach the white man's country in safety."

The moment I paused in this address Tom would answer me with a growl.

"Tom, I have laid in a great deal of food for you on shipboard: there are two hundred bunches of bananas and plantains, a great many pine-apples, a lot of sugar-cane, and many barrels of berries and nuts; so you will have plenty of food. But, Tom, you must try to eat the white man's food, for the bananas and the berries will not last all the voyage. Thus far I have not been able to cook you any of the white man's food, though I have nearly starved you, and kept you for days with hardly any food at all."

Another growl greeted this talk, as if to say, " I know what you say to me."

"The captain will take you, Tom." Then I looked at Captain Berridge.

"Yes," said he; "Tom, all I ask of you is to keep well, and to reach safely the country of the white men, so they may see how a young gorilla looks."

By the time I had ended this queer conversation with Tom we had reached our place of landing, and on the sea-shore several canoes were waiting for us. The breakers were high; several canoes had been upset, and their contents lost.

When I saw the state of the breakers, I concluded not to ship my photographs, and I tried to prevail on the captain not to go on board that day; "but," said he, "I have my life-preserver with me, and I will run the risk."

The large surf-canoe was got ready; Tom was put on board with his house, and the first thing he did was to get on top of it, where for a moment he yelled in affright at the foaming billows around him, and then hid himself in his house. The men had to be on the alert, and in the twinkling of an eye two stout fellows took Captain Berridge in their arms and put him in the canoe. They started off at once, passing the first breaker without accident; but the second, a huge one, broke over the canoe, filling it with water, and very nearly upsetting it. The wave went right over Master Tom, who gave a most terrific howl, and the bath, instead of cooling his rage, made him more violent than ever. The yellow wild boar gave several piercing screams, and the poor eagles were almost drowned, for the live-stock were all together.

I could not restrain my laughter at the rage of Tom; he did not seem at all to like the taste of salt water. When the canoe returned, for upon this attempt it was found impossible to pass the breakers, he jumped on the top of his house, shaking himself, and looking fiercely all around. No one dared to approach him after the canoe had landed, though really I could not help laughing to see poor Tom in such a plight—it was so unlike the woods where he had lived. I gave him a fine ripe banana, which he ate voraciously, and he became more quiet afterward.

In the afternoon, just at low tide, before the sea began to rise again, the captain, Tom, the wild pig, and the eagles went safely through the breakers.

I did not go on board. I took a bill of lading for Tom, and gave a draft for one hundred pounds sterling to the captain, to be paid to him by Messrs. Baring Brothers on the receipt of a live gorilla.

Would you like to hear the end of the story of Tom, which I heard on my return?

After three weeks all the bananas, plantains, berries, and nuts which he had not consumed were spoiled, and there was nothing left to give Tom but white man's food, though, as long as he could get his native aliment, the captain had tried in vain to make him eat of it. But when the fruits had been exhausted Captain Berridge called the cook, whereupon pies and puddings were made, and rice was boiled, plain and with molasses, but all these dainties Tom rejected. Crackers were offered him with no better result. Tom refused all kinds of food for three days, and the fourth day he died of starvation, and to the day of his death he was as ugly as the day he was captured.

A few days after the departure of the vessel, all the Commi chiefs met at my request, for I was ready to leave the country, and we held a grand palaver.

"I am your friend," said I to them; "I know that you love me. The vessel has gone, and now I am ready to go to the other side of your island" (I tried to make them understand that Africa was almost an island). "The journey will be a long one. I may have to go through a hundred tribes; there may be war; I may encounter hunger and starvation. We shall sail and paddle over many rivers; I shall cross over many mountains, and see many valleys and prairies. I am going toward the spot where the sun rises."

"Oh! oh! oh!" shouted the chiefs.

"Yes," said I, "I have told you the truth; and now I want some of your people to go with me. At the end of the long journey they will find all that they most desire— all the coats, all the hats, all the shirts, all the beads, all the guns, all the powder they want, and then a vessel will bring them back to you. It will be a rough journey, and perhaps some of those who go with me will never return again to you. But so it is with you when you go trading; one after another dies on the road, but it is not long before you go trading again. I want no man to come with me by force—sent by his chief or father; I want free men, with strong and brave hearts, who have heard all that I have said, so that when we are pinched for food there may be no grumbling. I do not go to make war, for war would stop our progress."

"What a talker our white man is!" they shouted. "Yes," said all the Commi chiefs at once, "we will not forbid any one to go with you. You have talked to us right; you have told us no lies. If a man comes back, he will come back rich."

Great excitement prevailed among the Commi for several days after my speech. Many young men wanted to follow me, but their families objected. In the meantime I was busy packing up my large outfit.

"I will be satisfied," said I to myself, "if I can get 25 Commi men to accompany me." But many had been frightened at my speech. Nevertheless, a few days after what I have related to you, there might have been seen several canoes on the river bank just opposite my settlement. Among them were two very large war-canoes, the largest in the country, which sat deep into the water, laden with the bulky equipment which was to be used by me in crossing the immense wilderness of Equatorial Africa. We were all ready to leave the country.

Many of the Commi people were to accompany me as far as Goumbi, while the men who were to follow me were but few; but we were great friends. My companions for the great expedition were 10 altogether.

There was Igala, whom I considered my righthand man, a warrior of great repute, one of the most famous hunters of the country. He was a negro of tall figure and noble bearing, cool and clear-headed in face of danger, fierce as a lion, but with me docile and submissive. Igala was to be my leader; he was to be foremost in the fight, if fighting had to be done. He or I were to lead the van into the jungle, and he was to keep a sharp lookout and see that the porters did not run away with their loads. With 20 such men as Igala I would have been afraid of nothing in Africa. Igala had a great reputation as a fetich-man, and his war and hunting fetiches especially were thought by the people to be very potent.

Next to Igala came Rebouka, a big, strapping negro, whose chief fault was that he always bragged about the amount he could eat; and he had really sometimes too good an appetite, for the fellow could eat an enormous quantity of food. But Rebouka had many good qualities, one of which was that he was a good fighting man, a very important one for me.

Igalo, bearing almost the same name with the fierce Igala, was a tall young man, full of spirit and dash, impetuous, excitable, and I had always my eye upon him for fear that he would get us into trouble. He could fight well too.

My good boy Macondai, a fellow I had almost brought up, the only sea-shore boy whom Quengueza had allowed to be with me in the country of the Bakalai in former times, was also of my party.

Then came Mouitchi, a powerful negro, not a Commi, but a slave, who had come in to the Commi country when a mere boy. Mouitchi had been a slave of Djombouai, Ranpano's nephew, but his freedom had been given him, and now he wanted to be five years on the road, and to see the white man's country. Mouitchi was very black, not very tall, a short-necked fellow, and was the very type of the negro, with thick lips, and a big nose almost as flat as that of a gorilla.

Another of my fellows was Rapelina, a short, stout negro, young, but strong as an ox. One of the chief faults of Rapelina was that he was sulky and obstinate, but I could always get along with him. He was a slave of Sholomba, another nephew of Ranpano, who did not want to be behindhand in manifesting an interest in my expedition, and, as Rapelina wished to accompany me, Sholomba gave him his freedom.

F

Retonda, Ngoma, Igala-Yengo, boys, were three other slaves that wanted to go to the white man's country, and so their freedom was also given them. Ngoma and Macondai were to be my servants; Ngoma was to be my cook, and Macondai was to wait upon me while eating.

Igala, Rebouka, Igalo, and Macondai belonged to the best blood of the country; they were descended from men who had been great in their tribe, but, as I said to them before we started, "Boys, there are to be no distinctions among you; we all have stout hearts, and the white men will thank us all alike if we succeed in our journey." I made Igala chief over them, and his orders were to be implicitly obeyed.

You have now a pretty good idea of the men and boys who were to follow me into that great equatorial jungle, and share my perils in countries so wild that we had not the slightest idea what we should meet with either in the people or in the wild beasts.

I had a nice outfit for each one of my boys (for so I called them). Each one of them had three thick blue woollen shirts, of the best quality that I could find, and, with care, these would last the whole of the journey.

They had, besides, each two pairs of thick canvas trousers, which they were to wear sometimes on the line of march, to protect them against the stings of insects, from thorns, and many other injuries; but ordinarily the trousers were to be worn only when making their appearance in the villages. At such times the boys were also to wear red worsted caps.

So they were not to look like the olomeiga (bushmen), as they called the interior people, whom they despised most thoroughly, being, they said, the class from which the slaves came.

Every man had a good thick blanket to keep him warm at night, and to protect him from the mosquitoes. I had given to each man a fine gun; besides, they had each a pair of pistols, a bag to contain their ammunition, and a huge hunting-knife.

For weeks before our departure I had drilled my men in the use of their guns, or in practising target-shooting, so that they might be splendid shots from the start; and in this, of course, a great deal of ammunition was wasted.

As the hour for our departure approached, the banks of the river were crowded with people. It was on the 2nd of October, 1864. That unfortunate shipwreck had caused me a great loss of time, but at last we were ready, and the people had come to see us off and say good-bye. Many a sad heart was on that shore; many a mother and sister thought it was the last time they should see the men and boys that were going with me. I felt the great responsibility I had assumed in taking away my men from their people.

Everything was ready, good-bye had been said a hundred times, the men had been in the canoes and had gone ashore again, when I said, "Boys, let us break off. I know it is hard to leave home. Don't you think it was hard for me to leave the white man's country?"

Igala, my right-hand man, my warrior, my hunter—Igala, with the heart of a lion, was the only one left ashore. He could not tear himself away from his little daughter, whom he tenderly loved, and who clung closely to her father, the tears streaming from her eyes, and begging him not to go with the white man on the okili mpolo (long road), for he would never come back. It was a great trial for Igala. I could see by the working of his face that his pangs at parting were severe. "Do not cry, ouana amée (my child); I am coming back; we shall reach the other side. I am going with Chally; I will bring plenty of beads from the white man's country." Then, by a sudden effort, he left her and jumped into my canoe; I gave the order for departure, and in the midst of tremendous shouting and firing of guns we got in motion. I hoisted the Stars and Stripes at the stern of my big canoe, and turned my head towards the mouth of the river as if to catch a glimpse of the sea once more.

As I looked at my men in that canoe my heart melted with love for them. What a strong faith they must have had in me! They had left father, mother, wife, sister to follow me. I swore to myself that their confidence in me should not be misplaced; henceforth they were to be brothers to me.

That night, as we stood by the fire in our camping-ground, I said, " Boys, you have left fathers, mothers, brothers, sisters, wives, your children, for me, because you would not permit me to go alone from tribe to tribe; for you said, ' If you get sick, who shall take care of you? if you are hungry, who shall get food for you? We will follow you to the end of the journey to the other side of the island, for we know that if you reach the white man you will bring us back to our country; we know that, even if one white man should be willing to give 10 ship-loads of goods for one of us, you would not sell us.' Boys, you have always heeded what I said to you; we are friends. When you come back and walk in your villages, the people will say, ' Here are the men with strong hearts; they went with Chally, and have seen what neither black men nor white men had ever seen before.' "

Where we had stopped for the night lived a celebrated doctor who the people believed could foretell events. His name was Oune-jiou-e-maré (head of a bullock); he was about seventy years of age, and a kind-hearted old man. As he enjoyed the reputation of being a great prophet, my people asked him whether our journey would be prosperous. He replied that we should go very far, and that a big chief would ask Chally to marry his daughter, and then, if Chally married her, and gave her all she asked, and made her heart glad, she would lead us from tribe to tribe until we reached the far-off sea where we wished to go.

" Chally, you must marry that girl," they all shouted; " yes, you must."

The next day Ranpano left us, but not before I granted a strange request of his. He wanted me to take off the garment I wore next to my skin; " not," said he, " that I want it to wear, but I will keep it, and then you will be sure to come back."

CHAPTER X.

AFTER a few days we reached the kingdom of Quengueza, and I received a royal welcome from the sturdy old chief, for he loved me more than anybody else. That evening we remained together all alone, and talked about my long journey. He said to me, " Chally, everybody is afraid ; none of my free men want to follow you. They think they will never come back ; but one of my slaves says he will go with you, and you can depend upon him.

" To make sure of your success," said the old king, " I want you to go where you like. I am an old man, but I am strong, and, though more than forty dry and forty rainy seasons have passed since I have been to the Ashira country, I will go there with you. I will put you myself in the hands of my friend Olenda, the Ashira king, and tell him to send you on."

Thirteen days after my arrival at Goumbi the beating of the kendo (the royal standard alarum) awoke me just before sunrise, and I heard the voice of the old chief invoking, in a loud tone, the spirits of his famous royal ancestors to protect us on our journey. The spirits he invoked were those of men who had been famous in war or as rulers, and their names had been handed down from generation to generation. Igoumbai, Wombi, Rebouka, Ngouva, Ricati, Olenga-Yombi—the skulls of all these great men were kept in the alumbi house of the king.

Quengueza was prouder than any chief I knew of the

powers of his deceased ancestors, and well might he be, for several had been great warriors, and some had been wise rulers.

At 10 o'clock on the 28th of October we left Goumbi, followed by a large array of canoes. We had had some trouble before the start, for Quengueza's slaves were alarmed, and many had hid in the woods. They were afraid that their master would give them to me, and they did not desire to go off into the far country.

"Good-bye" shouted the villagers on the shore; "good-bye, Chally; come back to us. Take care of our king; we do not like him to go so far away with you, for he is old; but he loves you, and will accompany you part of the way." And just as we disappeared from sight a wild shout rang through the air. It was the last farewell to me of the Goumbi people.

That evening we reached the junction of the Niembai and Ovenga Rivers, and resolved to pass the night on the shore. The rivers were low, for the dry season had been unprecedented in its length—indeed, the longest that the people could remember. In that country the rainy season comes from inland, and gradually makes its way to the sea-shore, while the dry season begins at the sea-shore, and gradually makes its way inland.

That evening our camp was a merry one, for the men who went out caught a great many fish (mullets and condos). The number was prodigious, for at that season of the year these fish ascend the river as the shad do in spring in America. The smoke of many a camp-fire ascended among the trees, and jokes, and laughter, and story-telling were carried far into the night. A negro is never happier than when he has nothing to do and plenty to eat.

My couch, made of leaves, was by the side of Quengueza's, and my brave companions were all around us.

Some funny stories were told that night, and one of them I wrote down. The long dry season was the subject of conversation. A man belonging to Goumbi got up. Nchanga means the wet, Enomo the dry season.

These two seasons are personified with the African. So the story went:—

Nchanga and Enomo had a great dispute as to which was the oldest, that is to say, which was the first to begin, and finally an assembly of the people of the air met to decide the question. Nchanga said, "When I come to a place, rain comes." Enomo retorted, "When I make my appearance, the rain goes." "Verily, verily," said the people of the air, who had listened to Enomo and Nchanga, "you must be of the same age."

These long dry seasons have a special name, and are called *enomo onguéro;* they last about five months. The showers coming at the close are very light, and produce no impression on the rivers.

Next morning we ascended the Ovenga, which was very low, being about 20 feet below the high-water mark. The narrow stream was encumbered with fallen trees and sand-banks, and the journey was difficult and slow.

We were getting among the Bakalai villages which lined the river banks from place to place, when suddenly we came to a spot where the river had been fenced or obstructed right across on accounted of some petty trade quarrel which the people of the village opposite had had with some other village higher up.

As soon as King Quengueza saw this his countenance changed, and wore the fiercest expression, and for the first time I could see that the terrible accounts I had heard of his warlike disposition when younger were true. The face of the man fairly changed its colour. He, the King of the Rembo, travelling with his ntangani (white man), saw that his river had been barred.

He got up and shouted, "Where are the axes and the cutlasses? where are the spears and the guns?" and he took up a gun himself, and fired into the air.

The fence was demolished in a few seconds, and onward we went. Our canoe took the lead, and just as we turned a bend in the river I saw five elephants crossing it, and before I had time to get a shot at them the huge creatures reached the bank and plunged into the forest, demolishing all the young trees which stood in the way of their flight.

Finally we reached the junction of the Ovenga River
and of the Ofoubou, and set up our camp there. Quengueza immediately despatched messengers to the Ashira
king, asking him to send us men. Our camp was close
by the village of friend Obindji, with whom you are
already acquainted, who came to see us every day.

You remember the description I gave you of Obindji,
and the fierce witchcraft-palaver that took place at his
cabin, Pende, his brother, having been accused of stealing
dead men's bones, &c.

I had brought with me a nice present for Obindji,
besides what I had sent him by Quengueza on my arrival.
The good old Bakalai chief was delighted.

We remained for several days at our encampment here,
till at last the Ashira people, sent by their King Olenda,
arrived.

The water was now so low that from the northern
bank of the Ovenga, on which our camp was placed,
there stretched a long point of beautiful sand, upon
which turtles would come during the night and lay their
eggs.

We soon found that the large number of men Olenda
had sent were not sufficient for repacking our baggage,
and I remained behind with Quengueza.

Three nephews of Quengueza—Adouma, Ouendogo,
and Quabi—went with the Ashira men, taking with them
all that the men could carry. When I saw that I had
really too much luggage, I gave to Quengueza nearly all
the salt I had, a great many brass rings, an additional
supply of powder, &c.

After a few days the Ashiras returned, and we concluded to take our departure the next morning.

Quengueza, besides being an illustrious warrior, was a
man who had a great deal of common sense, and after
everything was packed and ready, he ordered my men
to come to him. The old chief's countenance wore a
grave aspect, and after looking in the fire for some time,
smoking all the while as hard as he could, he said, "You
are going into the bush; you will see there no one of
your tribe; look up to Chally as your chief, and obey

him. Now listen to what I say. You will visit many
strange tribes. If you see on the road, or in the street
of a village, a fine bunch of plantains, with ground-nuts
lying by its side, do not touch them; leave the village at
once; this is a tricky village, for the people are on the
watch to see what you are going to do with them.

"If the people of a village tell you to go and catch
fowls or goats, or cut plantains for yourselves, say to
them, 'Strangers do not help themselves; it is the duty
of a host to catch the goat or fowl, and cut the plantains,
and bring the present to the house which has been given
to the strangers.' When a house is given to you in any
village, keep to that house, and go into no other; and if
you see a seat, do not sit upon it, for you know there are
seats upon which nobody but the owners are permitted
to sit.

"But, above all, beware of women; do not get in love
with any of them, for you will be strangers in a strange
land. I tell you these things that you may journey in
safety; I want you to have a smooth journey, and get
into no trouble. I need not tell you to take care of
Chally."

The speech of the old sage was listened to with great
attention, and Igala said, "*Rera* (father, king), we will
follow your advice, for we know that when salt or food is
left on the roadside it is to catch people; we know that
you must not go into other people's houses, for in some
no one but the owner can go; and as for sitting on somebody else's seat, we know better. We don't want to be
made slaves. Rera (father), we will remember what you
have said to us."

CHAPTER XI.

Bustle in the Camp—A Magic Horn—Quengueza's Idol—A Living Skeleton—Terrific Thunder-storm—A Gorilla Family—Stupendous Cataract.

THE next morning after this fine speech of Quengueza all was bustle in the camp, and everything was now ready. Quengueza stood by my side, wearing a coat, and having a green cloth around his loins; from his shoulder hung his bag, in which there was a large supply of tobacco and his kendo; close by him stood a slave and one of his nephews, carrying his gun and the sword I had given him. Adouma, Ouendogo, and Quabi were also near at hand.

I was in walking trim, with leggings on, carrying by my side a superb pair of revolvers. I bore also a double-barrelled rifle, and in my bag were 100 cartridges for my revolvers, and 150 bullets for my gun. Every man of my company was armed to the teeth, and they seemed greatly to enjoy looking formidable.

A gun is fired, the echo of which reverberates from mountain to mountain, and then more guns are fired by the Bakalai, who know that King Quengueza and his friend Chally are now on their journey.

We paddled up the Ofoubou for a little while, when we went ashore, and pursued our journey overland. That night we slept at the Bakalai village of Ndjali-Coudie.

The next morning we continued our journey, my dear friend Quengueza and I sticking close together. We had left Ndjali-Coudie a little before six o'clock, just at daybreak, and after a little more than two hours we reached the top of a steep hill (369 feet in height), called by the people Nomba-Rigoubou, where we stopped for breakfast. Immediately after breakfast we marched onward, and as toward four o'clock poor Quengueza appeared tired, I thought it best to stop for the night at the base of a hill called Ecourou. Here there were the remains of an Ashira encampment, which was nothing but an old shed, loosely covered with pieces of bark, in many places of which I could see through. I had not much faith in its excellence for shelter, and wanted to send the men to collect leaves, but they were so tired that I let them rest. It did not rain every evening, and perhaps it would not rain that evening; besides, we had an Ashira doctor with us, who blew his magic horn to drive the rain away.

Quengueza was an excellent companion on the march; full of pride, he would never complain of being tired, and disliked above all things to appear old. He was, indeed, an odd sort of person, and the eccentricities of his character were endless. Of course he never travelled without his idol, which was an ugly, pot-bellied image of wood, four or five inches in height, with a row of four cowries imbedded in its abdomen, and was generally carried, when travelling, in one of his coat pockets or in his bag. Walking or sleeping, the idol was never suffered to be away from him. Whenever he ate or drank, he would take the wooden image and gravely pass his tongue and lips over its abdomen, and before drinking any of the native beer he would always take it out of his pocket or bag, lay it on the ground, and pour a libation over its feet. Poor Quengueza! I used to talk enough to him about his superstitions; I tried to shake his blind faith in them, and to teach him to adore the true God and Creator. That evening he held a long parley with the idol.

The next morning old Quengueza appeared to feel stiff as he got up, but he took care not to tell it to anybody, and immediately we started. That day we reached the Ashira Land, which was the country to which Quengueza purposed to escort me himself on my way to the interior. It is a mark of great friendship here to accompany a man part of his journey, and Quengueza, though a man beyond threescore and ten, went with me over rough mountains, through rushing streams, and along thorny, bad roads, to show me how much he loved me.

As we emerged from the forest into the prairies of Ashira Land, the magnificent mountains of Igoumbi-Andelè and Ofoubou-Orèrè burst upon our view in the south, while in the north the lofty ridge of Nkoumou-Nabouali stood out in majestic grandeur against the sky.

Old King Olenda received us with great demonstrations of joy; he came to meet us beating his kendo, and seemed delighted to meet me again. How glad he was to see Quengueza! They had not seen each other for forty dry seasons and forty rainy seasons (forty years).

I have given you before in two of my works a description of old Olenda, the oldest man I ever saw. He was much the same now as when I last saw him: his cheeks sunken, his legs and arms thin and bony, and covered with wrinkled skin. He appeared, in fact, a living skeleton, yet retained his sight and hearing unimpaired.

After we had come to the ouandja (Palaver House), Quengueza said, "I have come to see you again, Olenda; I have come to see you, to bring you with my own hands my friend Chally, the spirit, and I want you to provide him with an escort to conduct him on to the next tribe."

Olenda promised everything. The Ashira came to us in great crowds, for they wanted not only to greet me, but to see the great Quengueza.

The next day presents of slaves were brought to Quengueza. I begged the old chief not to take them; but the trouble was that, according to the customs of the country it would be an insult for him to refuse them, for he was the guest. Nevertheless, I took the responsibility, and I said I did not desire Quengueza to take away any slaves from the country. Immense quantities of supplies were brought to us—goats, plantains, fowls, pea-nuts, sugar-cane, wild pine-apples, berries, and fruits of all sorts. After a few days I held a palaver, and said, "I must see the great waterfall of Samba-Nagoshi."

We started in light marching order, the only heavy baggage being my photographic apparatus, for I wanted to take accurate views of the splendid scenery which I expected to behold. I took only four of my faithful Commi boys — Rebouka, Igala, Macondai and Ngoma. The rest of my followers were Ashiras, among them were three of Olenda's grand-nephews—Arangui, Oyagui, and Ayagui.

We pursued a north-east direction till we struck the Ovigui River, crossing it on an immense tree which had been felled for the purpose, and which had lodged about 15 feet from the water. Then we took a path which was to lead us to the country of the Kambas. The forest was exceedingly dense. The first evening we had a fearful thunder storm, the rainy season had begun in these mountains. The thunder was terrific, and the flashes of lightning vividly illuminated the thick woods by which we were surrounded. The next morning we resumed our march along the western foot of a hilly range, and not a sound was heard as we trudged steadily along in Indian file. On the way we passed through a little bit of prairie, the name of which was Opangano, and before noon we came to a village of Bakalai. The village was fenced, that is to say, each side of the street was barred with long poles. The street was very narrow, and none of the houses had outside doors.

The Ashiras were afraid to go into the villages. They said that after the people were in sometimes the gates were shut, and then strangers were killed or plundered. A great panic seized the Bakalai as I entered the village, but their fears were somewhat allayed when they recognised Arangui. We remained but a little while, and continued our march northward, passing near several villages of the warlike Bakalai, two of which were entirely abandoned, and before sunset we reached a little prairie called the Lambengue. We had had a hard day's work; it had been raining all the afternoon, and we had been compelled to travel through the mire and over miles of slippery stones, so we built sheds, covering them with large leaves, and surrounded ourselves with roaring big fires to keep away the snakes and wild beasts.

The night's rest did little to refresh us, and the next

morning we still felt weary. For myself, I was quite unwell, and found my gun too heavy to carry. The feet of my men were sore on account of the pebbles with which the path was filled the day before. So I took the lead to cheer them up, and we were soon lost again in that great jungle. Oh, how wild it was! how desolate! how solitary! There was not an elephant to be seen, nor did the chatter of a monkey break the silence of the forest. I was ahead of the party trying to descry the future, when suddenly I was startled by a loud noise of the breaking of branches of trees. It was a family of gorillas. They had seen me, and began to hurry down the trees which they had ascended to pick the berries. How queer their black faces looked as they peeped through the leaves to see what was the matter! As they came hastily down the branches would bend with their weight. They were of different sizes. "It must be a family of gorillas," said I to myself. All at once I saw a huge black face looking through the foliage. There was no mistake—it was a huge male gorilla. He had caught sight of me, and I could distinctly see his hideous features, his ferocious eyes and projecting eyebrows. I was on the point of running away as fast as I could toward my men, when I heard their voices; they were coming up to the rescue. The shaggy monster raised a cry of alarm, scrambled to the ground, and disappeared in the jungle, going no doubt where his mate or family had gone before him.

A few days after meeting the gorillas I was seated on the banks of the river Rembo-Ngouyai, looking at a very grand and impressive scene. It was, indeed, a magnificent freak of nature. The great body of water rushed through a narrow gorge with headlong fury, and the whole stream was white with foam. To reach this spot we had gone through dense forests, having been led thither only by the roar of the rushing waters. We had passed two tribes before gaining the fall—the Kambas and the Aviia. The latter were our guides, and they said that the Fougamou, the real fall, was above; so we ascended the steep banks of the river for about a quarter of an hour, when we came upon the object of our search.

A Queer-looking Family.

The river here was about 150 yards wide. In the middle of it was an island, dividing the fall into two parts, and I could only see the half of the fall on our side. Between the island and the mainland, where I stood, the distance was not more than 70 or 80 yards. The fall was hardly greater than 15 feet, and that was broken in the centre by two huge granite boulders, which the water had not succeeded in wearing away or detaching from the bed of rock over which the river there descended. The water seemed to rush in an enormous volume down a steep incline. The cataract itself I thought was not imposing, but below it was one of the grandest sights I ever saw. A torrent of fearful velocity and great volume leaped madly along in huge billows, as though the whole river had dropped into a chasm, and bounded out again over ridges of rocks. The scene was rendered more magnificent by the luxuriant tropical foliage of the banks. Nothing could be heard but the noise of the cataract. The sky was cloudy, a fine rain was falling, and that day I could not take a photograph of the grand scene. I wanted to sleep that night near the fall, but my Aviia guides were frightened, and said that the great spirit Fougamou would come during the night and roar with such fury in our ears that we could not survive it; besides which, no one had ever slept there.

I gave you, in my Apingi Kingdom, the legend concerning the Samba-Nagoshi Falls just as I heard it from the Apingi, and the Aviia repeated it to me. I found that the Apingi had added nothing to it at all.

I had at last seen the famous Samba-Nagoshi Falls at the base of the towering Nkoumou-Nabouali Mountains. I was satisfied, and a few days after I was on my way back to Olenda's village.

CHAPTER XII.

The Death of Remandji—A Singular Superstition—Outbreak of the Plague—A Touching Incident—Dying off by Scores—Death of Olenda.

WHILE on my way from the Falls of Samba-Nagoshi to Olenda a secret deputation had been sent to him from the Apingi country, where, as you are aware, I had been made king, and where the people were so superstitious about me. The King of Apingi had sent word that Olenda must endeavour to dissuade me from going into Apingi Land

It appears that, after I had left the Apingi country, the people could not comprehend what had become of me. They would come to Remandji and ask him if he knew where I was. They declared that he had hid me in the forest for himself; that he was jealous, and did not want his people to see me. They came and asked for presents, but poor Remandji told them that the Spirit had not left him many things, and that really he did not know where I had gone; that they had seen me disappear in the forest, and had heard me say good-bye to the people just as he had.

A few days after my departure Remandji was found dead in his little hut, on his bed. A cry of anguish rose from one end of the village to the other when the news of Remandji's death spread; the people felt sorry, for they loved him. There was mourning and lamentation in the Apingi tribe.

A party among the people rose and exclaimed that some of the neighbouring people had killed their chief by aniemba (witchcraft), because they were jealous of him—jealous that he was my great friend—jealous that he possessed me.

Another party, and a very powerful one, having on its side the great doctors of the tribe, who had been consulted about Remandji's death, declared that the Spirit himself, meaning me, had killed Remandji, for I loved him so much I could not part with him, and I wanted to take his spirit with me wherever I went.

A few days after Remandji's death his son Okabi died also. Fear seized upon the Apingi people. "Surely," said they, "the Spirit has killed Okabi and Remandji," and many were oppressed with a presentiment of death, for many had been my friends, and from that day they believed that when I left a country I killed my friends in order not to part from them. The present chief of the Apingi Land, having heard of my arrival, sent a deputation to Olenda with the words "I do not want to see the Spirit. I do not want to follow him, as Remandji and his son have done, but rather prefer to stop at home and eat plantain. This present world is good enough for me."

The Apingi messengers were afraid of me, and had gone back to their own country without waiting for my appearance. So, after the departure of the Apingi messengers, a great council of all the Ashira chiefs was held to decide by which route I should be sent into the far country.

It was determined at last that I should go through the Otando country, and that messengers should be sent at once to the king of that far-off land, telling him that Olenda was to send me to him. Quengueza then made his preparations to return to Goumbi.

I sent my men out hunting every day to drill them and accustom them to fire-arms. I made them practise shooting every day, so that they might become better marksmen. I do not speak of Igala, who was what might have been called a dead shot.

A few days after what I have just related to you, a man called Elanga, a grand-nephew of Olenda, was taken ill with a disease which the natives had never seen.

G

Elanga lived a long distance from our village, but his people came to me to see what I could do for him. The description they gave me was that of the small-pox. I promised to go and see him the next day, but that day the news came that Elanga had died. There was a great deal of mourning and wailing among the people; they all went to Elanga's village except Olenda, my Commi men, and Quengueza's people.

Elanga had been to our camp to fetch our baggage, so immediately the people said Elanga had been bewitched. I went to see the body of Elanga; it could not have been recognised. I was not mistaken; the worst type of confluent or black small-pox had killed him. So when I saw the people around him I tried to dissuade them from touching him, and advised them to burn everything with which he had ever come in contact, even the house where he slept. Nevertheless, the mourning ceremonies took place as usual. My worst fears were realized. Soon after, two cases occurred among the mourners; then it spread like wildfire. Pestilence had come over the land. It came from the interior, and was working its way toward the sea.

The plague broke out with terrible violence all over the country. Olenda's village was attacked; Olenda's favourite wife was the first victim. Everybody who was attacked died. It was in vain that I begged them to stop their "mourning" ceremonies. Almost everybody who had attended Elanga's funeral had caught the plague and died. A cry of anguish rose over the land.

I established a quarantine camp, and forbid my men to move out of it. I was full of anxiety on account of poor Quengueza.

Half of the people of Olenda had died; half of the Ashira had gone down to their graves. Olenda is still well.

I implored Quengueza to go back to his country. "If you love me, Quengueza," I said, "go home." "No," said the old chief; "to leave you when you are in trouble! I, Quengueza, do such a thing! No, Chally; the people would laugh at me, and say 'Quengueza had no power to help Chally on his way.'"

Things had now become gloomy indeed; the storm is threatening. Rigoli, Quengueza's favourite little slave, had taken the plague, which had at last invaded our premises. Quengueza took him into his own hut. I was horror-struck at the idea, and cried, "Do you want to die, Quengueza?" His answer was beautiful. "I love Rigoli," said he; "he is the child of an old slave my brother Oganda left me. I can take better care of him here. If I get the plague it will be God's palaver." I looked at this savage king, and his noble reply made me love him more than ever. A few days afterward Rigoli was dead.

Three several times a gang of men had been sent for the transportation of my baggage to the Otando country; three times within a few days the plague had carried away the greater number of them.

I succeeded in making Quengueza send a large number of his people back to Goumbi. Then thirty Ashira men were mustered. I wanted them to go with my men to the Otando country with part of the luggage. To this my Commi men demurred. "How can we leave you here? Who, in the midst of this fearful disease, shall cook for you? Some of us must remain with you. These Ashira may poison you by putting the gall of a leopard into your food. Some of us will stay with you, come what may; if we are to die, we will die by you." Noble fellows!

So, with the thirty men which Olenda could now place at my disposition, I sent Igala, Rebouka, Mouitchi, Rapelina, Rogueri. Poor Olenda could only give me thirty men, for his people were either down with the plague or dead. Olenda promised solemnly to Quengueza that as soon as the men came back he would send them with me to the Otando.

In the meantime intelligence had been received that the plague had reached the banks of the Rembo-Ovenga, and that Bakalai and Commi were dying fast; so old Quengueza took his departure for Goumbi, but not before I took a good photograph of him.

Before he left us he said, "Chally, when you come back

with your people, bring me a big bell that rings ding, dang, dong, a silver sword that will never rust, a brass chest and plenty of fine things."

I accompanied Quengueza part of the way over the prairie. How sad I felt! for if I ever loved a friend I loved friend Quengueza, and just before we were to turn our backs upon each other there was a pause. "Chally, go back to Olenda," said Quengueza to me. Then he took my two hands in his own, blew upon them, and invoked the spirits of his ancestors to follow me as they had followed him. We looked in each other's face once more for an instant, and parted, he going toward the sea, and I toward the interior. I stood still as the old man moved away; he turned several times to get a glimpse of me, but soon disappeared in the tall grass of the prairie. He had but few of his people with him, for the plague had come heavily on Goumbi, and many had died of it.

Quengueza had hardly left the country when the plague became yet more terrible; not a day passed without its hundreds of victims. A cry of anguish was all over the land; the wailings, the mournful songs were heard everywhere.

At last there were not left well people enough to fetch food, and famine succeeded to the pestilence. My poor Commi men, who went in search of food in the neighbouring villages, were driven back, threatened with death by the terrified inhabitants, who shouted, "The Spirit with whom you came has brought this *eviva* (plague) upon us. What have we done to him?"

Not one of Olenda's numerous wives was well, but the king remained my steadfast friend. He said to his sick people that he remembered that when he was a boy the same thing had come over the land. How glad I was to have Olenda on my side!

A few days after the departure of Quengueza, if you had been in my little hut, you would have seen me seated on the side of my bed, my head resting on my hands, in utter loneliness and desolation of heart.

My boy Retonda had died and been buried that day.

How could I feel otherwise than unhappy when a whole country was cursing me, and the people were more afraid of me than of the plague itself?

In my own little hut Ngoma was lying near unto death; the crisis had come to him; his pulse was low. Was he to die also?

After a while I approached Ngoma, and said, "Ngoma, my boy, how do you feel?" He could hardly speak; the disease had gone also into his throat; he could not see—he was blind; mortification had set in, and the smell emanating from him was dreadful, and yet there I had to sleep.

In the next hut to mine lay Igala-Yengo; he too was taken with the plague. Poor Igala-Yengo was one of Quengueza's slaves, and had said to his master that he would go with me.

Those were indeed dark days for me. One morning, as I went to ask old Olenda how he was, he said, "My head pains me, and I am so thirsty." That day he laid him down on his bed never to get up again. For two days the fever increased, and part of the time I was by his bedside. The good chief, seeing my sorrowful countenance, would say, "Chally, do not grieve. It is not your fault if I am sick. You have not made me ill."

Oh, these words sounded sweetly to me. I left him toward nine o'clock in the evening to go to my hut to get a little rest, and found poor Ngoma a little better. I did not want Macondai to sleep in my hut; he was the only one besides myself that had not been seized by the plague.

As I lay wide awake on my couch, suddenly I heard a cry of anguish, a shriek from house to house. A shudder came over me. Olenda was dead—Olenda, my only friend, was dead.

As soon as that shriek was heard, Macondai, in despite of my former orders, rushed into my hut and said, "Chally, are your guns loaded? are your revolvers ready? for I do not know what the Ashira may do, since the great Olenda is dead."

I confess that I partook of Macondai's apprehensions, but I said to him, "Be of good cheer, my boy; there but one God, and he will battle for us.   Men can only kill the body."

This was a terrible blow for me, the consequences of which I could not foresee. Olenda, before dying, ordered his people to take care of me, and in a short time passed away as peacefully as if he had gone to sleep.

CHAPTER XIII.

Burial of Olenda—A Desolated Valley—Suspicions Aroused—Robbery—Paul in Perplexing Circumstances—Freeing a Man from the Stocks—Ravages of the Plague.

THE day of Olenda's burial had come, but there were hardly people enough left to bury him—such had been the devastations of the plague. Not far from the village stood in the prairie a little grove of trees, beneath whose shade the chiefs of the Ademba clan, to which Olenda belonged, were always buried; but it had been long since an interment had taken place there, for Olenda had outlived his brothers a score of years. All the people who could came to the funeral of their chief.

Olenda looked as if he were asleep. They had dressed him in the big coat I had given him, and came to ask me if I would give to my friend Olenda the umbrella I had. It was the only one I had, but I could not well refuse, and I said, "Take it."

They bore Olenda's body to the grove of trees with many manifestations of deep sorrow, shouting, "He will not talk of us any more; he will not speak to us any more. Oh, Olenda, why have you left us? Is it because we are all dying?" I followed the body to the grave, and I saw that they seated him on his big coat, and put over his head the umbrella I had given them for him. By his side was placed a chest containing the presents I had brought for him, and also plates, jugs, cooking utensils, his favorite pipe, and some tobacco; a fire was kindled, which was to be kept up from day to day for a long time, and food and water was brought, which was also to be daily replenished for an indefinite period.

Before dying, Olenda had told his people that he was not to leave them entirely; he would come back from time to time to see how they were getting on; so, for a few days after his death, the people would swear that they saw Olenda in the middle of the night walking in the village, and that he had repeated to them that he had not left them entirely.

The once beautiful Ashira, at the sight of which I had fallen into ecstacies, had now become the valley of death. Crazy men and women, made crazy only by the plague, wandered about till they died on the roadside. Every body was afraid of his neighbour; they had found out, at last, that the disease was contagious, and when one got it he was left to himself, and the poor creature would die of starvation; his wife, his father, his mother, his sister, his brother, if any such relatives had been left to him by the plague, would fly away from him as from the curse of God.

My Commi men did not come back; I wondered why, and began to feel very anxious about them. What had become of them? What a blunder I had made in letting these men go ahead of me! I would have given the world to see them again with me, for I did not know what those far-away people would do to them.

Strange rumours came from the Otando country: the news was that the people did not want me to come, as I carried with me the *eviva* (plague) wherever I went.

Several weeks passed away; no tidings of my men, no tidings of Arangui, or of the Ashiras who had gone with them. The plague was now diminishing in virulence for want of victims, for, except Macondai and myself, everybody had been attacked with it, and those who did not succumb had recovered or were fast recovering. In the beginning, everybody attacked was sure to die.

I began to feel suspicious, for three Otando men had come to me and told me they had important intelligence to communicate, but could not give it just then, and had promised to come back after two days. Three days had passed away, and I heard one night somebody talking in a hut; I listened outside, and was rewarded by finding out that the Ashiras had frightened away the three Otando men, who had gone back to Mayolo.

At length three of my Commi men suddenly made their appearance from Mayolo by themselves. I was thunderstruck; the Ashiras of the village were frightened. What did all this mean?

Rebouka, Mouitchi, and Rapelina were the good fellows. Though it had taken four days to come from the Otando country, they had found their way back. They were armed to the teeth, and looked like terrible warriors. Igala, tired of waiting for me, had sent them back to see what was the matter.

I now learned that the Ashiras had returned long ago, and, though weeks had passed away, I had seen none of them. I heard also that several of the loads had never reached Mayolo; that the porters had gone back to their plantations with them; that Arangui was at the bottom of all the thieving; and that Igala, with all his threats, could not make the porters sleep together near him at night. Then, to cap the whole thing, they told me that Arangui had seized one of the Otando men that had come to see me, and that this was the reason why the other two had fled.

"What is to be done?" said I to myself. "I must be crafty and cunning, and as wise as a serpent." It would never have done to get in a rage.

I told my men to keep quiet, and not to say a word about the robbery. I did not want to frighten them—I wanted more porters.

It did, indeed, require a great amount of self-control for me to keep cool when I was quite certain that all the men of the village knew that I had been plundered by their own people, and that probably most of them had been sharers of the plunder. Even Ondonga, who now was chief of the village and a cousin of Arangui, knew all about it. It is wonderful how savages can keep secrets: not a child, not a woman, not a man in the country had breathed to me the slightest word on the subject.

That night I kept revolving in my mind how I must

act to get out of the scrape. I said to myself, "I must become a hypocrite, and fight cunning with cunning, in order to win."

The next morning I said to my men, "Tell the Ashiras that you have not said a word to me about the robbery, for you were afraid that I might kill some of them if I knew it; and tell Ondonga, Mintcho, and their people that you know they are too great friends of mine and of Quengueza to have had anything to do with the plunder. Tell them that you were obliged to tell me about Arangui and the seizure of the man in order to give an excuse for your coming." I then dismissed them with saying, "Boys, mind and do just as I have told you."

To Ondonga, patting him on the shoulder, though I felt like blowing out his brains, I said, "Ondonga, I know that you are my friend; I know that the Olenda people are good people. I know that you never knew of the return of Arangui: if you had known it you would have surely told me."

Ondonga swore that it was so: he would have told me at once.

I shouted so that everybody could hear me, "Of course, Ondonga; I know that you would have told me, for you have a heart, and would not tell a lie. Why did friend Arangui do such a thing as to seize that Otando man—Arangui, whom I loved so much? The only thing Arangui can do is to give up the man. Must he not give up the man, Ashiras?" I cried.

"Yes!" exclaimed the people; "Arangui must give up the man."

I knew very well that no Ashira man would dare to go into the Otando country after having put in nchogo an Otando man, for they would all be seized, and then who should carry my baggage?

Mintcho and Ondonga said to me, "We will go at once to Arangui's plantation to see if he is there." "He must have been hiding from us," said Mintcho, with a laugh. "Hypocrite," said I to myself, "what a lying rascal you are!"

They went to Arangui's plantation, and on their return,

as soon as they saw me, they shouted, "That is so; Arangui is back. Arangui is a *noka* (rogue, liar), and none of us knew it."

"Ondonga, my friend," I whispered, "a necklace of beads shall be on your neck to-night" (and I felt very much like putting a rope around his neck and choking him). "Now tell me the palaver."

Ondonga said, "Two dry and two rainy seasons ago, the Otando people seized a relative of Arangui because Arangui owed them two slaves and had not brought the goods, and the man is still kept in nchogo (the native stocks). Arangui wanted his relative back, and by keeping that man he thought they would send back his relative."

I knew that, according to African fashion, this palaver would last several years. That would never do for me, for I must be off.

My men said that what Ondonga had said was true; they had heard so in the Otando country; so I sent Mintcho back, and said to him, "Tell friend Arangui that he must give up the man. If I had not to take care of my people I would go and see him. Tell him that he must do that for his friend Chally. Did not Arangui take Quengueza and myself from Obindji's place to come here?"

The two rascals Mintcho and Ondonga went again, and several days elapsed before Arangui let the man go. He did not do it until he was taken ill with the plague; then he became frightened, and thought I was going to kill him, so he immediately gave up the man, and Ondonga and Mintcho brought him in triumph to me. Poor fellow! his legs were dreadfully lacerated.

The plague was in its last stage. Arangui had been the only one who had not taken it before. The Otando man had not had it, and I was afraid he would catch it. If he were to die of it in the country of the Ashiras, not one of them would dare to go into that of the Otandos, and that would be the end of my trip; so it was necessary that I should hurry my departure. If it had not been for the rascality of Arangui I would have been in the Otando country two months ago. The thought of this made my blood boil, and I felt very much like hanging Arangui to the nearest tree.

It was the first time that I had been robbed in Africa, and that by Olenda's people. I knew they would not have done it if their old chief had been alive.

What a sea of trouble poor Paul du Chaillu had to contend with! Indeed, these were days of trial; but I had to face them, and I faced them manfully, though several times I was on the verge of despair.

By some means news of the death of Olenda had reached Quengueza, and I was astonished one day to receive a messenger from him with word that, as Olenda had left no people to carry me and my goods to the next country, he was coming to take me to another Ashira clan that had people. This frightened Ondonga, and he tried hard to get porters for me.

Terrible tidings now came from Goumbi: all the Goumbi people that had come with Quengueza to the Ashira country had died of the plague; nearly all the nephews of Quengueza were dead; Obindji had died, and every Bakalai chief. In some of the Bakalai villages not a human being had been left. Death had come over the land. But Quengueza had been spared; the plague had not touched him, though his head slave, good old Mombon, was no more.

CHAPTER XIV.

Departure from Ashira Land—A Silent Leave-taking—Thievish Porters—A Cunning old Rascal—Misfortune on Misfortune—Without Food in the Forest—A Desperate Plot—Feasting on Monkey-meat—Out of the Woods.

THE threat of Quengueza had the desired effect. At last Ondonga succeeded in getting porters, who, with my own men, made the number of our company about thirty. No amount of pay could induce more to come. They were afraid of trouble. They could not tell what the trouble would be, but they had a vague fear that something dreadful was impending.

Everything that we could not take with us I either gave away or destroyed.

Early in the morning of the 16th of March I left Ashira Land. How I had suffered in that poor, unfortunate land! The plague had destroyed the people, and the survivors accused me of having destroyed the victims of the plague. Then things had looked so dark that many and many a time I thought the end had come; that no more explorations were to be made, and I fully expected to be murdered by the infuriated savages.

My party of 10 Commi men had been reduced to seven. Retonda had died; Rogueri, a slave, had run away, and it was he who had advised the Ashira to rob me, and who had tried to disabuse them of my power. The plague had disabled Igala-Yengo. He was going back to Goumbi now that he was much better, and he was to take letters for me.

I felt thankful that God had spared the lives of so many of my men, for Rebouka, Mouitchi, and Rapelina took it on their return from Otando.

I was anxious about Mácondai; he was the only one who had not had the plague, as you are aware; and, leaving the Ashira country, I knew that I was going into a country where the plague had not yet disappeared.

This time there was no gun-firing as we left Olenda's village, no singing, nothing—we left silently. I had misgivings. I thought of mischief brewing ahead, and I was not mistaken.

That day we crossed the Ovenga, and followed a path which led to one of Olenda's large plantations; there I found a considerable village of Olenda's slaves, a slave himself being chief over the village. His name was Mayombo.

All the porters did not reach the place that evening. Ondonga himself had not come. The next morning he came with the news that several of the porters had run away, leaving their boxes in the path, and that he had been compelled to go back and fetch more porters.

Then I discovered that three boxes of goods were missing, and I became furious. Ondonga got frightened; I knew the rascal was at the bottom of the mischief, and once or twice I felt like making an example of him by calling a council of war, composed of my men and myself, and, upon the clear proof of his guilt, shooting him dead on the spot.

Ondonga swore that he would find the thieves; but the boxes came back, and they had been broken open, and many things were missing. Ondonga pretended to be in a violent rage, and declared in a loud voice that there should be war, and that the thieves should be sold into slavery. It was all I could do to restrain myself from breaking the fellow's head.

The acting was superb. The old chief and some of the slaves seized their spears, and shouted, "Let us go after the thieves!" They hurried out of the place shouting, cursing, and vowing death to the thieves. They were the thieves themselves; but I kept cool, and thought the day of reckoning would come.

Misfortune seemed to come upon misfortune. That

day Macondai complained of a violent back-ache. He
had the plague; this was one of the first symptoms.

What could I do? When we left the plantation the
dear good fellow tried to walk with us, but he became so
ill that we were forced to come to a stand in the woods.
No greater calamity could have befallen me. I felt as if
I could cry, for my fortitude was on the point of giving
way, and it seemed as though the hand of God was
against me.

When anything very important had taken or was
about to take place, it was always my custom to summon
my Commi men, and hold a council to see what was to
be done. So my faithful body-guard were now summoned to my side. As soon as we were seated together,
every one of us wearing an anxious look, I said, " Boys,
you will go ahead ; I will remain here and take care of
Macondai."

The men said, " No, Chally." Macondai himself said
no. " If we go without you," said the men, "they will
begin stealing again." " If you do not go," said Macondai
at once, " you will not have one porter left, for I heard
to-day some say they were afraid to follow you; they
were afraid on account of those who had robbed you;
and if you give them time to talk together, they will
agree to run away. Go now, Chally," said Macondai,
"for if you do not you will never reach Mayolo. I shall
get well."

After some consultation it was agreed that Igalo should
remain with Macondai on a small plantation near at hand,
and Ondonga said the Ashira would take care of him. I
could not bear parting with Macondai. I knew, of course,
that the Ashira would not dare to murder him, but then
he was ill.

After making every possible provision I could for the
comfort of the sick boy, and enjoining upon Igalo never
to leave him, and after weighing out medicine to be given
him at stated times, we continued our march; but I
was so wretched that I cannot describe to you my feel-
ings.

The travelling was exceedingly toilsome. The men

were overloaded, and I myself carried on my back in
my otaitai over 60lbs. of ammunition, besides having
my heavy revolvers slung by my side, and my most formidable double-barrelled breech-loader on my shoulder.
The path—for there was a path—lay through a most picturesque country, and along a mountain range, extending
north and south, which lies between the country of the
Ashira and the Otandos. The hills of this range were
very much broken up, so that we did nothing else than
make continuous ascents and descents. The forest was
dense, and impeded with numerous blocks of quartz which
lay strewn along the path nearly all the way, and quartz
crystals covered the beds of the sparkling rivulets that
flowed at the bottom of every valley.

It was very tiresome indeed, and I felt sad, very sad,
for I knew not how things would end. I kept thinking of
Macondai. I was not master of the position; they might
rob me. I could do nothing, for two of my men were left
in their hands—Igalo and Macondai.

The second day of our march we came to the river
Louvendji, which I had crossed, if you remember, in
former years going to the Apingi country; and very
beautiful the Louvendji is. The banks where we forded
the river were lined with beautiful palm-trees.

The porters began to lag behind under the pretext that
the loads were too heavy for them. For two days I had
succeeded in making all the porters keep up with me and
sleep in my bivouac; but there was not much sleep for
me or my men, for we had to keep a sharp look on the
porters, though they were not armed, lest they should have
given word to their people beforehand to hide spears and
bows and arrows somewhere in the forest near where they
knew we would camp for the night.

The third night, in despite of all my endeavours, some
of the men would not keep pace with us; so, when I
ordered the people to stop for the night, Mintcho and a
few men were missing. I knew at once that something
was wrong, and I said to the Ashira that were with me
that if I saw one of them move off I would shoot him on
the spot.

The next morning we waited for Mintcho and the men, and they made their appearance an hour after sunrise. Mintcho immediately affected to be very angry with them. " I waited for you," shouted he, " and you did not come, so I could not come and sleep by the side of my friend Chally. Where did you sleep? I blew the horn and you did not answer."

He raised some of the boxes from the ground, and cried, " Yes, these are not as heavy as they were; you have been stealing my white man's things; you are thieves." At this the culprits got frightened for fear of punishment from me, and, leaving their loads in the road, fled into the jungle.

Then came a tremendous excitement. The men openly declared that it was no use to go farther with the white man, for they would not get any pay, as some people had robbed him; that they had worked for nothing.

It was a plot; they were all in it. I saw that they wanted to leave me in the forest. Some had not dared to steal, but Mintcho was the chief thief. I forgot myself, and accused him of it. It was a mistake on my part. Mintcho appeared to be terribly angry at my accusing him. I saw the blunder at once, and I retracted and said that his people had stolen my property, and I did not see why he should not be responsible for them; that such was the law of the country. " But," said I, " Mintcho, I know that you are my friend, and that you would not do such a thing yourself." As we were talking, more porters ran away, leaving their loads on the ground.

This strange scene had taken place at a distance from any river. Things had come to a crisis; something was to be done at once, or I should be left alone in the woods. Mintcho and a few porters were the only ones left. I could not allow them to go: so, calling my Commi men, I said, pointing my gun at Mintcho, " If you make a step one way or the other, you are a dead man." In the meantime my men, pointing their guns at the Ashira, shouted, " You are dead men if you move." The fact was simply that, if Macondai and Igalo had not been left behind, there would have been bloodshed.

Apprehensions for their safety alone prevented me from resorting to very strong measures.

So I said, "Minchto and you Ashira men must take those loads and carry them to the river; then you will come back and take what remains to the same place, till every one of the packages has been carried thither. If you try to run away you will be shot;" and I ordered all my Commi men, who had now become furious, to shoot down the first man that tried to escape into the jungle. "Follow them," said I to Rebouka; "never let Mintcho move from you more than a step; shoot him dead if he goes two yards." Rebouka swore that he would shoot him dead. Mouitchi, Ngoma, and Rapelina followed the other Ashiras.

So they went, I remaining all alone to watch the goods. I had become furious, and it required all my self-command not to shoot Mintcho as a robber. I kept the sharpest look-out in every direction; my revolvers were ready, and all my double-barrelled guns were loaded and by me; but nobody came.

Rebouka, my Commi, and the Ashira came back a short time afterward. They had left the loads near a stream, and Mouitchi had remained behind watching them with six guns by his side. His orders were to fire on the first Ashira that came from the woods. Our blood was up, and we were getting desperate.

The Ashiras took each another load, and I repeated again to Rebouka and the Commi men to shoot them down as they would shoot a monkey if any should try to run away.

At last all the baggage was safely deposited on the margin of a little stream, where we were to build our camp.

The Ashiras then became really frightened, and began to think they should never get back to their country. That night I remained awake with my men, and they saw that they could not escape. I had become vindictive, and they knew it. Mintcho seized my feet, and shouted, "Do not kill us; let me go, and keep the other hostages. I will have all the things that have been stolen restored to you. I will make the porters come back." "No," said I, "Mintcho, there is no going away for you; if you move a step you are dead;" and, to frighten him, I fired a gun at a tree, and he saw that the bullet had made a great gash in the tree.

Then I ordered Mintcho and an Ashira, with one of my Commi, to go to Mayolo to get porters. At first they would not do it. They were afraid. The game they had played had not been quite as successful as they had expected.

We had no food; it rained every night, and we could find no large leaves to shelter us from the heavy fall of water. Oh dear, how far off was Mayolo? It was clear that strong measures must be taken immediately.

There was still with us our Otando prisoner, whom Arangui had given back to me. So I said, "Mouitchi, hurry to Mayolo with that man, and tell Mayolo to send men and food at once, so that we may go to his country." Mouitchi departed with the Otando man, taking with him a necklace of large beads for Mayolo.

I was now left with Mintcho and seven Ashira rascals, and had only two of my faithful Commi men with me— Rebouka and Ngoma—to keep watch over them. We were encamped in a small open space in the loneliest and gloomiest part of the forest, by the path leading to the Otando country. We were absolutely without food. Rebouka, Ngoma, and myself, agreed to keep watch over our eight Ashiras, who were now our prisoners. Now and then the rascals would pretend to be asleep, and snored hard. They lay on one side of the path, and we were on the other side, with the luggage piled by us. They saw there was no escape, for two of us were always wide awake, with all our guns by our side ready to fire into the first man who tried to run away.

The Ashiras felt that they were caught, and began to curse those who had robbed me. Mintcho was accused by two of them as having been at the bottom of the whole plot. Mintcho got angry, and swore that it was a lie. I knew that they had told the truth.

It was very plain that something must be done, or we

should die of hunger, unless the Mayolo men came with food. If it had been the season of the koola-nut, we should have had plenty to eat. So I determined to go into the bush in search of food, and ordered an Ashira to follow me to find berries for his people. I again instructed Rebouka and Ngoma to shoot Mintcho or the Ashiras if they tried to escape. I was getting very weak; for, besides the want of food, anxiety had almost killed me. I really could hardly walk when I left the camp. I came back without game. I had heard a gorilla, and if I could have killed him we should have had plenty to eat, but he ran away before I came up with him.

That evening I felt so exhausted that I said to my Commi boys, "I will rest a little. Keep watch; let not one of these rascals escape. Talk all the time; tell stories; then I will keep watch after I awake, and you shall go to sleep."

There was no sleep for me, and I began to think I was getting crazy for want of food. I thought of home, of dinners, of beef and mutton, and I recalled the hot turkey, and the fish, and the buckwheat cakes; I could remember distinctly several dinners that had taken place years before, and I could have named every dish that came on the table in those days of plenty.

I sent two Ashiras with Rebouka out to hunt, warning them that if they tried to run away they would be killed, and that I would put to death every Ashira that remained in my hands. I assumed a fierce look, and swore that I would do it.

They were more successful than I had been. They came back with two monkeys.

Mintcho and the Ashiras put the meat before me, and insisted that I should eat it all alone, saying that they were accustomed to starving, and could wait. How strange, I thought, these Ashiras were! They had tried to leave me in the woods; they had plundered me, no doubt thinking that I could get other goods; and in despite of the hard treatment they were now subjected to, their hearts yearned toward me in kindness.

I said, "Ashiras, we are all hungry together, and I will

divide the meat in exactly equal portions." This astounded the Ashiras, for with them the chief had always the lion's share.

Those monkeys made a delicious repast. How I enjoyed my share! they were so fat and so nice—only we could have eaten 10 monkeys instead of two.

As the Otando people appeared, the allayed fears of the Ashiras returned; they began to believe that I had sent word by Mouitchi for the Otandos to come in great force, and that I was to take them captive for their treachery. Once more some of them wanted to go back. I swore that they could not go; that I would shoot them down; and that, if any escaped, Quengueza would make war upon the Ashiras, and capture all those who had come to trade on the banks of his river, and then would call on all the Ashira people to destroy the clan of Olenda.

This talk was hardly ended when I thought I heard voices far in the distance. "Hark!" said I to my Commi, "I hear voices." Were they the Otando people, or were they the Ashiras coming back to rescue their men? I immediately placed the Ashiras in a group together, tied their hands behind their backs, and got the guns in readiness, for I was getting desperate. If the Ashiras dared to come, they were to be met with a warm reception of bullets.

I was mistaken; the Otandos were coming. A gun is fired—up bounded Rapelina to the rescue, followed by a long line of Otando men laden with food sent by King Mayolo. A wild hurrah from everybody, including the Ashiras, welcomed the party. That night we rested and feasted in order to be strong for the journey. I slept well, and it was the first good rest I had had for a long time. The next morning I awoke very much refreshed, and at sunrise the horns of the Otandos blew the signal for our departure. It had been raining hard during the night, and the rain-drops on the leaves of the trees glittered in the early sunlight. We marched off at great speed, for I was determined not to sleep another night in the forest. On the tramp we crossed a river called the

Oganga, on the banks of which the koola-trees were growing luxuriantly. Nuts in abundance were lying on the ground, and the men fed on them, after which we continued our journey. I remember well it was the 10th of March, in the evening, just at sunset, that we emerged from the solitude of the forest into the Otando prairie, so called because the Otandos lived on it. Never shall I forget how glad I felt when I came on the margin of the forest, and saw the blue sky appearing through the breaks in the tree-tops.

CHAPTER XV.

In the open Country at last—Interview with Mayolo—Igala falls
Sick—A Mutiny—the Otando Prairie on Fire—Return of Ma
condai and Igalo—Their Adventures—All together again.

A STRETCH of open undulating country was before
me. Guns were fired by my men, and soon after I
entered the first Otando village. It was the village of
Mayolo, who was the only chief that was willing to receive
me. We went right to the ouandja, and I seated myself
in the centre of the building. Soon after, the beating of
the kendo was heard; Mayolo, the chief, his body streaked
with alumbi chalk, was coming, muttering mysterious
words as he advanced toward me. When he came nearer,
he shouted, "Here is the great Spirit, with his untold
wealth." The language of the Otando people was the
same as that of the Ashiras, so I had no difficulty in un-
derstanding him. He looked at me with perfect astonishment for awhile, and then told me the trouble he had
with his people on my account, since they did not want
me to come into the country; "for," said they, "he
brings the plague and death wherever he goes." "I told
them that the plague had killed our people before we
ever heard of you, and that the plague was in our country
before it went to the Ashira Land to kill the people
there."

"That was right," said I; "Mayolo, I love you; I kill
no people—I send no plague. I will be your friend, and
the friend of your people."

As Mayolo was talking to me, I took a good look at
him. He was tall, broad-shouldered, and almost yellow
in colour; his eyes were small and piercing. When young

he had gone toward the sea, and in his trading had succeeded in buying a gun, and, not knowing how to load it,
it had burst and taken off three of his fingers while
firing at an elephant.

After Mayolo had retired, a large goat and two enormous bunches of plantains were brought before me. I
wish you could have seen the faces of my Commi men,
the prospect of a good meal made them grin so compla-
cently.

Immediately after Mayolo had taken leave of me I
went to see Igala. Poor Igala was very sick : the plague
had seized him ; his body seemed a mass of putrid flesh.
How glad he was to see me ! I do believe he would have
died if I had not come to take care of him. There he
lay in a large hut, with all my goods around him. I went
to him, took hold of both his hands, and looked him in
the face. He said, " Chally, are you not afraid to get the
plague by taking my hands?" "No," said I ; "Igala, I
will take care of you as if you were my brother." Immediately I warmed some water in a kettle, and then
washed him delicately, and he felt more comfortable.

Poor Igala ! he was my right arm, my fighting man,
I depended upon him.

The next morning, opening my packages and boxes, I
saw the sad havoc the Ashira thieves had made with my
goods. They had stolen a great deal, but, strange to say,
they had left a certain quantity in each parcel.

I felt furious at the discovery. Oh, how sorry I was
that Igalo and Macondai had remained behind ; for, if
they had not, the Ashiras would never have gone back
to their own country: I would have made porters of
them.

I boldly accused Mintcho of the robbery, and seized the
gun he had. The hypocritical rascal pretended to be in a
rage at the discovery I had made ; he foamed at the mouth,
and exclaimed, " Let me go back, Chally ; I will find the
robbers, and kill them if they do not give up everything
you have lost."

Just at this time his brother Ayagui came, with a gun
which Rebouka had foolishly lent him. I ordered him to

give up the gun; he was unwilling, and threatened to shoot the first man who approached him. When I heard this, I ordered my four Commi men to level their guns at him, and shoot him dead, if in an instant he did not lay it on the ground. The gun was handed to Mayolo.

The Ashiras thought the end of Ayagui had come, and fled in the direction of the forest. We pursued them, and captured one, whom I resolved to retain as a hostage for the restitution of my property; but it so happened that the captive was the son of Adingo, an Ashira chief who was a good friend of mine. The guilty Ashiras were terribly frightened, and I shouted, "Bring the things back, and the boy shall be returned."

Mintcho, in his flight, passed near Igala, who could have seized him, but, as his shelter was a little way off, Igala did not suspect his intentions, and let him escape, thinking that he was only going into the woods.

The Otando people had seen by our prompt action of what stuff we were made. I regretted the necessity for such measures, but it was the first time since I began my travels that the natives had dared to rob me on the road, and the news would spread. All this was Rogueri's doings.

In the meantime, Rebouka had secured our little prisoner so tightly with ropes that he fairly moaned with pain. As I came up to him, he said, "Chally, you are my father's great friend. I am but a child; I cannot run away. The Ashiras will come back with all your stolen goods. I am your boy; I did not leave you in the woods, but followed you here. Do loosen the cords which hurt me so much." I ordered Rebouka to slacken the cords, which he did; but he remonstrated firmly, saying that I was too kind; that I did not know negroes; that negroes were not children at that age. "Do you think," said he, "that a child could have come from the Ashira country here with the load this boy has carried?" We then secured him under the verandah of my hut, and I set a watch over him during the night. Mayolo recommended me to keep a good look-out on the boy, "for," said he, the goods are sure to come back." Adingo was a powerful chief, and, as soon as he should hear of the cause of his son's captivity, he would threaten war, and, in order to secure peace, everything would have to be returned.

The moon was full, and it was quite light, so that everything around could be easily seen.

Rebouka was right; I had loosened the cords too much, and the cunning little fellow escaped during that first night. I felt sorry, for I knew now that nothing that had been stolen would ever come back, especially with Macondai and Igalo in the hands of the Ashiras; but, after all, I did not feel so badly as if some others of the Ashiras had run away. If I had only secured Mintcho, I assure you he would never have run away. Happily I had a great many goods left, and all the scientific instruments necessary to make astronomical observations.

The next morning Mayolo, being the head man of his clan, ordered the chiefs of the different villages of the clan to come to see me. They came, and a grand reception took place. Mayolo made a great speech. I gave presents to the men who had come to fetch me out of the woods, and to all the leading men and women. Then Mayolo shouted, pointing to the goods, "This is the plague the Spirit brings."

We had hardly been four days in Otando Land when Mayolo fell ill. How sorry I felt! Fear seized upon his people. Surely I was an evil spirit. Olenda had died; I had killed him, and now I wanted to kill Mayolo. Night after night I was kept awake with anxiety, for Mayolo was very unwell. I found that he had a disease of the heart; his sufferings were intense at times, and his moanings filled me with distress. Surely if Mayolo was to die I could not advance a step farther inland.

A few days after my arrival I had an uncomfortable fright; the Otando prairie became a sheet of fire, and threatened the destruction of the village of Mayolo. Should the fire get into the village, I said to myself, what a terrible explosion would take place! So I immediately called the men and moved the powder into the woods. Happily the natives prevented the fire from reaching the village.

Time went on slowly, and one day, about noon, as I was wondering when Igalo and Macondai would come back to us, I heard guns fired in the forest. My Commi men at that time were round me. Perhaps the Ashiras were coming back with their plunder! We looked toward the path which led into the forest, when lo! what should we see but Macondai, my boy, and Igalo. They were safe. A wild cheer welcomed them, and they went directly to the olako or hospital, where Igala and Rebouka were confined with confluent small-pox, for, since my return, Rebouka had been seized with the malady. Igalo left Macondai with them, and continued his way to our village, to give me mbolo, "good-morning salutation." The Otando people seemed almost as delighted as ourselves. We were again all together. I had now learned wisdom, and promised myself never to divide our party again, happen what might. After I had heard the news from Igalo, I went to the camp, and there I looked at my boy Macondai, and took his hand into mine. What a sight! Poor Macondai was more frightfully disfigured than I could possibly have imagined, or than I can describe, and I shuddered as I gazed upon him. A chill ran through me as I thought he might not yet recover, but I felt so thankful that I had all the medicines necessary for his proper treatment.

"Macondai, my boy," I said, "you do not know how glad I am to see you. You do not know how often I have thought of you; indeed, several times I wanted to go back for you."

I seated myself on a log of wood, and all was silence for a little while. Then Macondai spoke and said, "Chally, I have been very ill; I thought I would die." The boy's throat was too full; he could say no more. Then Igalo, his companion, became the spokesman, and I give you the whole of his speech just as it was written out by me at the time. "Chally, after you left us we went to an olako in a plantation close by, where we slept. Ondonga took us there, saying that the head man was his ogoï (relation), and that he would take care of us. Then he said he was going to Ademba (Olenda village), to see how things were getting along in the village, and that he would return in two days. He borrowed from us our cutlass, saying that he would return it when he came back. This was the last we saw of him. Then the next day the chief came and said he wanted his pay for keeping us, as we stayed in his olako. Finally he agreed that he would wait till Macondai could get well.

"Four days after you had gone, some of the boys who had accompanied you returned. We knew that they could not have gone to the Otando country and got back in so short a time, and, being well aware themselves that we knew it, they said at once, 'We have left Chally with Mintcho and the other people one day's journey from the Otando country, for we have had palavers with the Otando people, and we were afraid to proceed farther for fear that the Otando people would seize us;' and they also went away. Some time afterward Ayagui and Etombi made their appearance. They said they had left you well, but that you said you would not pay them until Macondai had come to the Otando; and they added, 'Make haste, Macondai, and cure yourself, so that we may go. If you were well now, I would say we must go in two days; that would just give us time to rest and get food for the journey.' Then, as they were leaving, they said they would come back in two days. This was the last we saw of them. Then the chief wanted us to move off. Macondai said he was so ill that he could not move; 'I would rather die where I am.' I did not want," said Igalo, "to go back to the plantation or to the village. I had had enough of Olenda's village. Then the chief took another tack. 'What shall I do?' said he. 'Ondonga, who brought you to me, has not again shown himself here; he has deserted you.' And he added, 'These people have come back. Chally has seized two gangs of slaves because the Ashira stole some of his things, and Mintcho has come to see if he can get the things back, for one of the gangs seized belongs to him, and the other to Ondonga.' The chief left us after saying this, telling us that he was going to see a friend, and would come back in the evening, and we never saw him again. Three days afterward two old men and three young lads came; they slept near us, and said, ' Igalo, you must not stop washing Macondai's body; we see that you wash only his leg.' By seeing me taking great care of Macondai's leg, they thought we probably intended to leave, which we wanted to do as soon as Macondai was well enough to walk. Then they added, ' Go to the spring, and fetch plenty of water, and wash Macondai well, for this disease requires it.' Then," said Igalo, " I went to the spring, and during the time I was gone they plundered us of our things, seized the gun I had left behind, and Macondai's double-barrelled gun, a box containing beads and our clothes, and escaped to the woods, and when I came back with the water I learned our misfortune. They had come to the plantation under the pretext of getting plantains.

" When I saw how things stood—that we had not a gun with which to defend ourselves—mistrusting the Ashiras, I thought best to leave the place, and said to Macondai, ' Let us go.' Rebouka had told us the road before you left for the Otando, so we loaded ourselves with plantains which we got in the plantations, and left at once, with the utmost speed, the deserted olako, and we have been four nights and four days on the road."

" Well done!" we shouted with one voice; " well done, boys! Macondai and Igalo, you are men, you are men!"

" Then," added Igalo, " I forgot to tell you that the man of the olako had told us that Mintcho and Ondonga had made a plot for a general robbery, but that you watched them so closely that they could not accomplish it."

I was so angry that I felt very much like going to the Ashira country, all of us armed to the teeth, when my followers should have quite regained their health and strength, and carrying fire and sword through all the villages that belonged to the clan of Olenda, and raising the whole country against them. I know I could have done this easily, but then I had not come to make war.

After hearing the pitiful story of Macondai and Igalo I went back to the village, and heated some water in one of my huge kettles; then, returning to the camp, I gave poor

Macondai a tepid bath with a sponge, and ordered some chicken soup to be prepared for the sufferer.

How poor Macondai enjoyed his soup ! It did me good to see him lap it up. I had forbidden him to eat anything without my permission, telling him that I should feed him well, so that he might get strong, but that it would be some few days before I could let him eat to his heart's content, for he had been starved so long that I was afraid he would get ill if he was permitted to indulge his appetite to repletion.

Though filled with anxiety about Macondai, I slept well that night. We were all together again ; it was so nice, for getting all our party together again gave me a lively satisfaction.

CHAPTER XVI.

Terrible Storms of Thunder—Days of Anxiety—Shooting an Antelope—Brighter Prospects—Mayolo has a hard Time with his
  Doctors—Basket-making.

HOW strange the Otando prairie looks since the fire
has burnt the grass! Tens of thousands of gigantic
mushroom-like ant-hills are seen everywhere. I had never
met such a great number before. I have given you a
picture of these queer ant-hills in my "Apingi Kingdom."

We are in the season of tornadoes, of thunder and
lightning. Hardly a day passes that some terrible storm
does not burst upon us; and such thunder—how terrific!
We have not the slightest idea at home of what thunder
is. Among the mountains here it is perfectly appalling
and terrific. It is grand and sublime, and fills one with
awe. The whole of the heavens at times seems entirely
illuminated by the lightning; and I find that it rains quite
often during the day. The heaviest tornadoes in these
regions seem to occur in the month of April.

Days pass in the Otando country which are full of
anxiety for me. Mayolo is sick, and some of my Commi
men are down with the plague. Oh dear, how the time
is going! How far the head waters of the Nile are!
What a tremendous journey ahead! How many days of
hunger do I see looming before me; how many days of
sickness and of anxious care! But my heart is strong.
God has been kind to me. The plague has spared me; it
has been around me; it has lived with me, and in my own
dwelling; and I stand safe amid the desolation that it has
spread over the country. I am surrounded here by savage

men.   May I live uprightly, so that, after I have left, the
people may think well of me !

But when am I ever to leave this Otando country?
Just as I am wondering over this, and thinking of the
principal events that have taken place since I left the sea-
shore, my reverie is broken by the barking of my dogs in
the prairie.   I look, and what do I see?   A beautiful
antelope closely pursued by my six dogs.   Andèko, and
Commi-Nagoumba, and Rover cling to the neck of the
antelope, with their teeth in the flesh, while Turk, Fierce,
and Ndjègo are barking and biting the poor creature
wherever they can.   I run with the villagers in chase.
Soon I am on the spot, and, aiming carefully at the beast,
I bring it down with a single shot.   It is a very fine hart.
There is great joy in the village, and I divide the meat
among the villagers, giving a big piece to friend Mayolo,
who is delighted, for he says he is very fond of antelope's
meat.

By the end of April things began to look bright.
Mayolo was getting well ; Macondai was improving very
fast, and Igala and Rebouka were almost recovered.   But,
as soon as Mayolo got better, he was more afraid than
ever of witchcraft, and he and his people had a great time
in " pona oganga."   Pona oganga is a strange ceremony,
which I am about to describe to you.   It was performed
because Mayolo wanted to know who were the people who
had bewitched his place, and made the plague come among
his people.

A great doctor had been sent for, and, after his arrival,
he went into a hut, carrying with him a large bag.   Soon
afterward he came out, looking horribly.   He was dressed
in a most fantastic manner : his body was painted with
ochre of three different colours—red, white, and black ;
he wore a necklace formed of bones, the teeth of animals,
and seeds ; around his waist was a belt of leather, from
which dangled the feathers of the ogoloungoo ; and his
head-dress was made of a monkey's skin.   As he came out
he spoke in an unnatural and hollow voice, then filled a
large basin with water, looked intently into it, and shook
his head gravely, as if the signs were bad.   Then he

lighted a big torch, and looked steadily at the flame, as if
trying to discover something, moved the torch over the
water, shook his body terribly, smoked a condoquai, made
a number of contortions and gestures, and again spoke in
a loud tone, repeating the same words over and over. The
people, in the meantime, were silent, and looked at the
great man attentively. Then he gazed steadily into the
water again, and said, while the people listened in breathless silence, "There are people in your own village who
want to bewitch it, and bring the plague and kill people."
Immediately a great commotion took place. The crowd
shouted, "Death to the sorcerers!" and rose up and swore
vengeance. "The mboundou must be drunk!" cried
Mayolo; "we want no wizards or witches among us."
The paths leading to the village were closed. No strangers
were to be admitted.

The next morning the village was empty ; the people
had all gone into the woods. I could hear their voices ;
they had gone to make some of their number drink the
mboundou.

Poor Mayolo really had a hard time with his different
doctors. He was continually changing them, and they
came from all the adjacent villages. At last he gave up
the men doctors, and had a celebrated female doctor, an
old, wrinkled woman, who had gained a great reputation.
The visit of a physician among these people is very unlike that of a physician at home. This female doctor was
a very singular person. She appeared to be about sixty
years of age, and was short, and tattooed all over. When
she came to make her visit she was dressed for the occasion. Her body was painted, and she carried a box filled
with charms. When Mayolo expected her he was always
ready, seated on a mat, and with a genetta-skin by him.
The female doctor would come in muttering words which
nobody could understand ; then she would rub Mayolo's
body with her hand, and mark his forehead with the chalk
of the alumbi; then she made a broad mark with the
chalk on his chest, and drew stripes the whole length of
his arms, muttering unintelligibly all the time ; she then
chewed the leaves of some medicinal plant, and spat the

1

juice over Mayolo's body, especially on the affected part, near the heart, still muttering magical words. Afterward she lighted a bunch of a peculiar kind of grass, and as it burned, made the flames almost touch the body of poor Mayolo. Two or three times it seemed as if the fire was burning him. She began the fire-ceremony at the sole of his foot, gradually ascending to the head, and, when the flames ceased, she made the smouldering fire touch his person.

When I asked her why she used fire, she said that it was to prevent disease from coming into Mayolo's body from the outside.

All this time the Otando people were busy making *otaitais*, or porters' baskets. The otaitai is a very ingenious contrivance for carrying loads in safety on the backs of men. I have brought one of these baskets home, and preserve it as a keepsake. It is long and narrow; the wicker-work is made of strips of a very tough climbing plant; the length is about two and a half feet, and the width nine inches; the sides are made of open cane-work, capable of being expanded or drawn in, so as to admit of a larger or smaller load. Cords of bast are attached to the sides, for the purpose of securing the contents. Straps made of strong plaited rushes secure the basket to the head and arms of the carrier.

CHAPTER XVII.

Departure from the Otando Country—Talk with Mayolo—Living on Monkey-meat—Astronomical Studies—Lunar Observations —Intense Heat.

THE day of my departure from the Otando country was approaching. Mayolo was getting better and better every day. So, two days after the ceremony I have described in the preceding chapter, I summoned Mayolo and his people, and received them in state. I was dressed for the occasion, as if ready to start, with my otaitai on my back. I was surrounded by my body-guard, and they also were ready for the start, each man carrying his otaitai. I spoke to the people in similitudes, in the African fashion :

" Mayolo, I have called you and your people, that you may have my mouth. You black people have a saying among yourselves that a man does not stand alone—that he has friends. You Otando people have friends among the Apono and Ishogo people." "We will take you there !" shouted the Otandos. "I come to ask you the road through the Apono country. Come and show me the road. It is the one I like best; it is the shortest. I will make your heart glad if you make my heart glad. I have nice things to give you all, and I want the news to spread that Mayolo and I are two great friends, so that after I am gone people may say, 'Mayolo was the friend of the Oguizi.' " The last part of the speech was received with tremendous shouts of applause, and cries of " Rovano ! Rovano !"

Mayolo deferred his answer till the next day. I suppose he wanted to prepare himself for a great speech. The following morning he came before my hut, surrounded by his people. Mayolo began :

"When a hunter goes into the forest in search of game, he is not glad until he returns home with meat; so Chally's heart will not be glad until he finishes what he wishes to do." Then he continued to speak for more than an hour, and ended by saying, "Chally, we shall soon be on the *long road*, and go toward where the sun rises."

As soon as the recovery of Mayolo seemed certain, the people prepared to celebrate the event. Jar after jar of native beer came in, and in the evening the people of the village had a grand time. Mayolo was the most uproarious of all, dancing, slapping his chest, and shouting, "Here I am, alive! The Otando people said I should die because the Spirit had come, but here I am ! Here I am, Chally, well at last ! I tell you I am well, Oguizi !" and, to show me that he was well, he began to leap about, and to strike the ground with his feet, saying, "Don't you see I am well ? The Otando people said, the Apono said, as soon as they heard you had arrived in my village, 'Mayolo is a dead man !' As soon as I fell ill, they said, 'Mayolo will never get up again ! Has not the Oguizi killed Remandji and Olenda ?' But here I am, alive and well ! Fire guns, that the people of the villages around may know that Mayolo is well !" As he went, he shouted, "I knew that the Oguizi did not like to see me ill. I am Mayolo ! I will take him farther on !"

I never knew how good Mayolo was till I saw him in better health. He had a good, kind heart, though he was a savage, and we had nice talks together. He asked me all sorts of questions. When I told him that in my country we had more cattle than he, but that they remained on our plantations, just as his goats did, he seemed incredulous. Then I told him that as I went inland I would meet tribes of blacks who kept tame cattle. He said he had never heard of such people; he could not believe what I said. But when I told him that there were countries where elephants were tamed, and that the people rode on their backs, the astonishment of Mayolo and of his people became great. Then I showed him an illustrated paper. " Oh! oh! oh!" they shouted. In the evening Mayolo presented me with a splendid fat monkey.

I should tell you that all this time I had really splendid food. The monkeys were delicious, and so plentiful in the woods near Mayolo's village that we could have them wherever we pleased. It was in the season when they were fat. The nchègai, the nkago, the miengai, and the ndova were also abundant, and we enjoyed eating them, for those creatures seemed, in the months of April and May, to be nothing but balls of fat. It was the time of the year, too, when the forest trees bore most fruit, berries, and nuts. The miengai and the ndova were the species of animals which I preferred for food. I defy any one to find nicer venison in any part of the world. A haunch grilled on a bright charcoal fire was simply delicious. " Horrible!" you will say; "the idea of eating monkeys! It is perfectly dreadful!" and at the same time I am sure you will make a face so ugly that it would frighten you if you were to look at yourself in the glass. You may say, " Oh, a roast monkey must look so much like a roasted little baby! Fy!" Never mind. I can only say that if you ever go into the forests of Equatorial Africa, and taste of a monkey in the season when those animals are fat, you will exclaim with me, " What delicious and delicate food! how exquisite!" As I am writing these lines, the recollection of those meals makes me hungry. I wish I had a monkey here, ready for cooking. I would invite you to partake of it; and I think you could eat the monkey without being accused of cannibalism.

The first time after my arrival at Mayolo's village that I took my photographic tent out of its japanned tin box, I called him to look at it after I had fixed it ready for use, but it was not easy to get him to come. He had a suspicion that there was witchcraft in it. Finally I succeeded in getting him to look at the apparatus. I made him look at the prairie through the yellow window-glass by which the light came into the little tent while I was working with the chemicals or the plates. As he looked, the trees, the grass, the sunlight, the ant-hills, the people, the fowls, the goats, all appeared yellow to him. The good old fellow was frightened out of his wits. He thought I was practising witchcraft. I believe if he had gone into the tent he would have died of fright. He stepped back, looked at me with fear and amazement, and went away, raising his hands, and with his mouth wide open. After a while he said that I had turned the world to another colour. The next day all the people came to see the wonderful thing.

I had so little to do that I gave my whole heart to the contemplation of the heavens. Many hours of the night were spent by me looking at the stars. When every one had gone to sleep, I stood all alone on the prairie, with a gun by my side, watching. There was no place upon our earth where one could get a grander view of the heavens than that I now occupied, for I stood almost under the equator, and the months of April and May in Mayolo were the months when the atmosphere is the purest; for after the storms the azure of the sky was so intensely deep that it made the stars doubly bright in the blue vault of heaven.

At that period the finest constellations of the southern hemisphere were within view at the same time—the constellations of the Ship, the Cross, the Centaur, the Scorpion, and the Belt of Orion, and also the three brightest stars in the heavens, Sirius, Canopus, and α Centauri.

How fond I was of looking at the stars! I loved many of them; they were my great friends, for they were my guides in their apparently ascending and descending course. How glad I was when one of these lovely friends again made its appearance after a few months' absence! how anxiously I watched toward the east for its return! and at last, as it rose from the dim horizon, and became brighter and brighter in ascending the heavens, how it delighted my heart! Do not wonder at it when I say I love the stars, for without them I would not have known where to direct my steps. I watched them as a tottering child watches his mother.

" Oft the traveller in the dark
  Thanks you for your tiny spark ;
  Would not know which way to go
  If you did not twinkle so."

Venus shone splendidly, and threw her radiance all around ; red Mars, Jupiter, and Saturn were in sight ; the Southern Cross (so named on account of the four bright stars which form a cross) ; not far from the cross were the " Coal-sac," like two dark patches. No telescope powerful enough has ever been made to see any star there. There is no other spot of the kind in the starry heavens.

The Magellanic clouds were also seen ; they were like two white-looking patches—especially the larger one—brightly illuminated as they revolve round the starless South Pole. Then, as if the scene was not beautiful enough, there stood that part of the Milky Way between the 50th and the 80th parallel, so beautiful and rich in crowded nebulæ and stars that it seemed to be in a perfect blaze ; between Sirius and the Centaur the heavens appeared most brilliantly illuminated, and as if they were a blaze of light.

At the same time, looking northward, I could see the beautiful constellation of the Great Bear, which was about the same altitude above the horizon as the constellation of the Cross and of the Centaur, some of the stars in the two constellations passing the meridian within a short time of each other : γ Ursæ Majoris half an hour before α Crucis, and Benetnasch eleven minutes before β Centauri.

Where could any one have a grander view of the heavens at one glance ? From α Ursæ Majoris to α Crucis there was an arc of 125° ; and, as if to give a still grander view of the almost enchanting scene, the zodiacal light rose after the sun had set, increasing in brilliancy, of a bright yellow colour, and rising in a pyramidal shape high into the sky, often so bright that the contrast between the blue sky and this yellow glow was most beautiful. It often became visible half an hour after the sun had disappeared, and was very brilliant, like a second sunset ; it still increased in brilliancy, and often attained a bright orange-colour at the base, gradually becoming fainter and fainter at the top. It could be seen almost every night during the months of April and May. So if, under the equator, I had not the splendid Aurora Borealis to behold, I had the soft zodiacal light to contemplate.

I would take astronomical observations whenever I could, so that I might know my latitude and longitude, and I took a great many at Mayolo. In the evening I would bring out my sextant, my policeman's lantern, my artificial horizon, my thermometer, and would work for hours.

I will explain to you the use of the artificial horizon. It is so called on account of being an imitation of the natural horizon. Quicksilver is the best material. The heavenly bodies are reflected upon it, and you must lay your artificial horizon in such a way that the object you are watching is reflected on it, and then, with your sextant, you bring the direct object to its reflected image on the quicksilver, and the reading of the sextant gives you the number of degrees, minutes, and seconds of altitude.

It is always good to take two stars, one north and the other south of the zenith of the place. While at Mayolo I would often take one of the stars of the constellation of the Great Bear and one of the constellation of the Cross the same evening. You have to watch carefully when the star has reached its highest altitude, that is to say, when it appears neither to ascend or descend.

But the most difficult observations were those of the lunar distances for longitude. In those observations I generally used three sextants, one for the altitude of the moon, another for the altitude of a star, and another for the distance between the moon and the star. My watch, my slate, my pencil, and my policeman's lantern were also placed near me. The two artificial horizons were in front of me, and when everything was ready I would take an altitude of the moon, then that of the star, then look at my watch, and note down the exact time of each observation; then take four distances, and note the exact time each distance was taken, and then again the altitude of the star and moon in the reverse order of the first portion of the observation.

The following example will show you how a lunar distance is taken with a sextant :

OBSERVATIONS FOR LUNAR DISTANCES.

Date.	Place.	Time.	Object.	Alt. and Distance	Index Error.	Temp.	Resulting Longitude, E.
		H. M. S.		° ′ ′	′ ″	Fahr.	° ′ ″
1865. May 6	Máyolo (continued).	11 1 30	Moon Alt.	121 12 40	on 6 30		
		11 4 30	Jupiter Alt.	62 44 20	on 5 20		
		11 7 25	Distance	85 43 40	}		
		11 9 42	Distance	85 42 50	on 0 40		11 7 15
		11 11 53	Distance	85 42 20			
		11 13 27	Distance	85 42 20	}		
		11 15 10	Jupiter Alt.	67 31 0			
		11 18 2	Moon Alt.	113 5 10		77·0	Planet E. of Moon.
″	″	11 19 44	Moon Alt.	112 10 0	on 6 50		
		11 22 7	Jupiter Alt.	70 37 40	on 5 20		
		11 24 24	Distance	85 38 0	}		
		11 26 18	Distance	85 37 50	on 0 40		11 11 15
		11 31 43	Distance	85 37 0			
		11 33 10	Distance	85 36 0	}		
		11 35 8	Jupiter Alt.	70 22 0			
		11 36 40	Moon Alt.	103 59 30		77·0	Planet E. of Moon.

Take as many lunar observations as you can east and west of the moon—the more the better—and you will be able to know your exact longitude with more certainty. It would be here too complicated to tell you how to make the calculations, but I am sure that after a while many of you would be able to make them.

By lunar observations, if sickness or some other cause has made you forget the day of the month, or even the year, you can find it again. Several times I lost my days while travelling.

The heat was intense at Mayolo. The rays of the sun were very powerful, and raised the mercury nearly to 150°. Just think of it! In order to know the heat of the sun, the thermometer was only a glass tube supported by two little sticks. I had to take care that the rays of the sun fell always perpendicularly on the mercury.

CHAPTER XVIII.

ON the 30th of May, early in the morning, there was great excitement in Mayolo's village. That morning we were to leave for the Apono country. Mayolo himself was to take me there, and we were all getting ready, the men carefully arranging their otaitais. The horns were blown as the signal for our departure, and we took the path in single file, Igala leading, and Mayolo and I bringing up the rear.

"Good-bye, Oguizi!" shouted the people. "Don't forget us, Oguizi! Come back, Oguizi!"

Following a path in the prairie, we travelled directly east. Our road lay among the ant-hills, which could be counted by tens of thousands, of which I gave you a description in my "Apingi Kingdom." After a march of seven miles we came to Mount Nomba-Obana. Mayolo once lived on the top of this mountain, but moved his village to its base, and afterward went to the place where I found him. At the foot of Nomba-Obana, on the somewhat precipitous side, were great quantities of blocks of red sandstone, and in this neighbourhood we saw the ruins of Mayolo's former village. Mayolo is always changing his home, for he fancies that the places he occupies are bewitched.

At a distance of about three miles from Nomba-Obana we came to a stream called Ndooya, which we forded, but in the rainy season it must be a considerable body of water. We were approaching the Apono villages, and I felt somewhat anxious, for I did not know what kind of reception the people would give me. Groves of palm-trees were very abundant, and I could see numerous cala-bashes hanging at the tree-tops, ready to receive the sap, which is called palm wine.

At last we came in sight of the village of Mouendi, where we intended to stay. The chief was a great friend of Mayolo. As soon as the inhabitants saw me a shout rent the air. All the people fled, the women carrying their children, and weeping. The cry was, " Here is the Oguizi! Oguizi! Now that we have seen him, we are going to die." I saw and heard all this with dismay.

We entered the village. Not a soul was left in it; it was as still as death. I could see the traces of hurried preparations for flight as we continued our march through the street of this silent village till we came near the ouandja. There I saw Nchiengain, the chief, and two other men who had not deserted him. These were the only inhabitants we could see. The body of the chief was marked, striped, and painted with the chalk of the alumbi. He seemed filled with fear; but the sight of Mayolo, his *nkaga*, "born the same day," seemed some-what to reassure him.

Mayolo said, "Nchiengain, do not be afraid; come nearer. Do not be afraid. Come!" Then we went under the ouandja, and seated ourselves. In the mean-time, I had taken a look at Nchiengain. He was a tall, slender old negro, with a mild and almost timid expression of countenance.

Then Mayolo said, "I told you, Nchiengain, that I was coming with the Oguizi. Here we are. The Spirit has come here to do you good—to give you beads, and many nice things. Then he will leave you after awhile, and go still farther on."

Then I spoke to Nchiengain in his own language, for the Aponos speak the same language as the Ashira and Otando people. I said, "Nchiengain, do not be afraid of me. I come to be a friend; I come to do you good. I come to see you, and then will pass on, leaving beads and fine things for your women and yourselves. Look here"

—pointing to all the loads which my Otando porters had laid on the ground—"part of these things will be for your people," and immediately I put around his neck a necklace of very large beads, and placed a red cap on his head. I then gave necklaces of smaller beads to the two other men, and said, "Nchiengain, you will have more things, but your people must come back: I do not like to live in a village from which all the people have run away. Mayolo's people did not run away, and you do not know what great friends we are. Call your people back."

I then went around the village and hung a few strings of beads to the trees, and Nchiengain shouted, "Come back, Aponos; come back! Do not be afraid of the Spirit. As you come back, look at the trees, and you will see the beads the Spirit has brought for us, and which he will give to us." The two men then went out upon the prairie and into the woods, and before sunset a few men and women, braver than the rest, returned to the village, taking with them the beads which they had seen hanging from the branches of the trees.

In the evening the bright fires blazing in all directions showed that the fears of the people had been allayed, and that many of them had returned to their homes.

How tired I felt that evening! for not only had I been excited all day, but I had left Mayolo's village in the morning, with a heavy load on my back. Besides my revolvers, I carried a double-barrelled gun, and in my bag I had fifty cartridges for revolvers, ten bullets for a long-range Enfield rifle, ten bullets for smooth-bore guns, ten steel-pointed bullets, and more than twenty pounds of small shot, buckshot, powder, &c. In all, I carried a weight of over sixty pounds, besides my food, and my aneroids, barometers, policeman's lantern, and prismatic compass. I was so weary that I could not sleep. I resolved not to carry such big loads any more.

But my work was not yet done: in the evening I had to make astronomical observations. As I was afraid of frightening the people, I had to do this slyly. I was glad when I had finished it, but I found by my observations that we had gone directly east from Mayolo's village.

The next morning I walked from one end of the village of Mouendi to the other. The street was four hundred and forty-seven yards long, and eighteen yards broad. The soil was clay, and not a blade of grass could be seen. The houses were from five to seven yards long, and from seven to ten feet broad; the height of the walls was about four feet, and the distance from the ground to the top of the roof was seven or eight feet. Back of the houses were immense numbers of plantain-trees. In the morning many of the people returned. Mayolo and Nchiengain had a long talk together. Nchiengain was fully persuaded that I could do anything I wished; consequently, that I could make any amount of goods and beads for him. A grand palaver took place, and Mayolo began the day by making a speech. He said,

"The last moon I sent some of my people to buy salt from you Apono. You refused to sell salt, and sent word that you did not want the Oguizi to come into your country, because he brought the plague, sickness, and death. So I said to the Oguizi, 'Never mind; there is a chief in the Apono country who is my *nkaga* (born the same day); I will send messengers to him; he has big canoes, and I am sure he will let us cross the river with them.' Then I sent three of my nephews to you, Nchiengain, my nkaga, with beads and nice things, and I said to them, 'Go and tell Nchiengain that I am coming with the Oguizi, who is on his way to the country of the Ishogos.' You sent back your kendo, Nchiengain, with the words, 'Tell Mayolo to come with his Oguizi.' Here we are, Nchiengain, in your village, and I am sure you and your people will not slight us " (*mpouguiza*).

I gave to Nchiengain one shirt, six yards of prints, one coat, a red cap, one big bunch of white beads and one of red, a necklace of very large beads, files, fire-steels, spoons, knives and forks, a large looking-glass, and some other trinkets, and then called the leading men and women, and gave them presents also. This settled our friendship, for the people were pleased with the wonderful things I gave them.

The news of my untold wealth spread far and wide. People from a neighbouring village, who had been very much opposed to my journey through their country, made their appearance. When Nchiengain saw them, he said, "Go away! go away! now you come because you have smelt the *niva* (good and nice things). You are not afraid now."

After two or three days the people of Mouendi began to say, "How is it that two or three days ago we were so afraid of the Spirit? Now our fears are gone, and we love him. He plays with our children, and gives beads to our women." When I heard them utter these words, I said, "Apono, that is the way I travel. Those fine things that I give you are the plague I leave behind me! I bring not death but beads; so do not be afraid of me." They replied, "Rovano! Rovano!" ("That is so!")

A few days passed away, and then the Apono and I became great friends. They began to wonder why they had been so frightened by the *Ibamba* (a new name given me by the Apono), and soon all the people had returned to the village. Good old Nchiengain and Mayolo had at last a jolly frolic together, and got quite tipsy with palm wine. I wish you had heard them talk. The way they were going to travel with me was something wonderful. Such fast travelling on foot you never heard of before. Tribe after tribe were to be passed by them. They were not afraid; they did not care. We were even to travel by night over the prairie, for the full moon was coming.

After a few days at Mouendi, Nchiengain with his Aponos, and Mayolo with his own people, took me farther on; but before our departure Nchiengain and the Apono went out before daylight to obtain the palm wine which had fallen into their calabashes during the night. By sunrise they were all tipsy, and Nchiengain was reeling, but he was full of enthusiasm for the journey; Mayolo also was tipsy, but not quite so far gone as his friend Nchiengain. When I saw this state of things I demolished all the *mvomi* (calabashes), spilling on the ground the palm wine they contained, to the great sorrow of the Aponos.

"Where is Nchiengain?" I inquired, when we were ready to start. He could not be found; and, suspecting that he was somewhere behind his hut, drinking more palm wine before starting, I went to hunt for him. The old rascal, thinking I was busy engaged in looking after my men, was quietly drinking from the mbomi itself, with his head up and his mouth wide open. Before he had time to think, I seized his calabash, and poured the contents on the ground. Poor Nchiengain! he supplicated me not to pour it all away, but to leave a little bit for him. "I will go with you at once," he said; "give me back my mug" (a mug I had given him); "oh, Spirit, give it back to me!" By this time all the villagers had gathered about us. I put the mug on the ground, and told Nchiengain's wife to come and take it; and this gave great joy to the people, who exclaimed, "Nchiengain, go quick! go quick!"

When we left I went to the rear, to see that all the porters were ahead ; but old Nchiengain lagged behind, for he could not walk fast enough.

Three quarters of an hour afterward we found ourselves on the banks of a large river, the same which is described in my "Apingi Kingdom"—that kingdom being situated farther down the stream than the point at which we were now to cross. The river could not be seen from the prairie, for its banks were lined with a belt of forest trees. We found on the banks of the stream Nchiengain's big canoe waiting for us, together with some smaller ones. The large canoe was very capacious, but before all my luggage could be ferried over it was necessary to make seven trips. I sent Igala, Rebouka, and Mouitchi to the other side with the first load to keep watch. The canoe had just returned from its seventh trip, and the men were landing, when suddenly I heard the voice of Nchiengain in the woods shouting, "I am coming, Spirit! Nchiengain is coming!" It was half-past four P.M. A whole day had been lost.

Not caring to take his majesty Nchiengain reeling

drunk into my canoe, I jumped into it and ordered the men to push from the shore with the utmost speed. We started in good time, for we were hardly off when I began to distinguish the king's form through the woods, and when he reached the shore we were about fifty yards distant. We heard him shout "Come back! come back to fetch me;" but the louder he called the more deaf we were. "Go on, boys!" I ordered. As our backs were turned to the king, of course we could not see him. Finally we landed, and taking my glass I saw poor Nchiengain gesticulating on the other side, apparently in a dreadful state, thinking that I had left him. The canoe was sent back for him, and a short time afterward he was landed on our side of the river to his great delight. Two or three times during the passage he lost his equilibrium, but he did not fall. When he joined us he was about as tipsy as when I left him in the morning.

Poor Mayolo, who had been continually tipsy since we had left his village, fell ill during the night, and a very high fever punished him for his sins.

We built our camp where we had landed. A thick wood grew on the bank of the river, and firewood was plentiful. In the evening Nchiengain was sober again, and before ten o'clock everybody was fast asleep except three of my Commi men, who were on the watch. The dogs were lying asleep, and almost in the fire. Everything now promised well, and I was anxious to hurry forward as rapidly as possible on the following day.

At a quarter past six o'clock, A.M., we left our encampment, everybody being perfectly sober. Soon afterward we emerged from the woods into a prairie, and passed several villages, the people of which seemed to have heard wonderful stories of my wealth. They came out, and followed me with supplies of goats and plantain, and begged Nchiengain and his people to remain with the Oguizi. In the villages they went so far as to promise several slaves to Nchiengain if he would do this. Hundreds of these villagers while following us gazed at me, but if I looked at them they fled in alarm. Finally, seeing that it was useless to follow, they went back shouting to

Nchiengain and to Mayolo that it was their fault if I did not stop. My porters joined them in their grumbling, for the fat goats tempted them.

About midday we halted in a beautiful wooded hollow, through which ran a little rivulet of clear water, and by its side we seated ourselves for breakfast. I was really famished. After spending an hour in eating and resting we started again. When we came out of the wood we saw paths leading in different directions, one going directly east to several Apono villages. Nchiengain was opposed to our passage through them, and therefore we struck a path leading in a more southerly direction, or S.S.E. by compass. For three hours we journeyed over an undulating prairie dotted with clumps of woods, and then crossed a prairie called Matimbié irimba (the prairie of stones), the soil of which was covered with little stones containing a good deal of iron. The men suffered greatly as they stepped upon them.

CHAPTER XIX.

Rumours of War—Through a Burning Prairie—Imminent Peril—
Narrow Escape from a Horrible Death—A Lonely Night-
watch.

WAR began to loom up as we reached the southeast
end of the Matimbié irimba. We came to a village
called Dilolo, the path we were following leading directly
to it, and as we approached we found that the place had
been barricaded, and that it was guarded outside by all its
fighting men. On the path charms had been placed, to
frighten away the Aponos. The men were armed with
spears, bows and arrows, and sabres. When we came
near earshot, having left the path with the intention of
passing by the side of the village, they vented bitter curses
against Nchiengain for bringing the Oguizi into their
country—"the Oguizi who comes with the *eviva* (plague)
into villages," they shouted. "Do not come near us; do
not try to enter our village, for there will be war!" The
war-drums were beaten, and the men advanced and
retired before us, spear in hand, as if to drive us away, for
they thought we had come too near. We marched forward, nevertheless. So long as the Apono porters did not
show the white feather, I felt safe; they also had their
spears and their bows, and my men held their guns in
readiness. Suddenly fires appeared in different parts of
the prairie. The people of Dilolo had set fire to the grass,
hoping that we might perish in the flames. The fire
spread with fearful rapidity, but we soon came to a place
where our path made a turn by the village, and we
reached the rear of the place. At that moment we observed a body of villagers moving in our direction,

evidently intending to stop our progress. Presently two poisoned arrows were shot at us. I thought we were going to have a fight, but ordered my men to keep cool, and not to fire. Nchiengain walked all along the line to cheer up his men, and shouted that "Nchiengain's people were not afraid of war," but at the same time he begged me not to fire a gun unless some of our people were hit with the arrows.

We continued our march, keeping close together, so that we might help each other in case of need. My men were outside the path, between Nchiengain and the Dilolo people, with their guns ready to fire when I gave the word. The villagers, mistaking our forbearance for fear, became bolder, and the affair was coming to a crisis. A warrior uttering a fierce cry of battle, came toward us, and, with his bow bent, stood a few yards in front of Rapelina, threatening to take his life. I could see the poison on the barbed arrow. My eyes were fixed upon the fellow, and I felt very much like sending a bullet through his head. Plucky Rapelina faced his enemy boldly, and, looking him fiercely in the face, uttered the war cry of the Commi, and, lowering the muzzle of his gun, advanced two steps, and shouted in the Apono language that if the Dilolo did not put down his bow he would be a dead man before he could utter another word. By this time all my Commi men had come up, with the muzzle of their guns pointing toward the Dilolo, awaiting my order to fire. The bow fell from the warrior's hand, and he retreated.

Nchiengain behaved splendidly. He began to curse the Dilolo people, and said to them, "You will hear of me one of these days;" and my Aponos threw down their loads and got ready to fight.

"Let us hurry," I said to the men; "don't you see the country is getting into a blaze of fire? We must get out of it."

I fired a gun after we had passed the village, and the inhabitants were terrified at the noise. Nchiengain was furious, and again shouted to the enemy, "You will see that I am not a boy, and that my name is Nchiengain!"

The discomfited warriors of Dilolo gradually left us, probably thinking that the fire, so rapidly spreading, would do the work they could not perform; and, indeed, while we had escaped a conflict through our good common sense, we were now exposed to a far greater danger. The fire was gaining fearfully. The whole country seemed to be in a blaze. Happily, the wind blew from the direction in which we were going; still the flames were fast encircling us, and there was but one break in the circuit it was making. I shouted, "Hurry, boys! hurry! for if we do not get there in time, we shall have to go back, and then we must fight, for we will have to get into the village of Dilolo." So we pressed forward with the utmost speed, and finally our road lay between two walls of fire, but the prairie was clear of flames ahead. Although the walls of fire were far apart, they were gaining upon us. "Hurry on, boys!" I exclaimed; "hurry on!" We walked faster and faster, for the smoke was beginning to reach us. The fire roared as it went through the grass, and left nothing but the blackened ground behind it. We began to feel the heat. The clear space was getting narrower and narrower. I turned to look behind, and saw the people of Dilolo watching us. Things were looking badly. Were we going to be burned to death? Again looking back toward Dilolo, I saw that the fires had united, and that the whole country lying between ourselves and Dilolo was a sheet of flame.

Onward we sped, Nchiengain exhorting his men to hurry. We breathed the hot air, but happily there was still an open space ahead. We came near it, and felt relieved. At last we reached it, and a wild shout from Nchiengain, the Aponos, and my Commi rent the air. We were saved, but nearly exhausted.

I said to my Commi men, "Are we not men? There is no coming back after this! Boys, onward to the River Nile!" They all shouted in reply, "We must go forward; we are going to the white man's country."

Between four and five o'clock we came to another wood, in the midst of which was a cool spring of water. We encamped there for the night, and not far in the distance on

the prairie we could see the smoke coming out of a cluster
of Apono villages. They dreaded our approach. In the
silence of the twilight, the wind from the mountains
brought to us the cries of the people. We could hear the
shrieks and the weeping of the women, and the beating of
the war-drums. Afterward the people came within speaking distance, and shouted to us, " Oh, Nchiengain, why
have you brought this curse upon us ? We do not want
the Oguizi in our country, who brings the plague with
him. We do not want to see the Ibamba. The Ishogo
are all dead; the Ashango have all left; there is nothing
but trees in the forest. Go back ! go back !" They yelled
and shouted till about ten o'clock, and then all became
silent, and soon afterward my people were asleep by
the fires which they had lighted. They all suffered
from sore feet. Igala, Mouitchi, and Rapelina were to
keep watch with me, while my other Commi men were
resting; but they, too, after a while, went to sleep.
Even our poor dogs were tired, and were also sound
asleep.

I stood all alone, watching over the whole camp,
so anxious that I could not sleep. Things did look
dark indeed. A most terrible dread of me had taken
possession of the people. Something had to be done
to allay their fears, or my journey would come to
an end.

How quiet every thing was ! The rippling of the water
coming from the little brook sounded strangely in the
midst of the silent night. I looked at the strange scene
around me. Each of my men had his gun upon his arm,
but I thought of how useless the weapons would be in the
hands of men so weary and sunk in deep sleep. If, that
night, any one of you could have been there, you would
have seen Paul Du Chaillu leave the camp and the woods
and then have seen him all alone upon the prairie, standing like a statue, no one by him, his gun in one hand, his
revolvers hung by his side. The stars shone beautifully
above his head, as if to cheer him in his loneliness, for
lonely and sad enough he felt. Then, with an anxious
feeling, he looked through his spyglass in the direction

of the Apono villages to see if anything was going on there. No.   All there, too, was silent as death.

At three o'clook in the morning I awakened Igala and some of my Commi boys, and told them to keep watch while I tried to get a little sleep.

CHAPTER XX.

A Deputation from the Village—A Plain Talk with them—A
Beautiful and Prosperous Town—Cheerful Character of the
People—More Observations.

BEFORE daylight I arose, and again went out upon the
prairie, but saw no one there from the Apono villages, and heard no war-drumming. After a while a
deputation of three men came from the village to Nchiengain, and said, "Why have you brought this Oguizi to
us? He will give us the eviva."

"No," said Nchiengain; "months ago the eviva was in
the country. I myself got it; people died of it, and others
got over it. The eviva has worked where it pleased, and
gone where it pleased, and that when the Spirit had never
made his appearance. He has nothing to do with the
eviva. Go and tell your people that Nchiengain said so,
and that the Spirit has only been a few days in our country."
The men went off without seeing me, for Nchiengain was
afraid they might be frightened.

Toward ten o'clock Nchiengain and Mayolo were sent
for, and, a short time after they had gone, some of
Nchiengain's people came for me, saying that the Aponos
wanted to see me, and that Nchiengain was talking to
them; so, followed by all my Commi men, armed to the
teeth, I started. We left the wood and entered the
beautiful prairie, and soon I saw Nchiengain standing up,
and by him, seated in rows upon the ground in a semi-
circle, were several hundreds of Aponos. As I approached
they began to move backward, each row trying to hide
behind the other. Then Nchiengain said, "Do not be
afraid," and they stopped.

Nchiengain said to me, in a loud voice, so that every one could hear, " The Aponos sent for me this morning to ask me to tell you to come out of that wood. They want to see you, the great Spirit. Then they want you to go on the top of that hill " (pointing to it), " and stay there three days, so that the people may come and look at you, and bring you food."

" No," said I, in a loud voice, " no, I shall not go on the top of that hill. I am angry with the Apono people, for they curse me by saying that I bring the eviva with me. Has not the eviva been here long? Did not the people die of it long before they ever heard of me?"

" Rovano! Rovano!" (" That is so!") shouted the Aponos.

" Aponos," I resumed, " do not be frightened; I will make you hear a noise you never heard before," and I ordered my men to discharge their guns. The Apono chiefs stood by me, and I said to them, " Do not be afraid." Nevertheless, a good many of the people fled. The chiefs did not move. Then, putting beads around their necks, I said to them, " Go away in peace; the Spirit loves the Aponos." The people departed, and I went back into the wood, for the heat was intense on the prairie.

In the afternoon the Aponos became emboldened, and hundreds of them came to get a look at me, taking care not to come too near. Presents of goats, fowls, ground-nuts, sugar-cane, and plantains were sent to me. Afterward a deputation came to ask me to leave the wood, and to come to a wood nearer their villages, which I did. Then the different chiefs of the adjacent Apono villages begged me to become their guest, and to remain in their villages.

After consultation with Nchiengain, it was arranged that we were to go to a village called Mokaba, and accordingly we left our encampment, and were received in the midst of the most intense excitement by the villagers, who exclaimed, " The Spirit is coming!" How frightened they seemed to be!

The chief came and walked around me, fanning me

with a fan made of the ear of an elephant, and saying,
"Oguizi, do not be angry with me; Oguizi, do not be
angry with me. Oguizi, I never saw thee before; I am
afraid of thee. I will give thee food; I will give thee all
I have!"

That night the village of Mokaba was as silent as the
grave. The next morning immense crowds of Aponos
came to see me. The noise was perfectly deafening. The
people hid themselves behind the trees, in the tall grass
around the villages, and behind the huts, or wherever they
could see me without being seen by me. If perchance I
cast my eyes upon one of them, he ran away as fast as his
legs could carry him.

I spent the evening in making a great number of astronomical observations. The Aponos, when they saw me
do this, were seized with fear, and the next morning they
came to ask me to go back into the wood, promising that
they would bring food to me. I refused, saying, "I was
in the wood, and you told me to come to Mokaba; and
now that I am here, you ask me to go back into the wood.
I will not go. Do not be afraid; I am not an evil spirit.
I love to look at the stars and at the moon."

The chief of Mokaba, named Kombila, seemed to be a
nice fellow, of medium height, black as jet, with several
huge scars of sabre wounds on his back and arms, showing
that he was a great fighter. I liked him very much.

The village of Mokaba was beautiful. It was situated
on a hill in the prairie, just at the foot of the woody mountains which form a part of the immense equatorial range.
From the mountains came a stream of clear water, which
ran at the foot of the hill upon which Mokaba was built.
The mountains in the background seemed to be very high,
and the country was picturesque. The village was not
large, but its houses were nice, and each family possessed a
square yard, around which the dwellings were built. The
whole place was adorned with three squares, in the midst
of which grew many gigantic palm-trees. Back of the
village there were also great numbers of palm-trees, which
were planted by the parents of the present inhabitants.
Goats and chickens were abundant. The plantain, how-

ever, is the food of the country, and the hills surrounding
Mokaba were covered with plantain groves. Handsome
lime-trees, covered with little yellow blossoms, were also
to be seen everywhere.

The grass of the prairie was yellow and tall, and reminded me of the wheatfields at home when ready for
the scythe. Each of the palm-trees around the village,
grown from seeds planted by the people, had its owner.
The palm is a precious tree, for each man draws from it
his palm wine, and makes oil from the nuts, which, when
they are ripe, are of a beautiful rich dark yellow colour.

There was an atmosphere of comfort about Mokaba,
and the whole country adjacent to it, which did my heart
good. The Mokabans are a jolly people when they do
not fight with their neighbours. They are fond of dancing,
and the ocuya is one of the principal amusements.
This is a queer pastime, and I will try to describe it for
you.

One day, while I was quietly seated with Kombila, I
heard at the end of the village a great noise, caused by
loud singing, and immediately afterward saw a crowd of
people walking backward, beating their hands and
singing, with their bodies bent almost double, and all
shouting, dancing, and singing at the same time. Then I
saw a tall figure suddenly emerge from behind a house
and come into the street, and Kombila exclaimed, " The
ocuya! the ocuya!"

The tall figure seemed to be about twelve feet in height.
It wore a long dress made of grass-cloth, and reaching
nearly to the ground. The creature's face was covered
with a white mask painted with ochre. The lips of the
mask appeared to be open, showing that the two upper
and middle incisor teeth were wanting. The funniest part
of the costume was that the mask had a head-dress, looking
for all the world like a lady's bonnet, made of a monkey's
skin, with the tail hanging on the back, while the part of
the bonnet around the face was surrounded with feathers.
The figure was a man on stilts.

But troubles and cares again came to destroy the enjoyment I had in their lively village. Mayolo fell ill once

more, and grew worse so rapidly that his people determined to take him back to his village. A litter was made on which to carry him. But his own people said he had become jealous, and did not want any of them to get my fine things ; he wanted them all for himself.

The party left early in the morning. In the afternoon news came that the chief of the village of Dilolo had died that day. Fortunately, the people of Mokaba did not like him, and they shouted with joy when they heard the news. He wanted war when he tried to prevent the Oguizi and his people from passing, and if war had come at that time he would have been killed. They all shouted, "He had aniemba, and aniemba has killed him ! He will give us no more trouble ; he will prevent no more people from coming to us ! He will not stop the people who come to sell us salt !"

Two days after the departure of Mayolo, some of the Otandos, with some of the Mouendi people, came back to Mokaba. They came for Nchiengain. He was wanted. I never learned the reason. No doubt his people were afraid to leave him longer with me. Mayolo's life was now despaired of, and the Otando people told me slyly that they had mpoga-oganga, and that the oganga had said that the Nchiengain people had put things in the palm wine Mayolo drank in order to kill him.

Nchiengain came to me with a frightened air to tell me he had to go. He seemed to be afraid of me. I believe he thought I was going to kill him, as I had killed Remandji, Olenda, and Mayolo, and that now his turn had come. I said to him, "We are great friends. Make a good speech to the Apono for me, and I will give you such nice presents !" He promised to do it.

So all the Mokaba people were called. Nchiengain came out, and made a great speech. He said, "Kombila and Mokaba people, let the people who are to go with the Spirit come before me." They came and seated themselves on the ground, and I then gave to each a present, or his pay in goods, beads, trinkets. Then Nchiengain said, "Kombila, the Oguizi was brought to me by Mayolo, and before he reached Mayolo's village he passed through many countries of the black man. Now I leave him in your hands; pass him to the Ishogos. Then, when you leave him with the Ishogos, tell them they must take him to the Ashongos. After you leave him with the Ishogos your hands will be cleared, for you will have passed him over your tribe and clans. I am going; I leave him in your hands!" They all shouted, "We will take the Oguizi to the Ishogos! we will start the day the Oguizi wishes to start! We are men! the Mokaba people are men!"

Then Nchiengain added, "Wherever he goes, let the people give him plenty of goats, fowls, plantains, and game!" There was a great shout of "Rovana!"—"That is so! that is so!" "Do not be afraid of him," shouted Nchiengain; "see how well he has treated us! At first we were afraid of him; after a while our fears ceased. He will treat you just the same. He paid us when we left the village, and when we leave he gives us a parting present. Take him away to-morrow. Start for the country of the Ishogos. Hurry, for he does not want to tarry."

Then, in the presence of the people, he returned to me the brass kettle I had lent him for cooking his food, and the plate I had given him, and said to me, "Oguizi, good-bye! I have not *mpouguiza* (slighted) you; I go because I must go." As he disappeared behind the palm-trees he shouted again, "Oguizi, I have not *mpouguiza* you!" I answered, "No, Nchiengain, I am not angry with you; I am only sorry we part."

CHAPTER XXI.

Great Excitement in the Village—A Deserted Town—The Inhabitants Frightened Away—Afraid of the Evil Eye—The Author
taken for an Astrologer—Lost among the Plantations.

ON the morning of the 10th of June there was great
excitement in the village of Mokaba. The Apono,
headed by Kombila, were ready to take me to the Ishogo
country. All the porters wore the red caps I had given
them, and had put on their necklaces of beads. At a
quarter past ten o'clock, just as we started, I ordered guns
to be fired, to the immense delight of the Mokaba people.
Kombila gave the word for departure, and one by one we
took the path leading to the hills, which lay directly east
of the village, and soon afterward we were in the woods,
passing plantation after plantation that had been abandoned,
for they never planted twice in the same place. We
finally arrived at a plantation called Njavi, where thousands
of plantain-trees were in bearing, and where sugar-cane
patches were abundant. Fields of pea-nuts were also all
around us soon afterward. We rested to take a meal, and,
as Njavi was situated on the plateau, I had a good view of
the country.

When we resumed our march eastward the Apono were
in great glee, for they had become accustomed to me.
Kombila was filled with pride at the idea that he was going
to take the Spirit to the Ishogo country. The men were
talking loudly, and I saw that there was no chance for
killing game. The country was splendid. The hills had
been getting higher and higher till we had reached Njavi,
but since leaving that point we had been going down the
slope. We crossed a dry stream with a slaty bottom, and

soon afterward came to a stream called Dougoundo, the
Apona porters walking as fast as they could. Toward
four o'clock we reached the large Ishogo village of Igoumbić, but found it deserted. The few men who saw us ran
into their houses and shut their doors—for they had doors
in Igoumbić. The people reminded me of frightened
chickens hiding their heads in dark corners. A few men
had been so alarmed that they had lost the power of
walking, and as I passed did not utter a single word nor
move a step. We walked through the whole length of the
street, then got into the woods, and stopped. Kombila
said to me, "Let me, Spirit, go to the village;" and he
went with a few of his men. Soon afterward an Ishogo
man came with Kombila, and asked me to remain in his
village. "The Mokaba people are our friends," he said;
"they marry our daughters; how can we let them pass
without giving them food?" Rebouka being lame (one of
my heavy brass kettles having fallen on one of his feet),
I consented.

Now I found that I could no more know who was the
chief of a village. Kombila, I began to suspect, was not
the chief of Mokaba. The chiefs had a superstition that
if I knew who they were I would kill them.

In the Ishogo village I was among a new people, and,
indeed, their appearance was strange to me. Little by
little they came back to the village, for the Mokaba people
were great friends of theirs, and they told the Ishogos
not to be afraid. Many of the villagers, as they had to
pass by me, would put their hands over their eyes so as
not to see me. They were afraid.

I took a walk through the long street of that strange
Ishogo village, and counted one hundred and ninety-
one houses. The houses were much larger than those
of many other tribes, and were from twenty to twenty-
two feet in length, and from nine to twelve feet in width.
Each had a door in the middle from two to two and a
half feet in width, and about three and a half feet high.
The height of the lower walls was four and a half feet,
and the distance to the top of the roof eight or nine feet.
The doors of the houses were very tasteful. Each owner

seemed to vie with his neighbour in the choice of the prettiest patterns. Each door was carved and painted in different colours.

As I walked through the village, I thought what a great Spirit I must have seemed to the savage people of the interior of Africa. When I passed the houses of Igoumbié, some of the people, thinking I was not looking at them nor at their dwellings, partially opened their doors to get a peep at me; but if I happened to glance at them they immediately retired, evidently believing that I had an "evil eye."

I remained a day in the village of Igoumbié to make friends, so that the news might spread among the Ishogos that I was not an evil spirit; but most of them were so shy that when they had to pass the door of my hut they put their hands up to the side of their face so that they might not see me. Yet, in spite of their shyness, I made friends with many, and gave them beads.

One night the village was filled with fear. The people could not understand my doings. They were unable to discover what I meant by looking at the stars and at the moon with such queer-looking things as the instruments I held in my hand, and with dishes of quicksilver before me in which the moon and the stars were reflected. The aneroids, barometers, thermometers, boiling barometers, watches, and policemen's lanterns puzzled them extremely. They could not see why I should spend the greater part of the night with all those things around me.

I could not afford to lose much time in this village, for I had been so much detained before by the plague and other impediments, which have already been described, that it became necessary for me to go. I had still to pass through the territory of tribe after tribe; the Congo River was far to the eastward of us; the sources of the Nile were far away. So I said to Kombila, "Let us hurry. Take me to the farthest Ishogo village that you can. There we will remain a little while, and then I shall know all about the Ishogos."

We left Igoumbié, and once more plunged into the great forest. As I lost sight of the village, I heard the inhabitants crying loudly, "The Spirit has gone! the Spirit has gone!"

Suddenly, toward midday, the Apono porters stopped. I saw that a palaver was about to take place. I ordered my Commi men to be in readiness in case of any trouble. Kombila said, "Spirit, the people of Igoumbié wanted to have you among them. We said *nèshi* (no). The loads you have are heavy, and my people do not want to go farther unless you give them more beads, for their backs are sore."

I answered, "I have a heart to feel, and eyes to see. I intend to give to each of you a present before we part. Go ahead." The four elders or leaders of the party shouted, "It is so! it is so!" So we continued our march, and passed several villages, but the people were dumb with astonishment and fear.

In the country through which we were travelling, paths led from village to village, and when we came to a settlement we had to go through the whole length of it. Some of the villages in which the people had heard of my approach were perfectly deserted. In others the inhabitants had hidden themselves in their huts, and we saw none of them.

Once we lost our way, having taken the wrong path, and, being bewildered among the plantations of the natives, we had a hard time. Finally we came to a stream which the men recognised, and ascended it; but the day was then far advanced, and we concluded to build our camp. We all felt very tired, the men having sore feet on account of little ferruginous pebbles which covered the ground. After our fires had been lighted, and the men had smoked their pipes, and put the soles of their feet as near the fire as they could without burning them, we began to have a nice talk, and I asked the Aponos many questions.

CHAPTER XXII.

First Sight of a Village of the Dwarfs—A Strange and Interesting
Spectacle—An Abandoned Town—A Reverie beside a Stream—
The Leaf, the Butterfly, and the Bird—The Blessing of Water.

EARLY the next morning we started again on our
journey through the great forest, passing many hills
and several rivulets with queer names. Suddenly we
came upon twelve strange little houses scattered at
random, and I stopped and asked Kombila for what use
those shelters were built. He answered, "Spirit, those
are the houses of a small people called Obongos."

" What!" said I, thinking that I had not understood
him.

" Yes," repeated Kombila, " the people who live in such
a shelter can talk, and they build fires."

" Kombila," I replied, " why do you tell me a story?
How can people live in such little places? These little
houses have been built for idols. Look," said I, " at
those little doors. Even a child must crawl on the ground
to get into them."

" No," said Kombila, " the Dwarfs have built them."

" How can that be?" I asked; " for where are the
Dwarfs now? There are no plantain-trees around; there
are no fires, no cooking-pots, no water-jugs."

" Oh," said Kombila, " those Obongos are strange
people. They never stay long in the same place. They
cook on charcoal. They drink with their hands, or with
large leaves.

" Then," I answered, " do you mean to say that we are
in the country of the Dwarfs?"

" Yes" said Kombila, " we are in the country of the

L

Dwarfs. They are scattered in the forest. Their little villages, like the one you see before you, are far apart. They are as wild as the antelope, and roam in the forest from place to place. They are like the beasts of the fields. They feed on the serpents, rats and mice, and on the berries and nuts of the forest."

"That cannot be," I said.

"Yes, Oguizi, this is so," replied the porters. "Look for yourself;" and they pointed to the huts.

"Is it possible," I asked myself, "that there are people so small that they can live in such small buildings as those before me?"

How strange the houses of the Dwarfs seemed! The length of each house was about that of a man, and the height was just enough to keep the head of a man from touching the roof when he was seated. The materials used in building were the branches of trees bent in the form of a bow, the ends put into the ground, and the middle branches being the highest. The shape of each house was very much like that of an orange cut in two. The frame-work was covered with large leaves, and there were little doors which did not seem to be more than eighteen inches high, and about twelve or fifteen inches broad. Even the Dwarfs must have lain almost flat on ground in order to pass through. When I say door I mean simply an opening, a hole to go through. It was only a tiny doorway. But I managed to get inside one of these strange little houses, and I found there two beds, which were as curious as everything else about the premises. Three or four sticks on each side of the hut were the beds. Each bed was about eight inches, or, at the most, ten inches in width. One was for the wife and the other for the husband. A little piece of wood on each bed made the pillows. It was almost pitch dark inside, the only light coming from the opening or door. Between the two beds were the remains of a fire, judging by the ashes and the pieces of burnt wood.

These huts did really look like the habitations of men— the homes of a race of Dwarfs. But had Kombila told me a falsehood? Were not these huts built for the fetichs

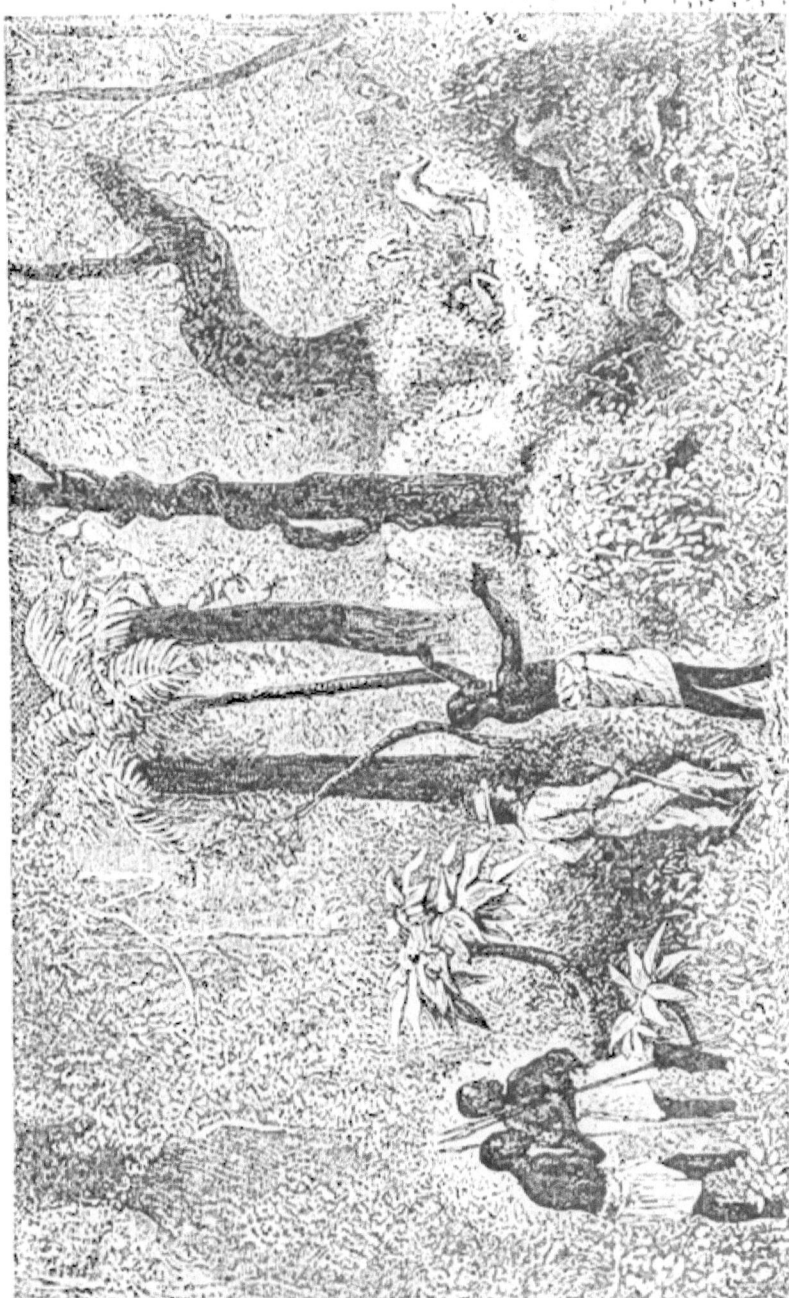

Huts of the Dwarfs.

and idols? It was true the great historian Herodotus had
described a nation of Dwarfs as living on the head-waters
of the Nile; Homer had spoken of the cranes and of the
land of the Pigmies; and Strabo thought that certain
little men of Ethiopia were the original Dwarfs, while
Pomponius Mela placed them far south, and, like Homer,
spoke of their fighting with cranes; but then nobody had
believed these stories. Could it be possible that I had
discovered these people, spoken of thousands of years
before, just as I had come face to face with the gorilla,
which Hanno had described many centuries before?

How excited I became as I thought this strange matter
over and over! Finally, however, my mind became settled,
and I said to myself, "No, these mean shelters could
never have been built by man, for the nshiegombouvé
builds as good a house. Kombila tells me a story. These
houses are built for a certain purpose, and he does not
want to tell me the reason."

So we left the so-called abandoned village of the
Dwarfs, and onward we travelled toward the east, and
soon came to a river called Ogoulou, on the bank of
which was situated an Ishogo village of the name of
Yengué.

We entered, but the villagers received us in profound
silence. Kombila all the time said to them, "Do not be
afraid. We have come here as friends." At last we
reached the ouandja, and there I seated myself. I could
not find out who the chief was, but the people evidently
knew the Mokaba tribe. The old men, after a while,
gave me a house for myself and my Commi, while my
Aponos went to lodge with their friends. I heard that
the chief had fled.

Nothing important took place that day. In the evening, while in my hut, in the midst of a profound silence,
I heard a voice exclaiming "Beware! We have an
oguizi among us! Beware! There is no *monda* (fetich)
to prevent us from seeing him during the day, but let no
one try to see him in his house at night, for whoever does
so is sure to die." So no one dared to come. After
hearing this speech, in order to give the savages an idea

of my great power, I fired a gun. Its report filled the people with awe.

After resting in Yengué we made preparations to cross the beautiful Ogoulou River, and when I stood upon its bank I said, "Ogoulou—such is thy Ishogo name; but, as I am the first white man who sees thy waters, I call thee Eckmühl, in remembrance of a dear friend!"

We crossed the river in canoes, and then continued our way, and after about six miles' journeying came to an Ishogo village called Mokenga. It was the last Ishogo village to which the Apono were to take me. They had fulfilled their mission, and had led me toward the east as far as they could go.

Mokenga was a beautiful village, with a wide and clean street; but as we walked through it we saw that the doors of the houses were all shut, and there was not one Ishogo to be seen. Nevertheless, we marched through the village until we came to the ouandja. A few men were then seen peeping at us from afar with frightened looks. Kombila called to them, saying, "How is it that when strangers come to your village you do not hasten to salute them?" Then they recognised some of my porters, and shouted back, "You are right! you are right!" Some of the elders came to us, and saluted us in the Ishogo fashion—that is, by clapping the hands together, and then stretching them out again, showing the palms.

Kombila made a speech, and other Aponos also spoke. Kombila cried out, in his stentorian voice, "If you are not pleased, tell us, and we will take the Spirit to another village where the people will be glad to welcome us." Then the elders of the village withdrew together, and presently came back, saying, "We are pleased, and gladly welcome the Oguizi;" and then huts were given to us.

The Ishogos have really good large huts, many of which were adorned with roomy piazzas. The forest round the village of Mokenga was filled with leopards, so that the people could not sleep outside their huts in very warm weather, and every goat was carefully guarded in order not to become the prey of those beasts. In the centre of the village were two goat-houses, built so strongly that the leopards could not get in, and every evening the goats were shut up. The Ishogos not only have goats, but also a small species of poultry, and almost every house has a parrot of the grey variety with red tail. Beehives were also plentiful.

Not far from the goat-house were found two large trees that were planted when the village was built, and upon them were thousands of birds' nests with myriads of birds, which made a fearful noise. These birds lived all the year round in Mokenga. I have given you a description of their colony in " Wild Life under the Equator."

One morning, before the people were up, I took the road leading to the spring from which the villagers got their water, for I wanted to see it. The path led down the hill, and soon a charming sight met my eye. The landscape was lovely. A rill of water, clear, cold, and pure, leaped from the lower part of a precipitous hill, and, with a fall of about nine feet, fell into a crystal basin filled with beautiful pebbles. From the basin a rivulet crawled along a bed of small pebbles down to the lower level, winding through a most beautiful forest. The scene was very beautiful.

One day, when I had seated myself below the fall, the rays of the sun, peeping through an opening, happened to shine upon the water, and made it look like running crystal. Below the cascade, the bed of the little stream, filled with pebbles of quartz, sparkled as if the pebbles had been diamonds; they might have been taken for gems while the sun was shining upon them. Water-lilies, white as snow, grew here and there, and moved to and fro, tossed by the water flowing toward the great river Rembo. The water looked like the water of life, and so it was. I said to myself, " When God is good to man, he is good to all; for all kinds of living creatures come to this stream, and drink of the water which is life to them."

The gentle ripple of the stream, as it glided down, sounded like music, and made me think. I could not help it. My thoughts wandered far over the mountains, and the lands I had crossed and discovered, and far beyond the sea, to the land where the great Mississippi flows. I looked intently at the water. Now and then I could see a little pebble rolling along; then it would stand still for a while, and again roll on, and every roll wore it away and rounded it. As it kept rolling down the stream day after day, year after year, it would become daily less and less in size. I said to myself, " What does keep still ? Since the beginning of the world nothing has stood still; everything goes on and on, and will continue to do so till the end."

Just as I was beginning to think deeply on the subject, a leaf fell from a tree into the water, and was carried away down the stream. Now it would strand on the shore, or on some little island which seemed to have been made for a resting-place, and then it would be carried away again by the swift current. I wondered what would be the journey of that little leaf. Would it be carried all the way to the sea? Surely it could not tell, neither could I tell how long a time it would take to get to the sea, nor what would happen to it during the passage. Our life, I thought, is very much like the journey of that little leaf: it knew not what was before it, nor do we know what will happen to us.

Such is life. From the day we are born we known not how we shall be carried on by the stream of life. We may strand on the shore, or we may glide gently down the current; but, like this little leaf, on our journey we must meet with whirlpools and rocky shores, rapids and precipices, and many obstacles. Storms may overtake us and strand us, but the end of the journey is sure to come, and then the great and the learned, the rich and the poor, the Christian and the heathen, the Moslem and the Jew, are sure to meet.

I followed the little leaf till it disappeared from my sight for ever. Another came and followed it, and another, and another, and they all vanished after a while never to come back to the same spot. So it is with man, I thought. One disappears from sight—Death has taken him. Another comes and takes his place; another and another follow each other, as these leaves did, and all go to the same goal—Death.

I said to myself, "I have drifted away like one of these leaves; sometimes tossed by the sea, sometimes by the wind, going to and fro, carried down the journey of life, meeting storms and breakers. I cannot tell where I shall drift, for no man can tell what the future has in store for him. God alone knows whither the little leaf and I are drifting."

As I continued my reverie, thinking of life and its mysteries, and of the future, a beautiful butterfly made its appearance. Its colours were brilliant—red and white, blue and gold. It went from lily to lily, caring apparently for nothing but the sweets of life. I could not help saying to myself, "How many are like this little butterfly! but how little we know, for I am sure this butterfly has its troubles, and so have those who have made the world and its pleasures the flowers upon which they live."

The butterfly had hardly disappeared from sight when a bird came—what a sweet little bird! I see it still by that little stream of Mokenga, though years have passed away. Down the tree he came fluttering from branch to branch, looking at the water, calling for his mate, as if to say, "I have found water; come and let us drink together;" but the absent one did not come. Soon afterward the bird was on the shore, its little feet leaving prints upon the sand. It came to one spot and stopped, gave a warble of joy, then drank, and between each sip sang, as if to tell how happy he was, and to thank God for that beautiful water. After drinking, it spread its wings and bathed its little body in the spring of Mokenga, then flew away, hid in the thick leaves out of my sight, and for a while I heard it singing.

"How grateful you seemed to be, little birdie, to that God who gave you this nice water to drink!" I said; "but, though you are happy just now, I know that you have your sorrows and troubles,* like every creature which God has made, from man down to the smallest insect."

---

* See chapter on "The Sorrows of Birds," in "Wild Life under the Equator."

After the little bird had gone I went to the spot where it had drank. Nothing could be seen but its footprints, and even these would remain but a short time, and after a while no one would ever know where its feet had been. So it is with the footprints of man—who can tell where they come upon the highways?

Not far from where I stood the stream was deeper. The little pebbles looked so pretty, the water so clear, so pure, and so cool, that I could not withstand the temptation, and, like the little bird, I drank, and thought there was not a beverage that ever was so good, for God had made it for man and for his creatures. Many times, in these grand and beautiful regions of Equatorial Africa, I have exclaimed, on beholding the beautiful water which abounds everywhere, and after I had quenched my thirst, " There is nothing so good and so harmless as the water that God created!"

CHAPTER XXIII.

Grotesque Head-dresses—Curious Fashions in Teeth—A Venerable
Granite Boulder—Interior of a Hut—A Warlike Race of Savages
—Giving them an Electric Shock.

HOW strange were those Ishogos! They were unlike
all the other savages I met. What a queer way to
arrange their hair! It requires from twenty-five to thirty
years for an Ishogo woman to be able to build upon her
head one of their grotesque head-dresses. But you
will ask how they can arrange hair in such a manner. I
will tell you:—A frame is made, and the hair is worked
upon it; but if there is no frame, then they use grass-
cloth, or any other stuffing, and give the shape they wish
to the head-dress. A well-known hairdresser, who, by
the way, is always a female, is a great person in an Ishogo
village, and is kept pretty busy from morning till afternoon. It takes much time to work up the long wool on
these negroes' heads, but, when one of these heads of hair
or *chignons*, is made, it lasts for a long time—sometimes
for two or three months—without requiring repair. I
need not tell you that after a few weeks the head gets
filled with specimens of natural history. The Ishogo
women use a queer comb: it is like a sharp-pointed needle
from one to eighteen inches in length, and, when the
insects bite, the point is applied with vigour.

A great quantity of palm oil is used in dressing the
hair, and, as the natives never wash their heads, the odour
is not pleasant. When a woman comes out with a newly-
made *chignon*, the little Ishogo girls exclaim, "When
shall I be old enough to wear one of these? How beautiful
they are!"

Every morning, instead of taking a bath, the Ishogos rub themselves with oil, mixed with a red dye made from the wood of a forest tree.

All the people have their two upper middle incisor teeth taken out, with the two middle lower ones, and often the four upper incisors are all extracted. They think they look handsome without front teeth. Their bodies are all tattooed. Their eyebrows are shaved at intervals of a few days, and their eyelashes are also pulled out from time to time.

Many who can afford it wear round the neck a loose ring of iron of the size of a finger, and if they are rich they wear on their ankles and wrists three or four loose iron or copper rings, with which they make music when they dance. Not an Ishogo woman has her ears pierced for earrings. This is extraordinary, for all savages seem fond of earrings.

The days passed pleasantly while I was in the village of Mokenga. I loved the villagers, and, besides, the country was beautiful. The mountains were lovely; the streams of clear water were abundant; around the village were immense groves of plantain-trees, in the midst of which, giant-like, rose gracefully a great number of palm-trees; the lime-trees were covered with ripe yellow limes; wild Cayenne pepper grew everywhere; and back of all stood the great tall trees of the forest, with their dark foliage, and with creepers hanging down from their branches, while underneath the trees was the thick jungle, into which man could hardly penetrate. All was romantic and wonderful.

Not far from the village stood a very large solitary boulder of granite. How did it come there? The people looked at the huge stone with veneration. They said a spirit brought it there long, long ago. This boulder stood by the path leading to the spring which supplied the villagers with drinking water, and the women of the village were constantly going with their calabashes to get the cool water. When I ascended the hill in returning from my walks, I was fond of stopping to rest upon this boulder, and it was a perpetual wonder to me.

But one day there was a great excitement in Mokenga. The people would go toward the boulder, and then come back with a frightened aspect, and look toward my hut apparently in great fear. Indeed, they were so alarmed that they fled from me when I looked at them. The Oguizi, they said, had got up from his slumber during the night, and had gone to the boulder, and taken it upon his shoulders and moved it away; for all said it was not in the same place that it had formerly occupied. "How strong is the Oguizi!" they said; "he can move mountains!" During the day they came, covered with the chalk of the alumbi, and danced around my hut while I was in the forest, shouting, "Great Oguizi, do not be angry with us!"

The hut which the Mokenga people gave me was quite a sight. The furniture of an Ishogo house is unique, and I am going to give you an inside view of it.

My own house was twenty-one feet long and eight feet wide. In the middle there was a door, with twelve carved round spots, painted black; the outside ring was painted white, and the background was red. The door was twenty-seven inches in height. The house had three rooms, and from the roof were suspended great numbers of baskets and dishes of wicker-work, made from a kind of wild *rotang*. Baskets and dishes constitute a part of the wealth of an Ishogo household, and great numbers of them are given to the girls when they marry. Hung to the roof were also large quantities of calabashes which had been hardened by the smoke. A large cake of tobacco had also been hung up, and all around were earthenware pots and jars, used for cooking purposes, with cotton bags, several looms, spears, bows, arrows, battle-axes, and mats.

The Ishogos and I gradually became very friendly. We had many nice talks together, and I heard strange tales, and more stories about the Dwarfs.

"Yes," said the Ishogos, "but a little while ago there was a settlement of the Dwarfs not far from Mokenga, but they have moved, for they are like the antelope; they never stay long at the same place."

" You are in the country of the Dwarfs, Oguizi," they continued ; " their villages are scattered in our great forest, where they move from place to place, and none of us know where they go after they leave."

An Ashango man was in Mokenga on a visit while I stayed there. An Ishogo had married his daughter. He, too, said that there were many settlements of Dwarfs in his country, and he promised that I should see them when I went there. The name of his village is Niembouai, and he said he should tell his people that we were coming ; for the Ishogos were to take me there, and leave me in the hands of the Ashangos, who in their turn, were to take me, as the Ishogos often say, where my heart led me.

After a very pleasant time in Mokenga, we left that place for the Ashango country, inhabited by the new people, who were said by the Isohogos to speak the same language as the Aponos. The villagers had begun to love me, for I had given them many things ; having too much luggage, I was rather generous with them, and had given the women great quantities of beads. There was great excitement in Mokenga before we left, and, as my Ishogo porters, headed by Mokounga, took up their loads, the people were wild with agitation.

During the day we crossed a mountain called Migoma, and saw Mount Njiangala. From Migoma I could see the country all around. As far as my eye could reach I saw nothing but mountains covered with trees. " There," said the Ishogos to me, " live gorillas, chimpanzees, Dwarfs, elephants, and all kinds of wild beasts."

The travelling was hard, but on we went, still toward the east, and before dark of the first day we came to a mountain called Mouïda. At its base was a beautiful stream called Mabomina. We encamped for the night, all feeling very tired. We had to keep watch carefully over our fires, for leopards were plentiful. The next morning we started, glad to get out of the haunts of these animals, which had been prowling around our camp all night.

After some severe travelling we arrived at the bank of

a river called Odiganga. After crossing the stream we came upon a new tribe of wild Africans called the Ashangos. There was a scream of fear among them when I made my appearance; but the Ishogos cried out, "Ashango, do not be afraid; we are with the Oguizi." I could see at a glance that the Ashangos were a warlike race. The village was called Magonga, meaning "spear." Back of it was a mountain, towering high in the air, called Madombo. We spent the night in the village, and after leaving it we had an awful task in ascending Mount Madombo. The path was so steep that we had to aid ourselves by using the bushes and creepers hanging from the trees. It was all we could do to succeed. I would not have liked any fighting at that spot.

On our journey we found that these wild Ashangos were very numerous in these mountains. Village after village was passed by us in the midst of a profound silence, sometimes broken by the people who had heard of our approach, and were hiding themselves in their huts. At other times, after we had passed, they would shout, "The Oguizi has black feet and a white face!" (They thought my boots were my own skin.) "He has no toes! What queer feet the Oguizi has!"

My seven Commi were perfectly delighted with their journey; our misfortunes were forgotten.

After a long journey over the mountains and through a wild region, we came at last to the village of Niembouai. I was glad to reach it, for there seemed to be no dry season in that part of the world. It rains all the year round. The people, though shy, did not run away, but were very difficult of approach. Our Ashango friend, whom we had met at Mokenga, had done his best to allay their fears, and he and a deputation of the Niembouai had come to Magonga to meet us, and to take us to their own country. So everything was ready for my reception. When I reached Niembouai the best house of the village was given to me. It belonged to the elder who had seen me at Mokenga, and who claimed the right to have me as his guest.

The next day after my arrival the supposed chief came.

I had no way of knowing if he was the true chief. A grand palaver was held, and I gave presents of beads, trinkets, &c., to him, and to forty-three elders, and to the queen and other women. After the presents had been given I thought I would show them my power, and ordered guns to be fired. This filled them with fear. " He holds the thunder in his hand !" they said. " Oh, look at the great Oguizi ! look at his feet ! look at his hair ! look at his nose ! Look at him ! Who would ever have thought of such a kind of oguizi, for he is so unlike other oguizis ?"

After the excitement was over I told the Ashangos to keep still. I then went into my hut and brought out a Geneva musical box of large size, and when I touched the spring it began to play. I moved off. A dead silence prevailed. By instinct the Ashangos moved off too, and a circle was formed by them around the box. They all listened to " the spirit," to " the devil that was inside of that box" talking to me. Fear had seized upon them. I walked away. They stood like statues, not daring to move a step. They were spell-bound.

After a few moments I took the box back into my hut, and brought out a powerful electric battery. Then I ordered the forty-three elders and the king to come and stand in a line. They came, but were evidently awed. The people dared not say a word. Everything being ready, I told them to hold the ninety feet of conducting wire. " Hold hard !" I cried.

The people looked at the old men with wonder, and could not understand how they dared to hold that charmed string of the Oguizi. The Ishogos, my guides, were themselves bewildered, for they had not seen this thing in their village. My Commi men did not utter a word, but their faces were as long as if they never had seen anything.

" Hold on !" I repeated ; " do not let the string go out of your hands." I then gave a powerful continuous shock. The arms of the elders twisted backward against their will, and their bodies bent over ; but they still held the wire, which, indeed, now they had not the power to drop. Their mouths were wide open ; their bodies trembled from the continuous electric shock ; they looked at me and cried, "Oh! oh! oh! Yo! yo! yo!" I had really given a too powerful shock. The people fled.

In an instant all was over. I stopped the current of electricity. The wire fell from the elders' hands, and they looked at me in perfect bewilderment. The people came back. The elders explained their electric sensation, and then a wild hurrah and a shout went up. "There is not another great oguizi like the one in our village," was the general exclamation ; and they came and danced around me, and sang mbuiti songs, bending their bodies low, and looking at me in the face as if I had been one of their idols. "Great Oguizi, do not be angry with us," they cried repeatedly.

"Don't be afraid, Ashangos," I said. I then ordered my men to fire their guns again, and to add to the noise, our dogs began to bark ; so that, with the barking, the shouting, the firing, and the beating of drums by the natives, Niembouai was very lively for a few minutes.

"Come again !" shouted the Ishogos. "The Oguizi we brought to you has more things to show you." Then I came out with a powerful magnet, which held many of the implements of iron used by the Ashangos. Up and down went the knives; the magnet sometimes held them by the end, sometimes by the blade. The people were so afraid of the magnet that not one of them dared to touch it when I asked them to do so.

That night I hung a large clock under the piazza, and the noise it made frightened the Ashangos very much.

My power was established. The electric battery had been effective. How droll the sight was when they received the shock ! You would have laughed heartily if you could have seen them.

CHAPTER XXIV.

Visit to a Village of the Dwarfs—Walk through the Primeval Forest
—An Ancient Account of this Strange Race—A Great Ashango
Dance—A Watch and a tremendous Sneeze—First view of the
Dwarfs—Queer Specimens of Humanity.

THE day after I had done before the Ashangos the
wonderful things I have described to you, as I was
seated under the veranda of the king with Mokounga and a
few Ashango elders, I began to talk of the country, and
I said to them, "People say that there are Dwarfs living
in the forest. Is it so, Ashangos? How far are they
from Niembouai?" "At no great distance from this
spot," said the chief, "there is a village of them; but,
Oguizi, if you want to see them you must not go to them
with a large number of attendants,. You must go in a
small party. Take one of your Commi men, and I will
give you my nephew, who knows the Dwarfs, to go with
you. You must walk as cautiously as possible in the
forest, for those Dwarfs are like antelopes and gazelles;
they are shy and easily frightened. To see them you
must take them by surprise. No entreaty of ours could
induce them to stay in their settlements if they knew you
were coming. If you are careful, to-morrow we shall see
them, for as sure as I live there are Dwarfs in the forest,
and they are called Obongos."

Early the next morning the Ashango chief called one
of his nephews and another Ashango, and ordered them
to show me the way to the country of the Dwarfs. So
we got ready to start, I taking three of my Commi men
with me—Rebouka, Igalo, and Macondai. I had put on
a pair of light indiarubber boots in order not to make

any noise in the forest. Before leaving I gave a large
bunch of beads to one of the Ashango men, and told him
as soon as we made our appearance in the village to
shout, "Obongos, do not run away. Look here at the
beads which the Spirit brings to you. The Spirit is
your friend; do not be afraid; he comes only to see
you."

After leaving Niembouai we walked through the forest
in the most cautious manner, and as we approached the
settlement the Ashango man who was in the lead turned
his head toward us, put a finger on his lips for us to be
silent, and made a sign for us to walk very carefully, and
we advanced with more circumspection than ever. After
a while we came to the settlement of the Dwarfs. Over a
small area the undergrowth had been partially cut away,
and there stood twelve queer little houses, which were the
habitations of these strange people, but not a Dwarf was
to be seen. They had all gone. "Nobody here," shouted
the Ashangos, and the echo of their voices alone disturbed
the stillness of the forest. I looked around at this strange
little settlement of living Dwarfs. There was no mistake
about it. The fires were lighted, the smoke ascended from
the interior of their little shelters; on a bed of charcoal
embers there was a piece of snake roasting; before another
were two rats cooking; on the ground there were several
baskets of nuts, and one of berries, with some large wild
fruits that had been gathered by the Dwarfs in the woods;
while near by stood several calabashes filled with water,
and some bundles of dried fish.

There was, indeed, no mistake: the huts I had seen on
my way to Niembouai were the same as these, and had
been made surely by the same race of Dwarfs. The
Ishogos had told me no idle stories. I wish you could
have seen the faces of Rebouka, Igalo, and Macondai.
"Oh! oh! oh!" they exclaimed. "Chally, what are we
not going to see in the wild countries you bring us to?
These people must be *niamas* (beasts); for, look," said they,
pointing to their huts, "the shelters of the nshiegombouvé
are quite as good."

I lingered a long while in the hope that the Dwarfs

M

would return, but they did not. We called for them, but our voices were lost; we followed some of their tracks, but it was of no use. "You cannot overtake them," said the Ashangos, "for they can run through the jungle as fast as the gazelle and as silently as a snake, and they are far off now. They are afraid of you." Before leaving their settlement I hung on the lower branches of trees surrounding their village strings of beads of bright colours which I carried with me in my hunting-bag, for I always had some ready to give away whenever I wanted to do so. I had red, white, and yellow beads with me that day, and the trees looked gay with these strings hanging from them. We had taken goat-meat for the Dwarfs, and I hung up three legs of goats also, and several plantains, and I put a little salt on a leaf near a hut, and we departed. So I hoped that the Dwarfs, seeing what we had left behind us, would become emboldened, and see that we did not desire to do them harm, and that the next time they would not be afraid of us.

I was pleased to perceive on our arrival in the evening at Niembouai that the Ashangos seemed glad to see us again, though the chief was quite disappointed that we had not seen the little Obongos.

That evening the Ashangos clustered around me, and wanted me to talk to them, not in their own language, but in the language of the oguizis (spirits). So I talked to them, and their wonder was great, and I read to them from a book, all of them listening the while with their mouths wide open. Then I took my journal, and read to them aloud in English, and after reading the part which related to what I had done in the Ishogo village of Mokenga, I translated it to them, to the great delight of the Ishogos. The part I read related to my arrival in Mokenga; how the people were afraid of me, and what warm friends we became, and how the villagers said I had moved the big boulder of granite. At this there was a tremendous shout. Then I said, "Ashangos, the oguizis do not forget anything. What I write will always be remembered. Now I will read you something we have from an oguizi who wrote about Dwarfs. The name of that oguizi was Herodotus." "And yours," shouted the Ishogos, " is Chally !"

" That oguizi, Herodotus," I continued, " wrote about what he heard and what he saw, just as I do. Long, long ago, before any tree of the forest round you had come out of the ground" (I could not count in their language, and say about 2300 years ago), "that oguizi, Herodotus, travelled just as I am travelling to-day"—" *Oh ! oh !*" shouted the Ashangos. " Mammo! mammo!" shouted the Ishogos. " Listen! listen!" said my Commi men in English, for they all now could talk a little English—" and he writes :—

" ' I did hear, indeed, what I will now relate, from certain natives of Cyrene. Once upon a time, when they were on a visit to the oracular shrine of Ammon, when it chanced in the course of conversation with Etearchus, the Ammonian king, the talk fell upon the Nile—how that its source was unknown to all men. Etearchus, upon this, mentioned that some Nasamonians had come to his court, and, when asked if they could give any information concerning the uninhabited parts of Libya, had told the following tale (the Nasamonians are a Libyan race who occupy the Syrtes and a tract of no great size toward the east). They said there had grown up among them some wild young men, the sons of certain chiefs, who, when they came to man's estate, indulged in all manner of extravagances, and, among other things, drew lots for five of their number to go and explore the desert parts of Libya, and try if they could not penetrate farther than any had done previously. (The coast of Libya, along the sea, which washes it to the north throughout its entire length from Egypt to Cape Soloeis, which is its farthest point, is inhabited by Libyans of many distinct tribes, who possess the whole tract except certain portions which belong to the Phœnicians and the Greeks.) Above the coast-line and the country inhabited by the maritime tribes, Libya is full of wild beasts, while beyond the wild-beast region there is a tract which is wholly sand and very scant of water, and utterly and entirely a desert. The young men, therefore, despatched on this errand by their comrades, with a plentiful supply of water and provisions, travelled at first through the inhabited region, passing which they came to the wild-beast tract, whence they finally entered upon the desert, which they proceeded to cross in a direction from east to west. After journeying for many days over a wide extent of land, they came at last to a plain where they observed trees growing: approaching them and seeing fruit on them, they proceeded to gather it; while they were thus engaged there came upon them some *dwarfish men under the middle height*, who seized them and carried them off. The Nasamonians did not understand a word of their language, nor had they any acquaintance with the language of the Nasamonians. They were carried across extensive marshes, and finally came to a city in which all the men were of the height of their conductors, and dark complexioned. A great river flowed by the city, running from west to east, and containing crocodiles. Etearchus conjectured this river to be the Nile, and reason favours this idea.'"

"Oh! oh!" shouted my Commi men. "It is no wonder that the white man forgets nothing. Chally, will what you write about the strange things we see be remembered in the same manner with what that man Herodotus wrote?"

"I do not know," said I. "If the white people think that what we saw is worthy of preservation, it will be remembered; if not, it will be forgotten. But never mind," I said; "let us see for ourselves, and what a tale we shall have to tell to our people on our return; for what we see no other men have ever seen before us."

After my story of Herodotus the shades of evening had come, and a great Ashango dance took place. How wild, how strange the dancing was in the temple or house of the mbuiti (idol)! The idol was a huge representation of a woman, and it stood at the end of the temple, which was about 50 feet in length, and only 10 feet broad. The extremity of the building, where the mbuiti was kept, was also dark, and looked weird by the light of the torches as I entered. It was painted in red, white, and black.

Along the walls on each side were Ashango men seated

on the ground, each having a lighted torch before him.
In the centre were two mbuiti-men (doctor, priest) dressed
with fibres of trees round their waist; each had one side
of his face painted white and the other side red. Down
the middle of the breast they had a broad yellow stripe,
and the hollow of the eye was painted yellow. They
make these different colours from different woods, the
colouring matter of which they mix with clay. All the
Ashangos were also streaked and daubed with various
colours, and by the light of their torches they looked like
a troop of devils assembled on the earth to celebrate some
diabolical rite. Round their legs were bound sharp-
pointed white leaves from the heart of the palm-tree;
some wore feathers, others had leaves behind their ears,
and all had a bundle of palm-leaves in their hands. They
did not stir when I came in. I told them not to stop;
that I came only to look at them.

They began by making all kinds of contortions, and set
up a deafening howl of wild songs. There was an orchestra
of instrumental performers near the idol, consisting of
three drummers beating as hard as they could with their
sticks on two *ngomas* (tam-tams), one harper, and another
man strumming with all his might on a sounding-board.
The two mbuiti-men danced in a most fantastic manner,
jumping and twisting their bodies into all sorts of shapes
and contortions. Every time the mbuiti-men opened
their mouths to speak a dead silence ensued. Now and
then the men would all come and dance round the mbuiti-
men, and then they would all face the idol, dance before
it, and sing songs of praise to it.

I could not stand this noise long, so I left my
Ashangos to enjoy themselves, and, as usual before re-
tiring, ordered my men to keep their watch in a proper
manner.

"Don't be disheartened," said the chief of Niembouai
to me after my unsuccessful attempt to see the Dwarfs.
"I told you before that the little Obongos were as shy as
the antelopes and gazelles of the woods. You have seen
for yourself now that what I said was true. If you are
careful when you go again to their settlement, you will

probably surprise them, only don't wait long before going again, for they may move away."

Before sunrise the next morning we started again for the settlement of the little Dwarfs. We were still more cautious than before in going through the jungle. This time we took another direction to reach them, lest perhaps they might be watching the path by which we had come before.

After a while I thought I saw through the trunks of the trees ahead of us several little houses of the Dwarfs. I kept still, and immediately gave a sign to make my guides maintain silence. They obeyed me on the instant, and we lay motionless on the ground, hardly daring to breathe. There was no mistake about it; we could see, as we peeped through the trees, the houses of the Dwarfs, but there seemed to be no life there, no Obongos. We kept watching for more than half an hour in breathless silence, when lo! Rebouka gave a tremendous sneeze. I looked at him. I wish you had seen his face. Another sneeze was coming, and he was trying hard to prevent it, and made all sorts of faces, but the look I gave him was enough, I suppose, and the second sneeze was suppressed. Then we got up and entered the little settlement of the Dwarfs. There was not one of them there. The village had been abandoned. The leaves over the little houses were dry, and, while we were looking all round, suddenly our bodies were covered with swarms of fleas, which drove us out faster than we came. It was awful, for they did bite savagely, as if they had not had anything to feed upon for a whole month.

We continued to walk very carefully, and after a while we came near another settlement of the Dwarfs, which was situated in the densest part of the forest. I see the huts; we cross the little stream from which the Dwarfs drew their water to drink. How careful we are as we walk toward their habitations, our bodies bent almost double, in order not to be easily discovered. I am excited—oh, I would give so much to see the Dwarfs, to speak to them! How craftily we advance! how cautious we are for fear of alarming the shy inmates! My Ashango guides hold bunches of beads. I see that the beads we had hung to the trees have been taken away.

All our caution was in vain. The Dwarfs saw us, and ran away in the woods. We rushed, but it was too late; they had gone. But as we came into the settlement I thought I saw three creatures lying flat on the ground, and crawling through their small doors into their houses. When we were in the very midst of the settlement I shouted, "Is there anybody here?" No answer. The Ashangos shouted, "Is there anybody here?" No answer. I said to the Ashangos, "I am certain that I have seen some of the Dwarfs go into their huts." Then they shouted again, "Is there anybody here?" The same silence. Turning toward me, my guides said, "Oguizi, your eyes have deceived you; there is no one here; they have all fled. They are afraid of you." "I am not mistaken," I answered. I went with one Ashango toward one of the huts where I thought I had seen one of the Dwarfs go inside to hide, and as I came to the little door I shouted again, "Is there anybody here?" No answer. The Ashango shouted, "Is there anybody inside?" No answer. "I told you, Oguizi, that they have all run away." It did seem queer to me that I should have suffered an optical delusion. I was perfectly sure that I had seen three Dwarfs get inside of their huts. "Perhaps they have broken through the back part, and have escaped," said I; so I walked round their little houses, but everything was right—nothing had gone outside through the walls.

In order to make sure, I came again to the door, and shouted, "Nobody here?" The same silence. I lay flat on the ground, put my head inside of the door, and again shouted, "Nobody here?" It was so dark inside that, coming from the light, I could not see, so I extended my arm in order to feel if there was any one within. Sweeping my arm from left to right, at first I touched an empty bed, composed of three sticks; then, feeling carefully, I moved my arm gradually toward the right, when—hallo! what do I feel? A leg! which I immediately grabbed above the ankle, and a piercing shriek startled me. It

was the leg of a human being, and that human being a
Dwarf! I had got hold of a Dwarf!

"Don't be afraid; the Spirit will do you no harm,"
said my Ashango guide.

"Don't be afraid," I said, in the Ashango language,
and I immediately pulled the creature I had seized by
the leg through the door, in the midst of great excitement among my Commi men.

"A Dwarf!" I shouted, as the little creature came out.
"A woman!" I shouted again—"a pigmy!" The little
creature shrieked, looking at me. "Nchendé! nchendé!
nchendé!" said she. "Oh! oh! oh! Yo! yo! yo!"
and her piercing wail rent the air.

What a sight! I had never seen the like. "What!"
said I, "now I do see the Dwarfs of Equatorial Africa—
the Dwarfs of Homer, Herodotus—the Dwarfs of the
ancients."

How queer the little old woman looked! How frightened she was! she trembled all over. She was neither
white nor black; she was of a yellow, or mulatto colour.
"What a little head! what a little body! what a little
hand! what a little foot!" I exclaimed. "Oh, what
queer-looking hair!" said I, bewildered. The hair grew
on the head in little tufts apart from each other, and the
face was as wrinkled as a baked apple. I cannot tell
you how delighted I was at my discovery.

So, giving my little prize to one of the Ashangos, and
ordering my Commi men to catch her if she tried to run
away, I went to the other little dwelling where I thought
I had seen another of the Dwarfs hide himself. The
two little huts stood close together. I shouted, "Nobody
here?" No answer. Then I did what I had done before, and, getting my head inside of the hut through the
door, again shouted, "Nobody here?" No answer. I
moved my right hand to see if I could feel anybody,
when, lo! I seized a leg, and immediately heard a shriek.
I pulled another strange little Dwarf out of the door.
It was also a woman, not quite so old as the first, but
having exactly the same appearance.

The two Dwarf-women looked at each other, and began

to cry and sing mournful songs, as if they expected to be killed. I said to them, " Be not frightened !"

Then the Ashangos called to the last Dwarf who had hid to come out; that it was no use, I had seen them all. They had hardly spoken when I saw a little head peeping out of the door, and my Ashangos made the creature come out. It was a woman also, who began crying, and the trio shrieked and cried, and cried and shrieked, wringing their hands, till they got tired. They thought their last day had come.

" Don't be afraid," said the Ashangos ; " the Oguizi is a good oguizi." " Don't be afraid," said my Commi men.

After a while they stopped crying, and began to look at me more quietly.

For the first time I was able to look carefully at these little Dwarfs. They had prominent cheek-bones, and were yellow, their faces being exactly of the same colour as the chimpanzee ; the palms of their hands were almost as white as those of white people ; they seemed well-proportioned, but their eyes had an untamable wildness that struck me at once ; they had thick lips and flat noses, like the negroes ; their foreheads were low and narrow, and their cheek-bones prominent ; and their hair, which grew in little, short tufts, was black, with a reddish tinge.

After a while I thought I heard a rustling in one of the little houses, so I went there, and, looking inside, saw it filled with the tiniest children. They were exceedingly shy. When they saw me they hid their heads just as young dogs or kittens would do, and got into a huddle, and kept still. These were the little dwarfish children who had remained in the village under the care of the three women, while the Dwarfs had gone into the forest to collect their evening meal—that is to say, nuts, fruits, and berries—and to see if the traps they had set had caught any game.

I immediately put beads around the necks of the women, gave them a leg of wild boar, and some plaintains, and told them to tell their people to remain, and not to be afraid. I gave some meat to the little children, who, as soon as I showed it to them, seized it just in the same manner that Fighting Joe or Ugly Tom would have done, only, instead of fighting, they ran away immediately.

Very queer specimens these little children seemed to be. They were, if anything, lighter in colour than the older people, and they were such little bits of things that they reminded me—I could not help it—of the chimpanzees and nshiego-mbouvés I had captured at different times, though their heads were much larger.

I waited in vain—the other inhabitants did not come back; they were afraid of me. I told the women that the next day I should return and bring them meat (for they are said to be very fond of it), and plenty of beads.

CHAPTER XXV.

AFTER several visits to the settlement of the Dwarfs we became friends, but it took time. My great friend among them was Misounda, an old woman, the first one I had seen, and whom I pulled out of her own house; but I had some trouble before I could tame friend Misounda.

One day I thought I would surprise the Dwarfs, and come on them unawares, without having told my friend Misounda I was coming. When I made my appearance I just caught a glimpse of her feet as she was running into her house. That was all I saw of Misounda. At all the other huts little branches of trees had been stuck up in front to show that the inmates were out, and that their doors were shut, and that nobody could get in. These were, indeed, queer doors. I had never seen the like. They were of little use except for keeping out the dogs and wild beasts. When I went in Misounda's hut and got hold of her, she pretended to have been asleep. "So, after all, these little Dwarfs," said I, "know how to lie and how to deceive just as well as other people."

Upon one of my visits to the village I saw two other women, a man, and two children; all the other Obongos had gone. So I made friends with them by giving them meat and beads. I saw that the women were not the mothers of the children. I looked at the doors of all the huts; they all had branches put at the entrance to signify that the owner was out. I do not know why, but I began to suspect that the mother of the children was in the settlement, and close by where they stood. I had my eyes

upon one of the little houses as the one where she was
hiding.; so I put aside the branches at the entrance, and,
putting half of my body into the hut, I succeeded in discovering in the dark something which I recognised, after
a while, as a human being.

"Don't be afraid," I said. "Don't be afraid," repeated
my Ashango guides. The creature was a woman. She
came out with a sad countenance, and began to weep.
She had over her forehead a broad stripe of yellow ochre.
She was a widow, and had buried her husband only a few
days before.

"Where is the burial-ground of the Dwarfs?" I
asked of my Ashango guides. "Ask her," said I to
them.

"No, Spirit," said they, "for if you ask them such a
question, these Dwarfs will fear you more than ever, and
you will never see them any more. They will flee far
away into the thickest part of the forest. We Ashango
people do not know even where they bury their dead.
They have no regular burial-ground. How could they?"
added my guide, "for they roam in the forest like the
gorilla, the nshiego-mbouvé, the kooloo-kamba, and the
nshiego. I believe," said the Ashango, "that all these
Dwarfs have come from the same father and the same
mother long, long ago."

Another time I came to the village of the Obongos with
two legs of goats, a leg of wild boar, ten house-rats which
had been trapped, a large dead snake, and two land-turtles,
which I intended to give as a feast to the Obongos.
Rebouka, Macondai, and Igalo were with me, and several
Ashango women accompanied us. We had several bunches
of plantain, for I had resolved to give them a regular
banquet, and we had set out to have a good time in
their settlement. I had brought beads, a looking-glass,
some spoons, knives, forks, and one of my little Geneva
musical boxes. Guns were also to be fired, for I was
going to show the Dwarfs what the Oguizi could do.
When they saw us with food they received us with great
joy. "What a queer language," I thought, "these Dwarfs
have!" There was a wild Dwarf hurrah, "Ya! ye! yo!

Oua! oua! Ké! ki-ke-ki !" when they saw the good things that were to be eaten.

Nearly all the Dwarfs were here; very few of them were absent. Misounda, who was my friend, and who seemed to be less afraid of me than anybody else, stood by me, and kept her eyes upon the meat. There were fifty-nine Dwarfs all told, including men, women, children, and babies. What little things the babies were! Smoke came out of every hut, fires were lighted all round, nuts were roasting, berries and fruits had been collected in great abundance, and snake-flesh was plentiful, for the Dwarfs had been the day before on a feeding excursion. Rats and mice had also been trapped.

"Obongos," said I, "we have come to have a good time. First I am going to give to every one of you beads." Then the Ashangos brought before them a basket containing the beads, and I asked who was the chief. I could not find him, and they would not tell me. Among them were several old people.

The Dwarfs were now eager for beads, and surrounded me, and, though I am a man of short stature, I seemed a giant in the midst of them; and as for Rebouka and Igalo, they appeared to be colossal. "Ya! ya! yo! yo! ye! qui! quo! oh! ah! ri! ri! ké! ki! ké! ki!" seemed to be the only sounds they could make in their excitement. Their appearance was singular indeed, the larger number of them being of a dirty yellow colour. A few of them were not more than four feet in height; others were from four feet two inches to four feet seven inches in height. But if they were short in size they were stoutly built; like chimpanzees, they had big, broad chests, and though their legs were small they were muscular and strong. Their arms were also strong in proportion to their size. There were grey-headed men, and grey-headed wrinkled old women among them, and very hideous the old Dwarfs were. Their features resembled very closely the features of a young chimpanzee. Some had grey, others hazel eyes, while the eyes of a few were black.

As I have said before, their hair was not like that of the negroes and Ashangos among whom the Dwarfs live, but grew in little short tufts apart from each other, and the hair, after attaining a certain length, could not grow longer. These little tufts looked like so many little balls of wool. Many of the men had their chest and legs covered with these little tufts of woolly hair. The women's hair was no longer than that of the men, and it grew exactly in the same manner.

I could not keep my eyes from the tiny babies. They were ridiculously small, and much lighter in colour than the older people. Their mothers had a broad string of leather hanging from their shoulders to carry them in.

There was great excitement among them as I distributed the beads, and they would shout, " Look at his djivie (nose); look at his mouna (mouth); look at his diarou (head); look at his nchouié (hair); look at his mishou (beard)!" and, in spite of my big moustache, they would shout, " Is he a bagala oguizi (man spirit), or an oguizi mokasho (woman spirit) ?" Some declared that I was a mokasho, others that I was a bagala. I did not forget my friend Misounda.

After I had given them beads I took out a large looking-glass which I had hidden, and put it in front of them. Immediately they trembled with fright, and said, " Spirit, don't kill us !" and turned their heads from the looking-glass. Then the musical box was shown, and when I had set it playing the Dwarfs lay down on the ground, frightened by the brilliant, sparkling music of the mechanism, and by turns looked at me and at the box. Some of them ran away into their little huts. After their fears were allayed I showed them a string of six little bells, which I shook, whereat their little eyes brightened, and their joy was unbounded when I gave them the bells. One, of course, was for friend Misounda, who hung it by a cord to her waist, and shook her body in order to make it ring.

After this I ordered Igalo to bring me the meat, and taking from my sheath my big, bright, sharp hunting-knife, I cut it and distributed it among the Dwarfs. Then I gave them the plantains, and told them to eat. I wish you had seen the twisting of their mouths; it would have made you laugh. Immediately the little Dwarfs scattered round their fires, and roasted the food I had given them, and it was no sooner cooked than it was eaten, they seemed to be so fond of flesh.

When they had finished eating, the Obongos seemed more sociable than I had ever seen them before. I seated myself on a dead limb of a tree, and they came round me and asked me to talk to them as the spirits talk. So I took my journal, and read to them in English what I had written the day before. After speaking to them in the language of the Oguizis, I said, "Now talk to me in the language of the Dwarfs;" and, pointing to my fingers, I gave them to understand that I wanted to know how they counted. So a Dwarf, taking hold of his hand, and then one finger after another, counted one, moï; two, beï; three, metato; four, djimabongo; five, djio; six, samouna; seven, nchima; eight, misamouno; nine, nchouma; ten, mbò-ta; and then raised his hands, intimating that he could not count beyond ten.

One of them asked me if I lived in the soungui (moon), then another if I lived in a niechi (star), another if I had been long in the forest. Did I make the fine things I gave them during the night?

"Now, Obongos," I said to them, "I want you to sing and to dance the Dwarf dance for me." An old Dwarf went out, and took out of his hut a ngoma (tam-tam), and began to beat it; then the people struck up a chant, and what queer singing it was! what shrill voices they had! After a while they got excited, and began to dance, all the while gesticulating wildly, leaping up, and kicking backwards and forwards, and shaking their heads.

Then I fired two guns, the noise of which seemed to stun them and fill them with fear. I gave them to understand that when I saw an elephant, a leopard, a gorilla, or any living thing, by making that noise I could kill them, and to show them I could do it I brought down a bird perched on a high tree near their settlement. How astonished they seemed to be!

"After all," I said to myself, "though low in the scale

of intelligence, like their more civilized fellow men, these little creatures can dance and sing."

"Now, Obongos, that you have asked me about the Oguizis," I said to them, "tell me about yourselves. Why do you not build villages as other people do?"

"Oh," said they, "we do not build villages, for we never like to remain long in the same place, for if we did we should soon starve. When we have gathered all the fruits, nuts, and berries around the place where we have been living for a time, and trapped all the game there is in the region, and food is becoming scarce, we move off to some other part of the forest. We love to move; we hate to tarry long at the same spot. We love to be free, like the antelopes and gazelles."

"Why don't you plant for food, as other people do?" I asked them.

"Why should we work," said they, "when there are plenty of fruits, berries, and nuts around us? when there is game in the woods, and fish in the rivers, and snakes, rats, and mice are plentiful? We love the berries, the nuts, and the fruits which grow wild much better than the fruits the *big people* raise on their plantations. And if we had villages," they said, "the strong and tall people who live in the country might come and make war upon us, kill us, and capture us."

"They do not desire to kill you," I said to them. "See how friendly they are with you! When you trap much game you exchange it for plantains with them. Why don't you wear clothing?"

"Why," said they, "the fire is our means of keeping warm, and then the *big people* give us their grass-cloth when they have done wearing it."

"Why don't you work iron, and make spears and battle-axes, so that you might be able to defend yourselves, and be not afraid of war?"

"We do not know how to work iron; it takes too much time; it is too hard work. We can make bows, and we make arrows with hard wood, and can poison them. We know how to make traps to trap game, and we trap game

in far greater number than we can kill it when we go
hunting; and we love to go hunting."

" Why don't you make bigger cabins ?"

" We do not want to make bigger cabins ; it would be
too much trouble, and we do not know how. These are
good enough for us; they keep the rain from us, and we
build then so rapidly."

" Don't the leopards sometimes come and eat some of
you ?"

" Yes they do !" they exclaimed. " Then we move off
far away, several days' journey from where the leopards
have come to eat some of us ; and often we make traps to
catch them. We hate the leopards !" the Obongos shouted
with one voice.

" How do you make your fires ? tell me ;" and I could
not help thinking that, however wild a man was, even
though he might be apparently little above the chimpanzee, he had always a fire, and knew how to make it.

They showed me flint-stones, and a species of oakum
coming from the palm-tree, and said they knocked these
stones against each other, and the sparks gave them
fire.

Then, to astonish them, I took a match from my match-
box and lighted it. As soon as they saw the flame a wild
shout ran through the settlement.

" Obongos, tell me," said I, " how you get your wives,
for your settlements are far apart, and you have no paths
leading through the forest from one to another. You
never know how far the next settlement of the Dwarfs
may be from yours."

" It is true," said they, " that sometimes we do not
know where the next encampment of the Obongos may be,
and we do not wish to know, for sometimes we fight among
ourselves, and if we lived near together we should become
too numerous, and find it difficult to procure berries and
game. Our people never leave one settlement for another.
Generation after generation we have lived among ourselves, and married among ourselves. It is but seldom we
permit a stranger from another Obongo settlement to come
among us."

N

"How far," said I, pointing to the east, "do you meet Obongos?"

"Far, far away," they answered, "toward where the sun rises, Obongos are found scattered in the great forest. We love the woods, for there we live, and if we were to live anywhere else we should starve."

"As you wander through the forest," I asked, "don't you sometimes come to prairies?"

"Yes," said they, and here an old Obongo addressed himself to my Ashango interpreter. "When I was a boy, we had our settlement for a long time in the forest not far from a big *prairie*, and farther off there was a big river. Since then," said the old Obongo, "as we moved we have turned our backs upon where the sun rises, and marched in the direction where the sun sets" (which meant that they had been migrating from the east toward the west).

"Did you not see," said I, continuing my questions, "birds with long legs and long beaks in those prairies?"

"Yes," said all the Obongos; "sometimes we kill them, for we love their flesh."

I could not but remember the description Homer gave of the Cranes and the Pigmies, and I here give it to you in the translation of a man of whom every American should be proud as one of the greatest poets of the age. Mr. William Cullen Bryant's translation reads as follows:

> "As when the cry
> Of cranes is in the air, that, flying south
> From winter and its mighty breath of rain,
> Wing their way over ocean, and at dawn
> Bring fearful battle to the Pigmy race,
> Bloodshed and death."—*Iliad*, iii. 3-8.

Of course our friend Homer, the grand old bard that will never die, did not see the Dwarfs, and only related what he had heard of them, and, like everything that is transmitted from mouth to mouth, and from country to country, the story has become very much exaggerated.

Beyond a doubt, at certain seasons of every year the cranes left the country of which Homer spoke, for cranes are migratory, and their migration was toward the Nile thence they winged their flight toward the Upper Nile, and spread all over the interior of Africa; and, as they came to the country of the Dwarfs, the Dwarfs came out to kill them, instead of their coming to kill the Dwarfs. The dwarfs of Homer's time killed them for food, as they still kill them in Equatorial Africa in certain seasons of the year.

I am now going to tell you what I wrote about these big cranes before I had even heard of the Country of the Dwarfs, or that such people as the Obongos ever existed:

"This account of Homer has been thought fabulous; for 'How,' it has been asked, 'could cranes attack a race of men?'

"Where were these pigmies to exist? I will try to show that Homer had some reason to say what he wrote. In the first book which I published (called 'Explorations in Equatorial Africa'), I did not mention what Homer had written. I had heard of the Dwarfs, but I dismissed the account given to me by the Apingi as fabulous. In chap. xiv. p. 260, I say:

"'The dry season was now setting in in earnest, and I devoted the whole month of July to exploring the country along the sea-shore. It is curious that most of the birds which were so abundant during the rainy season had by this time taken their leave, and other birds in immense numbers flocked in to feed on the fish, which now leave the sea-shore and bars of the river mouth, and ascend the river to spawn.'

"In the four paragraphs in advance on the same page I said, 'Birds flocked in immense numbers on the prairies, whither they came to hatch their young.

"'The ugly marabouts, from whose tails our ladies get the splendid feathers for their bonnets, were there in thousands. Pelicans waded on the river's banks all day in prodigious swarms, gulping down the luckless fish which came in their way.'

"In the next paragraph, page 261, I continue:

"'And on the sandy point one morning I found great flocks of the *Ibis religiosa* (the sacred Ibis of the Egyptians), which had arrived overnight, whence I could not tell.

"'Ducks of various kinds built their nests in every creek and on every new islet that appeared with the receding waters. I used to hunt those until I got tired of duck-meat, fine as it is. Cranes, too, and numerous other water-fowl, flocked in every day, of different species. All came, by some strange instinct, to feed upon the vast shoals of fish which literally filled the river.

"'On the sea-shore I sometimes caught a bird, the *Sula capensis*, which had been driven ashore by the treacherous waves to which it had trusted itself, and could not, for some mysterious reason, get away again.

"'And, finally, every sand-bar is covered with gulls, whose shrill screams are heard from morning till night as they fly about greedily after their finny prey.'

"I terminated the description by saying, 'It is a splendid time now for sportsmen, and I thought of some of my New York friends who would have enjoyed the great plenty of game that was now here.'

"In chap. xiii. of the same book, p. 199, I wrote:

"'From Igalé to Aniambié was two hours' walk, through grass-fields, in which we found numerous birds, some of them new to me. One in particular, the *Mycteria Senegalensis*, had such legs that it fairly outwalked me. I tried to catch it, but, though it would not take to the wing, it kept so far ahead that I could not even get a fair shot at it.

"'These *Mycteria Senegalenses* are among the largest of cranes. They have a long neck, and a very powerful beak, from 8 to 10 inches in length, and I killed several of them, which I brought back. I had grand shooting with them, and many a time I gave up the chase; but when I killed one I took good care to see that the bird could not hurt me and was quite dead before I approached it.'

"Hence I conclude that the description of Homer is correct as regards the great number of cranes, and that he was right, for you see that they came in the dry season, and when the rains came they disappeared from the country.

"The dwarfish race of whom I speak are great hunters, and is it not probable that during the dry season, when the cranes came, there was rejoicing in the Pigmean race? for there would be food and meat for them; and they would fight also with the large crane, the *Mycteria Senegalensis*, which probably they could not kill at once, and hence it required on the part of the Dwarfs great dexterity to capture them. For myself, I was always careful in approaching the *Mycteria Senegalensis*, whose height is from 4 to 5 feet, as I have said, when quite clear. The natives, as I approached the first that I killed, shouted to me, 'Take care; he will send his beak into your eye.'"

CHAPTER XXVI.

A Modern Traveller's Account of the Dwarfs and their Habits—
Where and how they bury their Dead—Hunting for the Dwarfs
—How they make their Huts.

NOW that I have told you what Herodotus and Homer
wrote about the Dwarfs, let us come to a more
modern account of them. We read the following in Rev.
Dr. Krapf's "Travels and Missionary Labours in East
Africa :"—

"Noteworthy are the reports which in the year 1840
were communicated to me by a slave from Enarea, who,
by order of the King of Shoa, was charged with the care of
my house in Angolala during my residence in Onkobez.
His name was Dilbo, and he was a native of Sabba, in
Enarea. As a youth, he had made caravan journeys to
Kaffa, and accompanied the slave-hunters from Kaffa to
Tuffte, in a ten-days' expedition, where they crossed the
Omo, some 60 feet wide, by means of a wooden bridge,
reaching from thence to Kullu in seven days, which is but
a few days' journey from the Dokos, a Pigmy race of
whom Dilbo told almost fabulous stories" (p. 50).

Then Dr. Krapf gives an account of Dilbo, which does
not bear on the subject, and then continues :—

"He told me that to the south of Kaffa and Sura there
is a very sultry and humid country, with many bamboo
woods (meaning, no doubt palm-trees), inhabited by the
race called Dokos, who are no bigger than boys ten years
old ; that is, only four feet high. They have a dark olive-
coloured complexion, and live in a completely savage
state, like the beasts, having neither houses, temples, nor
holy trees, like the Gallas, yet possessing something like an

idea of a higher being, called Yer, to whom, in moments
of wretchedness and anxiety, they pray, not in an erect
posture, but reversed, with the head on the ground, and
the feet supported upright against a tree or stone. In
prayer they say, 'Yer, if thou really dost exist, why dost
thou allow us thus to be slain? We do not ask thee for
food and clothing, for we live on serpents, ants, and mice.
Thou hast made us, why dost thou permit us to be trodden
under foot?' The Dokos have a chief, no laws, no weapons.
They do not hunt nor till the ground, but live solely on
fruits, roots, mice, serpents, ants, honey, and the like, climbing trees and gathering the fruits like monkeys, and both
sexes go completely naked. They have thick protruding
lips, flat noses, and small eyes. The hair is not woolly,
and is worn by the women over the shoulders. The nails
on the hands and feet are allowed to grow like the talons
of vultures, and are used in digging for ants, and in tearing
to pieces the serpents, which they devour raw, for they are
unacquainted with fire. The spine of the snake is the only
ornament worn around the neck, but they pierce the ears
with a sharp-pointed piece of wood."

Then Dr. Krapf adds that they are never sold beyond
Enarea, and continues as follows:—

"Yet I can bear witness that I heard of these little
people not only in Shoa, but also in Ukambani, two degrees to the south, and in Barava, a degree and a half to
the north of the equator. In Barava a slave was shown
to me who accorded completely with the description of
Dilbo. He was four feet high, very thick set, dark complexioned, and lively, and the people of the place assured
me that he was of the Pigmy race of the interior. It is
not impossible, too, that circumstances, such as continual
rains from May to January, and other means, may con-
tribute to produce a diminutive people of stunted develop-
ment in the interior of Africa. *A priori*, therefore, the
reports collected from different and mutually independent
points of Africa cannot be directly contradicted, only care
must be taken to examine with caution the fabulous
element mixed up with what may be true by native
reporters. In the Suali dialect 'dogo' means small, and

in the language of Enarea 'doko' is indicative of an ignorant and stupid person."

Now I think, though Dr. Krapf was a long way from where I was, that his Dwarfs must be the same people as the Obongos, though they do not bear the same name; but you must remember that the Obongos are called by three different names by other tribes. It is true the Dwarf he saw was very black, but then there may be some Dwarfs much darker than others, just as some negroes are darker than others.

Then I said to the Ashango interpreter, "Ask the little Obongos where they bury their dead." I wanted to know, though I did not tell him why. I wanted the skeleton of an Obongo to bring home, and I would have been willing to give a thousand dollars for one.

"Don't ask such a question of the Obongos," said he.

"And why?" I inquired.

"Because," he answered, "they would be so frightened they would all run away. Even we ourselves, the Ashangos, who are their friends, know not where they bury their dead, and I will tell you why: they are afraid that the Ashangos would steal the skulls of the dead people for fetiches, and if they could procure but one they would always know where the Obongos were in the forest."

"Tell me," said I, "how they bury their dead."

"When an Obongo dies," said my Ashango friend, "there is great sorrow among the Dwarfs, and the men are sent into every part of the forest to find a tall tree which is hollow at the top. If they find one, they come back to the settlement and say, 'We have found a tree with a hollow.' Then the people travel into the forest, guided by the man who has found the hollow tree, and taking with them the body of the dead Obongo. When they have reached the spot, some of them ascend the tree, carrying with them creepers to be used as cords for drawing up the body, and the corpse is then drawn up and deposited in the hollow, which is immediately filled with earth, and dry leaves, and the twigs of trees."

"But," said I, "big hollow trees, such as you have been

speaking of, are not found every day. If they do not find
one, what then?"

"It is so, Oguizi. Sometimes they cannot find a big
hollow tree; then," said my Ashango guide, "they wander
into the forest, far from paths and villages, in search of a
little stream, which they turn from its natural bed, and
then dig in it a big, deep hole, wherein they bury the
body of the Obongo, after which they bring back the
water to its own bed again, and the water for ever and
ever runs over the grave of the Obongo, and no one can
ever tell where the grave of the Obongo is."

"Why," said I to myself, "this way of burying an
Obongo reminds me of the burial of Attila."

This is all I know of the way the Obongos bury their
dead, and this was told me by the Ashangos. The Obongos,
who had seen me holding so long a talk with the Ashangos,
began to appear frightened, and asked what we had been
talking about. The Ashangos answered that we had
been talking about hunting wild beasts. After a while
we departed, apparently good friends with them, but not
before promising the Obongos that I would come again
and see them.

The next day I went hunting in order to kill meat and
bring it to the Dwarfs, and their delight was great when
I brought them five monkeys. A little while after I had
put the monkeys on the ground I said, "Dwarfs, let us be
good friends. Don't you see that I do not desire to kill
you or capture you? I wish only to know you well.
Every time I come to see you I bring you food and nice
things." "That is so," said the Dwarfs, headed by my
friend Misounda.

The hours passed away, and as evening approached I
said, "Dwarfs, what do you say to my spending the night
in your settlement, and going back to morrow to Niembouai?" "Muiri! muiri!" said the Dwarfs, and immediately a little house was given me for the night. I was
glad, for I wanted to be able to say when I came back
home that I had slept in a house of the Dwarfs.

The little Dwarfs went into the woods to collect firewood
for me, and to look after their traps. After a while they

came back, and they, too, brought food. Misounda brought me a basket of wild berries, and the other Obongos presented me game, consisting of three beautiful fat rats, a nice little mouse, one squirrel, two fish, and a piece of snake. They laid these things before me. To please them, I ordered the squirrel to be cooked on a bright charcoal fire, and how delighted they were to see me eat it! how they shouted when they saw me take mouthful after mouthful!

The sun went down behind the trees, and soon after it was dark in the village of the Dwarfs. I could see that they were still afraid of me. They had an idea that probably I wanted to capture some of them. At last the time came for me to go to bed. I had some trouble to get through the door, and when I was inside I lay down on my bed made of sticks, and put my head on my revolvers as a pillow. I had a little fire lighted so that the smoke would drive the musquitoes away, and before lying down I looked round to see if there were any snakes. You must always take that precaution in that part of the world. The Dwarfs kept awake all night outside of their huts, for they were not yet certain that I had not come to capture some of them.

Their little huts were of a low, oval shape, like gipsy tents. The lowest part, that nearest the entrance, was about 4 feet from the ground; the greatest breadth was also 4 feet. On each side were three or four sticks for the man and woman to sleep upon. The huts were made of flexible branches of trees, arched over and fixed into the ground, the longest branches being in the middle, and the others successively shorter, the whole being covered with large leaves.

The next morning the Ashangos and the Dwarfs went into the forest to look after the traps they had made to capture game.

As the time of our departure from Niembouai had arrived, I said to the Dwarfs that I must bid them good-bye, for I was going away toward where the sun rises. "Now you see," said I, "you have always been afraid of me. Tell me, have I done harm to any one of you?"

'No, no," they exclaimed; "no, no," said my friend Misounda. So I shook hands with them, and they said to me in parting, "You will see more little Dwarfs in the countries where you are going. Be kind to them, as you have been to us."

As I walked on through the jungle, my mind kept dwelling on the strange Obongos. "If you want one of them to take away with you," said my Ashango guide, " we will capture one for you, if you will give us beads and copper rings." "No, no," said I, "the Spirit does not want to capture people; he wants only to see people."

Now I must tell you what I think of these Obongos. I think that they are the very same people of whom Herodotus and Homer had heard; that they are closely allied to the Bushmen of South Africa, for the hair on their heads grows in the same way; only they are darker in colour, and in that respect seem to be a shade between the negro and the Bushmen. They are also a little shorter in stature than the Bushmen, and I have a strong belief that in times past they belonged probably to the same nation.

And now we must take leave of the Dwarfs, for I am to talk to you of the great negro tribes in whose country the little creatures live. If I should learn anything more about the Dwarfs as I go forward, I will surely relate it to you.

CHAPTER XXVII.

SEVERAL days have passed away since I have left the
Pigmies and the village of Niembouai, and I am
travelling toward the rising sun. The country is getting
more and more mountainous as we advance eastward, the
forests are very thick, the jungle is very dense, and many
of the trees are of immense size. An apparently perpetual
mist shrouds the summit of many of the hills, where it
rains almost every day, though on the sea-shore it is the
dry season. Village after village of the wild Ashango
inhabitants of the country have been passed by us; many
are deserted. The people are afraid of me, and do not
wish to see me.

Some of the mountains we passed had queer names.
One was called Birougou-Bouanga. I remember well
Birougou-Bouanga; it was 2574 feet in height.

In order to know the elevation of the country as I
travelled along, I had two kinds of instruments with me—
aneroids, and an apparatus for ascertaining at what point
water boils. The boiling apparatus was a queer-looking
instrument, and was a great object of fright to the negroes.
I will endeavour to give you an idea of the instrument:
there is a policeman's lantern; in it is a lamp, and on the
top is a kind of kettle in which water is put when to be
used. To the kettle is attached by a screw a thermometer, the bulb of which is immersed in the water. A
short time after the lamp is lit, the water boils and forces
the mercury along the tube; then the degrees are read off

on the instrument. With this reading entered on the tables which are made for this instrument, the height of the place where you are is obtained.

The aneroid looks very much like a large watch, but having only one hand. The higher you ascend, the lower the reading, on account of the atmospheric pressure. This reading, referred to a table, gives the height, as by boiling water. Any one of you, procuring these instruments when going in the country, can amuse himself when he travels in taking the height of the hills and mountains he passes over.

On my return from the country of the Dwarfs I found improvements in the boiling apparatus, and also in the artificial horizon. There is now a very small artificial horizon, invented by my friend Captain George, of the British Navy, and it is very portable, especially when compared with the old one travellers had to use. It will be a great boon to explorers. I doubt that a more useful and safe one to the traveller can be made. Captain George, I am very happy to say, is the gentleman who taught me how to take astronomical observations, and how to calculate them.

At the foot of Birougou-Bouanga was the village of Niembouai-Olomba, which meant Upper Niembouai. The head men of Niembouai and of Upper Niembouai were two brothers, so the people consented to receive me, and we tarried there a few days. The village was situated just at the junction of two gorges or valleys, one of which ran almost directly north and south, and the other east and west. From the village, looking up, I could see the sun as it rose almost from the natural horizon. The wind during the day blew all the time from the south, and early in the morning the temperature was quite cool— 69° Fahrenheit.

After leaving Niembouai - Olomba, and travelling through the great and dense forest, we came to a village called Mobana, the inhabitants belonging to the Ashango tribe, for we were still in the Ashango territory. The chief of Mobana was called Rakombo. The village was situated at the summit of a mountain 2369 feet in height, at the foot of which ran a beautiful stream called Bembo. The Bembo was the first river I had reached which ran toward the east, toward where the sun rose. How glad I was! "It no doubt falls into the Congo River," I said, for I began to hear of a large stream in our line of march going toward the rising sun.

The great embarrassment now was that the people were so much afraid of me, not as a spirit who brings the plague, but as a spirit whose evil eye they dared not meet. I succeeded in leaving Mobana, as I had left scores of villages before without trouble, and Rakombo had taken me to a village farther east with the name of Mouaou-Kombo. The name of the village proper was Mouaou, and the chief's name was Kombo. If the people of the wild tribes I had passed before had been afraid of me, the people of Mouaou-Kombo stood in still greater dread of my coming. The people of Mobana, who had taken me to that village, had disappeared one by one, and Rakombo himself, their chief, had deserted me. So I was left all alone with my Commi men among the Mouaou-Kombo people.

A few days after my arrival at Mouaou-Kombo, if you had sought me or my Commi men in the village, you would not have found us there. Where were we? We were encamped by ourselves not far from the village, from which we had withdrawn to show the people that we were tired of remaining there, and impatient to take our departure. We had been busy that day in cutting down trees around our camp to serve as an abatis and safeguard, so that nobody could approach us without making us aware of it by their noise in penetrating the dense branches. We passed the night in reasonable security, though without much fire, for our dogs—Andèko, Commi-Nagoumba, Rover, Turk, Fierce, and Ndjègo—would have in an instant apprised us by their barking of any strange visitor attempting to enter the camp. All our luggage was by us. The path from Mouaou-Kombo to our retreat was very steep.

I had that day sent Igala, Rebouka, and Mouitchi, armed to the teeth, along the path leading eastward, telling

them to look sharp, and to ascertain, if they came to a
village, whether the inhabitants did not want us to pass
through their country; in fact, to learn all the news they
could, and make report to me. After two hours Igala
came back laughing, and saying that he had entered a big
village, from which the people had fled in perfect terror,
thinking I had come with him, but that finally he had
succeeded in holding a parley with some of the inhabitants,
and learned that they had trouble with the Mouaou-
Kombo people. Igala told them not to be afraid of me,
and that they must not be alarmed if they should see me
come to their village. So far all was right; we knew
exactly what was ahead of us. "Well done," I said, "my
boys."

The next morning a deputation of villagers of Mouaou-
Kombo came to our camp and begged us to come back,
saying that if I would return in two days they would
conduct me by another route to the south-east in order to
avoid the hostile villages. So we returned to the village,
the villagers helping my men in carrying our luggage
back. Now I regretted that I had no more Commi men
with me, so that we might have been independent of
strangers for the transportation of our luggage.

As I came back to Mouaou-Kombo, little did I know
what a dark cloud was hanging over us, for my heart was
filled with joy at the prospect of soon continuing our
journey. Little did I dream of the storm that in a short
time was to burst upon us. Little did I think as I ascended
the hill in the midst of the peals of laughter of my Commi
men and of the Ashangos, that there was fighting and
bloodshed in store; that I was soon to be engaged with
my men in defending our lives, and in beating a disastrous
retreat along the way we had come, and see the mournful
end of that glorious journey upon which I had set my
heart! Like the little leaf cast upon the stream of
Mokenga, I was drifting I knew not whither. I had no
knowledge then of the breakers ahead, and now I am
going to relate to you the sad story.

I had entered again the village of Mouaou-Kombo;
our luggage had been put back in the huts; Kombo, the

chief, headed by his elders, had come to receive me, beating his kendo as he advanced.   After a while the elders
departed, and the chief and his queen were seated by my
side in the street.   The people were passing to and fro to
their accustomed avocations, and everything was going on
as usual.

"Is it true," said Kombo to me, "that you Oguizis kill
people as we Ashangos kill monkeys and the wild beasts
of the forest?   We Ashangos believe you do it, and that
is the reason we are afraid of you.   We are even afraid
that your eye is an evil one, and that a look of yours can
bring death."   Then the chief stopped and looked at me.

"Nèshi, nèshi, nèshi," I repeated three times ("No, no,
no"), and I spat on the ground to show him how I hated
what he had said.   "No," said I, "Kombo, the Oguizi
loves people, loves the Ashangos, and kills no one."

As I was speaking, a goat, the peace-offering of the
king, stood before me, and several bunches of plantain lay
near by, which had been brought in a little before by his
people.   The king said, "Eat these, Spirit.   In two days
I will conduct you where you want to go.   I am so glad
to hear that you do not kill people, but surely us Ashangos
are afraid of you; but in a day's journey you will reach
the Njavi country."

Then the queen said, "I told you, my husband, that
the Oguizi did not kill people as the Ashangos kill
monkeys.   Now don't you believe me?" said she, looking
at the king right in the face.   Then, turning to me, she
said, "Oguizi, I am cooking a pot of *koa* (a root) for you
and your men; will you eat them?"

"Certainly," said I.

I had hardly uttered those words when there appeared
before us four warriors of a hostile village, who said they
would make war on the Mouaou-Kombo people if they
dared to take me through their village; that they did not
want me to pass that way.

Kombo, the chief, said to me, "Oguizi, go in your hut;
I do not want these people to see you," and he asked my
men to fire guns to frighten the warriors.   Igala fired,
advancing toward the four warriors, who fled.   I could

not help laughing. Other guns were fired, when I heard, back of where the king and queen and myself were seated, the report of another gun, and I was startled to see the Mouaou villagers, with affrighted looks and shouts of alarm, running away in every direction. The king and queen got up, and fled along with the rest.

"Mamo! mamo!" was heard everywhere.

I got up, and, looking back in the direction where the gun had been fired, I saw, not far from my hut, the lifeless body of a leading Ashango man.

Igalo had done the deed. He rushed toward me and shouted, "I did not do it on purpose; the gun went off before I had raised it."

Now, indeed, I might be sure that the Ashangos would believe that the Oguizi could kill people as they did monkeys.

What was to be done? I was hundreds of miles away from the sea.

I called the king back. "Do not be afraid," I said.

Kombo cried back to me, "You say you come here to do no harm, and you do not kill people. Is not this the dead body of a man?" and in an instant he was out of sight.

Oh, how sorry I felt! but there was but little time for melancholy reflections.

I shouted back, "Ashango people, I am very sorry. What can I do? I will pay you the price of twenty men for that man who has been killed."

In the meantime the war-drums began to beat furiously in every part of this large village, and the warriors came out by hundreds, armed with spears, bows and poisoned arrows, battle-axes, and other murderous implements of war.

My men held beads and goods in their hands, and shouted, "Come, we will pay you for that man that has been killed."

Then suddenly one of the elders, bolder than the rest, shouted, "Let there be no war; let us have peace. The Oguizi will pay for that man's life."

There was a lull. Some said, "Let us make war; let

o

us kill the people who have come with the Oguizi, for they have come to kill us," while another party shouted, "Let us have peace." The war-drums for a while ceased to beat, and the horns calling the warriors from the forest had ceased to blow.

There was a lull—just what I wanted. I knew it was utterly impossible to make those people believe that that man had been killed by accident. I might just as well have tried to make them believe that a spear would go through a man and kill him without being hurled by another man.

That lull was precious time to me, though it was but short. I encouraged my seven Commi men, who had come close to me for advice. "Don't be afraid, boys," I said. "We are men; we can fight. Not one of you will be delivered to the Ashangos for this palaver. We will fight our way back; get ready. Though they may be inclined for peace, let us prepare for the worst, and woe to our enemies if they want to fight." Then, turning toward Igalo, I said to him reproachfully, though kindly, "See what your carelessness has brought upon us."

In a very short time we had got out an additional supply of ammunition, 200 bullets extra for each man, and 6 one-pound cans of powder. We could not be taken unawares, for our guns had never left our hands, and by the side of each man hung always a bag containing 100 bullets and 2 or 3 pounds of powder; so you see we had ammunition enough to carry on a desperate fight, and we were bound to sell our lives dearly, but not before having exhausted every means of conciliation.

Then, pointing to seven otaitais, I said, "Get ready to put them on at an instant's notice." They contained my precious things—photographs, scientific instruments, and valuable notes.

We were ready for our retreat in case war should be decided upon by the Ashangos.

The appearances were hopeful, and I began to think that the palaver would be settled satisfactorily, when suddenly a woman, whom afterward I recognised to be the queen, came wailing and tearing her hair. Stripping off her garment of grass-cloth, she rolled herself on the ground before me, crying, "Oguizi, what have I done to you? Why have you killed my sister? What had she done to you? She gave you food—that is the harm she has done you. Go and see her body behind the hut," and she wailed aloud. Then from afar the friendly elder, who did not desire at first to make war, shouted, "Why have you killed my wife, oh wicked Oguizi?"

The fatal bullet had gone through the man, and then through a hut, killing the sister of the queen, who was busy behind her dwelling.

As the sad news spread, a general shout for war arose from the increasing multitude, and every man who had not his spear or bow rushed for it, and those who had them brandished them in sign of defiance. War was declared—there was no help for it. Oh dear, what was to be done? I had not come into that far country to kill these savages, but then my men, who had left their homes, their wives, fathers, mothers, brothers, sisters, children, must not be killed—they trusted in me. What shall we do? Is Paul Du Chaillu to run away from the enemy? Shall these savages call him a coward? Such thoughts made the blood rush to my head. I shall never play the coward, but then there are many ways besides fighting to show one's courage. My mind was made up; so I girded my loins for the fight, sad at heart. First I thought I would set fire to the house where my baggage was, but there was so much powder there—several hundred pounds—that in exploding it more Ashangos would be killed. We had shed the first blood; we must be careful to shed no more without being obliged to do so, and I offered a silent prayer to God to guide me in what was to be done.

My seven Commi men stood by me, ready to start with their otaitais on their backs. "Be not afraid, boys," said I; "we are men."

We had to go through the whole length of the village before we could reach the path by which we had come to Mouaou-Kombo.

I shouted, "Ashangos, all the goods I have I give to

you for the people that have been killed. Now we go
away. We did not come here to make war; we did not
come here to kill people. We don't wish to kill you, so
do not compel us to do so."

My Commi boys were cool and steady, and, keeping a
firm line, we marched through the street of the village.
A rain of spears and of poisoned arrows came from behind
the huts, and showered all around us. I am wounded—
a sharp-pointed arrow pierces me. Then Igala, my
right-hand man, is wounded. "Don't fire, boys; let us
shed no more blood in this village if we can help it," I
said. "Press onward; do not be afraid. There is but
one God, the ruler of the universe; all will be for the
best."

We advance steadily, the crowd ahead of us in the
street brandishing their spears and sending arrows at us;
but they keep far away, while, with guns pointed toward
them, we continue to advance, Rebouka and Mouitchi
looking around toward the huts, for our hidden enemies
were the ones we dreaded the most. Another shower of
spears and arrows fell in the midst of us. I look around
—no one is wounded; when, lo! Macondai is struck by
an arrow. The infuriated savages, shouting their terrific
war-cries, become bolder, and come nearer. Must more
blood be shed? And now Rebouka is wounded. Five
spears fall by me, and a perfect shower of them fly all
around.

Igala says, "Chally, do you think we are going to let
these savages wound you? A man in our country would
be put to death if he dared to raise his hand against you.
Don't you see our blood? May we not fire and kill some
of them?"

"Be patient, by boys. Remember we shed the first
blood. Wait a little while; perhaps they will desist.
They dare not come too near; when they do we will kill
them."

Oh dear, one of our dogs is killed—poor Andèko!
three spears go into him and lay him prostrate; he gives
a shriek of pain, and he is dead. Our other dogs are by
us. Commi-Nagoumba is in a great rage; he barks

furiously at the Ashangos; a spear has just wounded him slightly on the back. Rover, Fierce, Turk, and Ndjégo are ready to help us; we have trouble to keep them in check. They are going to be useful in the forest—they will discover the men in ambush. The Ashangos know this, and they try to kill them. Just as we reach the end of the village, Rover and Fierce are wounded, each receiving an arrow in his body.

CHAPTER XXVIII.

Retreat from Mouaou-Kombo—The Attack—Paul is Wounded—
A Panic—The Fight Renewed—The Enemy Reinforced—Lying
in Ambush —The Enemy Repulsed — A Poisoned Arrow —
Mouitchi Safe—Death of the Dogs.

WE enter the great forest; we are going to leave
the village of Mouaou-Kombo for ever. We are on
the path which we took on our way eastward. We are
going back. The forest near the village is filled with
savages waiting for us behind the trees.

We can only go single file. I give command. Igala
is to take the lead; then follow Rebouka, Rapelina,
Ngoma, Macondai, and Igalo, the cause of our trouble.
I guard the rear; the post of danger, of honour, must
belong to me, their chieftain, for I have sworn to them,
and their people when I left the sea-shore, to protect
them.

All at once I remember Mouitchi. I do not see him.
He is not with us. "Mouitchi, where are you?" I cry.
"He is dead," replied the Ashangos. "He will never
come to you. We have killed him. You will never see
him again."

Before plunging into the forest we turn back and
shout, "Ashangos, we do not want war. We did not
come to your country to kill people. Beware! We leave
your village; do not follow us, for if you do there will
be war." They answer by a fierce war-cry, and hundreds
of spears from afar are thrown at us as in defiance.

"Now," said I, "boys, no more mercy! blood for blood!
Fight valiantly, but kill no women, no old men, no children; for remember, you are with a white man, and we

never make war on these. I would not dare to raise my head in my country if I had killed women and children."

Three dogs are left. Poor Rover and Fierce have just been killed. More than fifty spears had been thrown at them. They fell bravely in our defence. The forest was filled with armed Ashangos. When we got into the path a large spear was thrown at me from behind a big tree; Macondai saw the man. "Do not kill him," said I; "he is an old man, and he is disarmed." He had no other spear with him. At this moment a poisoned arrow struck into me—a long, slender, bearded arrow, which first pierced the leather belt that held my revolvers. I had no time to take the arrow out; the fighting was too terrific. Six savages all at once rushed upon Macondai from behind a tree. Macondai fired at them, and I came to the rescue. Bang, bang, bang from my revolvers, and the miscreants troubled us no more. Igalo now received·a wound from a poisoned arrow, and we were almost surrounded.

My men quickened their speed. "Don't go so fast," I shouted from the rear; but they went on faster and faster. The shouts of the savages became more violent, and they were shooting at us from behind every tree. My Commi ran as fast as they could. Igalo and I remained behind. "Olome (men)," shouted I, "what are you doing?" A panic seized them; they ran faster and faster along the path, and I shouted in vain for them to stop. Wild shouts, and the tramp of scores of infuriated men thirsting for blood, were heard close behind us, and the Ashangos got bolder and bolder as they saw that we quickened our steps. They began to realize that my men were demoralized.

Just as I was raising my gun, an arrow cut the flesh of my middle finger to the bone, severing the small artery, and causing the blood to flow copiously on the path. A little after I heard the Ashangos shout, "Ah! ah! we see your blood on the track; you lose blood. Not one of you shall see the sun set to-day. We are coming; all the villages in front of you will fight you. You shall lie dead like the man you killed. We will cut you to pieces."

I rushed ahead, shouting to my Commi men to stop. Suddenly, as I advanced to overtake them, I see their loads strewn on the ground along the path. They had thrown down their baggage. It was now my turn to be infuriated. I rushed ahead, revolver in hand, and shouted, "I will shoot the first man of you that dares to move a step." They stopped for sheer want of breath. My breath was also almost taken away. I said, "Boys, what have you done? You have run away from the Ashangos. You have left me behind all alone to fight for you. You are to be called by those savages cowards; they will say that you do not know how to fight," and I looked Igala and the other men boldly in the face, and shook my head sorrowfully. "What have you done?" I added. "Where are my photographs? where my note-books? where my route maps? where are those mementoes of friends at home? where are my scientific instruments? Gone, thrown away; the toils of years irrecoverably lost. My boys, what have you done?"

The panic had lasted about ten minutes. Their flight had been so hurried that we had left all the savages somewhat in the rear. "Boys," said I, "think a little while and don't run away any more. Don't you see that the Ashangos have the disadvantage? They are obliged to stop every time they want to adjust an arrow and take aim, and as for their spears they cannot manage them in the thick jungle, for they have not space enough. Besides, we are often out of sight before they can deliver their shot, and the only people we have to fear are those who are waiting in ambush for us. Their bravest men will think twice before they come to us at close quarters, and if they do, have we not guns and revolvers? have we not guns whose bullets will go through four or five men, one after another? So be not afraid."

By the time I had finished this little speech, and had just taken breath, the infuriated savages were again upon us. Their hatred seemed to be now against Igala, whom they called *malanga*, cursing him. They dodged about, taking short cuts through the jungle, and surrounding us. "You have tasted blood," they cried;

"you are all dead men. It is no use for you to try to fight."

My men by this time had recovered from their panic, and sent back the Commi war-cry, and shouted, "Yogo gou-nou (come here)! We are ready; come here; we will make you taste death. Many of you will never go back by the path you came;" and we stood still. "Well done, boys!" I shouted. "Show the people what you can do;" and many Ashangos fell on the ground never to rise again.

In a little while we came to a village from which the people had fled. There I discovered the plan of the Ashangos. They wanted to flank us, while some of them were going forward to rouse the other villages ahead to fight us. If they could succeed in flanking us, they would soon finish us; if not, they could make all the population ahead hostile to us on our way back. There lay our great danger. If they succeed in rousing the population against us, it would be impossible for us to escape. We could not keep fighting for ever. I was already beginning to feel very weak. We had had no food since the day before, for the trouble came before our breakfast. The poisonous arrows began to show the effect of the poison in the blood, and I felt a raging thirst. My men were very much frightened at this. The Commi knew nothing of the poisoned missiles, but had heard of the dreadful effects of poisonous wounds from the slaves coming from the interior.

Poor Igala complained of great pain and great thirst. "I shall die, Chally," said he; "I shall never see my daughter again!"

"If God wills it, you shall not die, Igala," I said.

Let us get ready. The Ashangos are coming silently this time; we hear their footsteps; they are in sight. We hid at the extremity of the village, and I shouldered my long-range rifle. The Ashango leader advanced, and as he was adjusting his bow I fired. His right arm dropped down broken and powerless by his side, and the next man behind fell with a crash in the bush in the midst of fallen leaves and branches. Rebouka fired, and down came another man, and one by one my men kept up the fire. The Ashangos had now received a momentary check. The bravest among them had fallen in the dust, and my men shouted to the Ashangos that fell, "You will never return by the path you came." The panic was over; my Commi men were ashamed to have acted as they had done.

We jogged on now leisurely till we came to a rivulet. I could not stand; I lay flat, and drank, and drank as much as I could. How fervently I wished Mouitchi was with us! Poor Mouitchi! where was he killed? His body must have been hacked to pieces. Another dog was missing; two only were left. They had been killed for being our friends, and finding out our enemies behind the trees.

The Ashangos began to learn how to fight us. We had not gone far when suddenly they came again in great numbers without uttering a war-cry. The path was most difficult when we became aware of their appearance; steep hill lay beyond steep hill; stream after stream had to be crossed, and we increased our speed, for we were to be under a disadvantage; but it was fortunate that we knew the ground by having been over it before. Suddenly a paralyzing thud, accompanied by a sharp pain, told me that I had been struck from behind my back or in flank by an unknown enemy. This time it was in my side that I was wounded. We were just going up a steep hill, and I turned to see my assailant. Igalo, the poor good fellow, the unfortunate cause of our woe, was by my side, and turned round also to see who had launched the missile. Lo, what do we descry lying flat on the ground among the dry leaves, still as death? An Ashango, crouched as still as a snake in its coil, his bright eyes flashing vindictively at me. Igalo, in the twinkling of an eye, discharged his gun at him, and the too-skilful bowman lay low, never to rise again. I could not help it—I felt sorry; I deplored that fight with my whole heart from the beginning. This time I was wounded badly. The arrow was bearded, small, and slender, and had gone deeply into my stomach, and if the leather belt which held my revolvers, and through which it passed, had not weakened its force, I should have been mortally wounded; but a kind Providence watched over me, and, though another wound disabled that poor, tired, worn-out body of mine, I did not grumble. I had reached that state in which I did not care. The trouble was that I had to go with that arrow in my body, for there was no time to disengage it.

My men came around me, for they saw that the pain had turned me deadly pale, and, though not a cry of anguish was uttered by me (for I, their chief, must teach them how to suffer), they saw that my strength was gradually giving way.

How painful that little bit of bearded arrow was as part of it lay inside, and the other part in the leather!

We were now near Mobana, and the Mouaou warriors, and those that had been added to them, were still pursuing us. Happily, we knew every hill and every stream. We crossed the Bembo, a stream with which you were made acquainted on our way east, and the ascent of the steep hill on the other side was terrible. The Mouaou warriors were shouting all the time, "Men of Mobana, do not let the Oguizi pass! They have killed our people!"

Approaching Mobana, we could hear the war-drums beating in the village, but fortunately the path led us by the end of the street, and as we passed we saw the Mobanians in battle array, and heard them sending fierce war-cries at us.

The Mobanians made common cause with the Mouaou people, and they were like a body of fresh troops coming to the rescue—they were not tired. The situation was becoming grave, especially if the people ahead of us were also in sympathy with the Mouaou people.

We recognised the leading Mobana warrior, armed with his bow and several quivers of arrows. Happily they were at some distance from us, and I ordered my men not to fire at them, thinking that perhaps when they saw that we did not desire to make war they might remain quiet in their village, and not pursue us.

We had no time to lose, for I knew that Mobana was situated on the top of a very steep and high hill, and of course I did not want to be taken in the rear by those savages, and subjected to a plunging fire of spears and arrows from their high elevation, from which they could look down on us.

"Boys," said I, "let us go down this hill quickly, so that we may reach the bottom and ascend the other before they come; then we shall have a great advantage over our enemies." We descended the hill, the multitude of savages following us, shouting, "Ah! ah! you run away! You do not know this forest; you shall never leave it; we will kill you all; we will cut your bodies to pieces!"

My blood was getting up. At last we reached the bottom of the hill, and began to ascend the other by the path. "Boys," said I, "don't you remember that there is a big fallen tree near the path up this hill where the jungle is very thick? We are getting weak; let us lay in ambush there, and be as silent as if we were all dead, and wait for the Ashangos."

After a while we came to the place I had spoken of, and in the thick bushes just by the side of the path, not far from the big fallen tree, I ordered Igala, Rapelina, and Ngoma to lie down together. On the other side, in a position which I thought would be a good one, I put Igalo, Macondai, and Rebouka. I myself kept the centre, facing the path, and could see tolerably well what was going on around.

We lay almost flat on the ground, nearly hidden by the underbrush, with our bags of bullets hanging in front, our flasks of powder handy, and our cartridges ready. We kept as silent as the grave, moving not a muscle, and hardly daring to breathe, and waited for the slightest rustling of the leaves as a warning that the Ashangos were coming.

Hark! hark! we hear a very slight distant noise, which seems as if an antelope or gazelle was passing through the forest. We look at each other as if to say, "They are coming." As by instinct we look at our guns and our ammunition, and see that everything is ready for the fray.

We were indeed desperate, for now we knew it was a death-struggle—that we must either vanquish the Ashangos or be killed by them.

The rustling in the midst of the leaves becomes more distinct, and we glance rapidly in front of us, on the right of us, on the left of us, and behind us.

We see the sharp-shooters forming the Ashango vanguard advancing carefully, with their bows and arrows in readiness. They came in almost a sitting posture. Now and then the leaders would stop to wait for the men behind, their fierce, savage faces looking all around at the same time, and their ears erect to catch the slightest sound. Suddenly they stop, perhaps to listen and know where we are. They look at each other as if to say, " We don't hear anything," or perhaps they mistrust the bush ahead. Then I get a glimpse of the great Mobana warrior, and also of one of the leading Mouaou warriors. All at once they gave a cluck, the meaning of which I could not tell. Perhaps it meant danger.

I had been looking intently for a minute at these savages, when I cast a glance in the direction where Igala, Rapelina, and Ngoma were. Igala was aiming with an unerring and steady hand at the great Mobana warrior, and Rapelina was aiming at the Mouaou warrior; whether Ngoma was aiming at any one I could not see. It took only one glance for me to see what was going on in that direction. Then, turning in the other direction, I saw that Macondai, Rebouka, and Igalo were getting ready; they had also caught sight of some sly and silent enemy. I shouldered my rifle also. Not twenty seconds had passed after I had looked at Igala when I heard in his direction, bang! bang! The great Mobana warrior was shot through the abdomen, and uttered a cry of anguish, while Rapelina had sent a bullet through the lower jaw of the Mouaou warrior, smashing it completely. Ngoma fired, but I could not see the man he fired at. All at once, bang! bang! bang! I hear from Igalo, Macondai, and Rebouka's side. Bang! bang! bang! three guns from the other side. Bang! from my own gun.

"Well done, boys!" I cried. "Forward, and charge, and let us show the Ashangos we are men." We rush through the jungle in the direction from which the warriors had come. They are surprised; their leading chiefs are killed. Bang! bang! bang! from revolvers and guns; we are fighting like lions at bay. We are victorious; our enemies fly in abject terror.

We shouted to the fleeing Ashangos cries of defiance: "Come here! Come again; not one of you shall go back to your villages. We are coming; we will kill you all before night. You made war; we did not make it. Come and look at your dead in the forest. Come and fetch them if you dare! To-night we are coming to your villages, and will destroy them!"

The voices of the Ashangos became fainter and fainter, and there were no more answers to our cries of defiance.

Some of us had been wounded again. As we came to a little stream, my exhaustion was such that everything became dim before me; the trees of the forest seemed to be moving, and finally I fell almost unconscious to the ground. After awhile I drank copiously of the refreshing water of the stream, for the poisoned arrows had given me an unquenchable thirst. The men drank also; none of us seemed ever to be satisfied. A few minutes after, and we drank again. Now we breathed more freely, and rested a little while, keeping a sharp look out, however, at the same time. I examined the wounds of Igala and the others, and said, "Igala, don't be afraid; you are not going to die from the effects of the poisoned arrow. I am going to put in your wound something that will burn you, but do you good." It was ammonia. I applied it, and he gave a piercing shriek.

The slender, small, sharp-pointed, bearded arrow had remained in my body the whole of the day; two or three times I tried in vain to pull it out, but it seemed to stick fast in the flesh; so I took off the belt of my revolver, and said to Igala, "Pull that arrow out for me." He tried gently, but it would not come. I said, "Pull it with all your strength."

Oh how it pained! It was like a little fish-hook—a little bit of a thing, but it so tore the flesh that I felt like giving a cry of anguish. I became deadly pale, but did not utter a word; I wanted to set an example of fortitude to my men. Then I put ammonia in all my wounds and those of my men, for I always carried a little bottle of it to use in case of snake-bites. The blood had flowed freely from my finger, and I was sorry to see that my clothes were quite saturated, but the effusion of blood had carried off the poison.

I found that the effect of the poison was to bring on mortification of the flesh, and was not so dangerous as I had been led to believe, though I was very sick a few days after the fight.

After resting awhile, and after equalizing our munitions of war, we shouldered our empty otaitais. Just as we were ready to start we heard again a rustling of leaves. Are the Ashangos coming back? We are silent, and look in the direction of the noise. We see a man—our guns are directed toward him. I make a sign not to fire, I do not know why—God directs me. Now and then he hides himself—stops—watches—he is advancing, not in the path, but a little way from it. The man comes nearer; we see a gun in his hand—it is Mouitchi! I am the first to recognise him. "Mouitchi!" I shouted. "I am Mouitchi," the answer was. He rushes towards us; he is safe; he is not even wounded, and with tremulous voice I said, "Boys, God is with us; I thank thee, Father." I could say no more, but this came from the inmost depths of my heart.

Mouitchi's story was this: He had mistaken the path in the panic, and finally had gone through the jungle and followed us by the halloing of the fierce Ashangos, but kept at a good distance from them. He heard them crying out that the great warriors of Mobana and of Mouaou were killed. They had fled in the utmost terror.

Poor Commi-Nagoumba was the only dog left; all the others had been killed. If I could have collected their bodies I would have dug a grave for them at the foot of a big tree, and written on it the words,

HERE ARE BURIED

THE DOGS

ANDÈKO, ROVER, FIERCE, TURK, and NDJÈGO.

They were faithful unto death.

CHAPTER XXIX.

Travelling Westward—A Night in the Forest—Paul's Speech to his Men—Their Reply—The Retreat resumed—Taking Food and Rest—Meeting with Friends.

THIS meeting with Mouitchi revived for a while my failing strength. I saw in his safety the decree of a kind Providence. My warriors were by me; though wounded, none of us had been killed.

We continued our journey westward. The forest had resumed its accustomed stillness, undisturbed by the savage war-cries of the infuriated Ashangos. I felt so weak that it was with great difficulty I could walk. I had been obliged to get rid of my splendid formidable double-barrelled breech-loading rifle by breaking the butt-end and throwing the barrel into the woods. I had tried as hard as I could to carry two guns, but at last I had to give up. Now I had only a smooth-bore to carry.

A little after we had resumed our march, as we walked silently in the forest, we met suddenly two Mobana women. Igala at once was going to shoot them; I forbid him doing it. Poor Igala said he did not like this way of making war; he said it was not the white man's country, and we ought not to fight in the white man's fashion. He was for shooting every Ashango he saw; and, pointing to our wounds, he said, " Don't you think they would have killed all of us if they had been able?" I answered, "Never mind, Igala; they will tell their people that, after all, we did not want to kill everybody."

Poor women! they really thought they were going to be murdered, but they had no idea of what had taken place.

P

We went on, though I was becoming weaker and weaker. A high fever had set in, and my thirst continued to be intense; at the sight of a stream I thought I could drink the whole of the water. My men were pretty nearly in the same condition as myself.

Thus we travelled on till near sunset, when at last I said, " Boys, I cannot go any farther ; I cannot walk, I am so weak, so weary, so ill. There is that big village of Niembouai-Olomba near us; we are all too tired to go through it and fight our way if the people want to fight us. It will soon be dark; let us leave the path, and go into the forest and rest. At midnight, when the people are asleep, we will go through the village, and continue our way toward the sea."

" You are right," said the men. " You are our chief; we will do as you say."

We left the path and plunged into the woods, and after a while we halted in one of the thickest parts of the forest, where no one could see us but that good and merciful God whose eye was upon us in that day of our great trials, and who had given us strength to contend with our enemies. We were hidden from the sight of man, and hundreds of miles away from the Commi country— I was thousands of miles away from my own. It was, indeed, a day of tribulation. The men were afraid to light a fire, for fear that it might betray our hiding-place. We did not even dare to speak aloud; we were almost startled at the rustling of the leaves, for we knew not but that it might be the enemy. Our pride had left us with our strength. We were helpless, wounded, weak, hungry; the future before us was dark and gloomy. What a picture of despondency we presented !

After a while we lay on the ground to sleep, muzzling our only dog, that he should not betray our hiding-place. Darkness came on, and the silence of the night was only broken by the mournful cry of a solitary owl that came to perch near us. In a little time my exhausted men thought not of leopards, or poisonous snakes, or hostile savages, in the deep slumber that enwrapped them. Igala alone now and then moaned from pain. The night air was misty and cold. As I lay awake on the damp ground an intense feeling of sadness came over me. There was I, far from home. I thought of our northern climes, of spring, of summer, of autumn, of winter, of flakes of snow, of a happy home, of girls and boys, of friends, of school-mates. I knew that if any of them could have been made aware of my forlorn condition they would have felt the tenderest sympathy with me in my misfortunes, and I thought if I could see them once more before dying I should die happy.

Hours passed by, and at last I thought it must be time to start. I took a match from my match box, and lighted a wax candle (I always kept one in my bag), and looked at my watch. It was just midnight. We lay in a cluster, and I awoke my men in a moment. "Boys," said I, "it is time for us to start, for the hours of the night are passing away; the people of the village must have retired. Two of you must go as scouts, and see if the people of Niembouai-Olomba are asleep." Mouitchi and Igala at once started. "Be as cunning," said I, "as leopards, and noiseless as snakes."

After a while they came back, telling us that every-body was asleep in the village of Niembouai-Olomba, and that we had better start immediately, "for," said they, "the first sleep is the deepest."

They, calling my boys around me, I gave them what I thought might be my last words of admonition. With dead silence they waited for what I was going to say.

"Little did we know, boys, at sunrise this morning, what would happen to us to-day. Men cannot look into the future. I was leading you carefully across that big country of the black man toward the land of the white man. I did not defeat the journey—one of you has done it. Poor Igalo is sorry for it, but no one is more sorry than I am, for I had set my heart on taking you by the okili mpolo. I was leading you on well to the white man's country. Now all hope of this is over. We are poor; everything we had has been left behind, and we have nothing else to do but go back to the sea, following the road by which we came.

"In a little while we shall start. I have called you around me to give you advice, for I am ill and weary, and if there is much fighting to be done I am afraid I shall not have the strength to take part in it. If perchance you see me fall on the ground, do not try to raise me up; let me alone; don't be frightened. Stand close together; do not run, each man his own way. You have guns; you can reach the Commi country if you are wise as serpents, and then you will behold the beautiful blue sea and your Commi country once more.

"I have kept my word with your people. I have stood by you to the last. My boys, I have fought for you as resolutely as I could, but the time may be at hand when I shall be able to fight no more. I may be killed to-night, as I have said to you, or I may not be strong enough to raise my gun. Whatever happens, remain together; listen to Igala, your chief.

"We have lost nearly everything, but these books (my journal), in which I have written down all we have done, are yet safe. If I fall, take them with you to the sea, and when a vessel comes, give them to the captain, and tell him 'Chally, Chally, our friend, the great friend of the Commi, is dead. He died far away, calmly, without fear, and he told us to give these to the white man.'* Take also the watch I carry on my person, and that little box, which contains four other watches, aneroids, and compass, and give them to the captain. All the other things and the guns I give you to remember me by. You will give a gun to Quengueza, and a gun to Ranpano."

My men crept close around me as I spoke. I had hardly spoken the last words when they stretched their arms toward me, and these lion-hearted negroes wept aloud, and, with voices full of love and kindness, said, "Chally, Chally, you are not to die. We will take you alive to our

---

* On the first page of each journal I had written, "Copy of Du Chaillu's African Journal. Should death overtake me, and should these my journals find their way to a civilized country, it is my wish that Messrs. John Murray, of London, and Harper and Brothers, of New York, shall publish an account of my journey, if they feel inclined to do so.—P. B. Du Chaillu."

people. No, no; we will all go back to the sea-shore together. You shall see the deep blue ocean, and a vessel will come and carry you back home. Do you think that, even if you were killed, we would leave your body here? No; we would carry it with us, and tarry somewhere and bury you where nobody could find you, for we do not want the people to cut off your head for the alumba. Chally, Chally, you are not to die."

"Boys," I answered, in a laughing tone, in order to cheer them up, "I did not say I expected to die to-night, only that I might die. You know that Chally is not afraid of death, and many and many times he has told you that men could kill the body, but could not kill the spirit. Don't you know that Chally knows how to fight? We are men. If I have talked to you as I have, it is because I want to prepare you for the worst. Be of good cheer, and now let us get ready."

We got up and girded our loins for the fight, and swore, if necessary, to die like brave men. We examined our guns by the light of the candle, and refilled our flasks with powder, and replaced our cartridges and bullets. Ncommi-Nagoumba, our last dog, was looking at us. He seemed to understand the danger, and to say, "Don't kill me; I will not bark." I looked at him and said, "Ncommi-Nagoumba, don't bark. You have been our friend. You discovered many of our enemies behind the trees ready to spear us, and you have warned us of our danger. Our friends, the other dogs, have been killed; you alone now stand by us, but we are not ungrateful, and we shall not kill you, Ncommi-Nagoumba. Don't bark, don't bark," I said to the dog, looking earnestly at him.

Then, shouldering our bundles and guns, we struggled through the entangled thicket, tearing ourselves with thorns, into the path, and at last came to the village street. We here paused, and called to each other in a low tone of voice, to make sure that no one was left behind, for it was so intensely dark that we could not see a yard before us. It was necessary to guard against any possible ambush. We then stepped forward like desperate men, resolved to fight for our lives to the last, and, entering the village, took the middle of the street, our feet hardly touching the ground. Igala carried Ncommi-Nagoumba in his arms, for we were afraid that, if suffered to run loose, he might possibly bark. I shall never forget that night. We threaded the long street cautiously, with our guns cocked, and ready at the slightest warning to defend ourselves. Onward we went, our hearts beating loudly in our terrible suspense, for we feared a surprise at any moment. Now and then we could hear the people talking in their huts, and at such times we would carefully cross to the other side of the street. At one house we heard the people playing the wombi (native harp) indoors, and again we crossed lightly to the other side, and passed on without having alarmed the inmates. Then we came to an ouandja where three men were lying by the side of a fire stretched out on their mats, smoking their pipes, and talking aloud. I was afraid Ncommi-Nagoumba would bark at them, but we passed without being detected. It was no wonder that we were afraid of everybody, for we were so weak and helpless. Thus we continued our march through that long street, and it seemed as if we should never reach the end of it.

At last we came to the farthest confine of the village, rejoicing that we had so successfully avoided creating an alarm, when all at once a bonfire blazed up before us! As we stood motionless, waiting for the next move, a kind voice spoke out from the darkness, "It is the Oguizi people. Go on; you will find the path smooth. There is no more war for you." It was the voice of the old king of Niembouai-Olomba. But, being not sure that some treachery was not intended, we passed on without saying a word in reply to the kind speech of the chief. As it proved, however, instead of a death-struggle we had found friends.

On we went in the darkness of the night, losing the path at times, and finding it again; in swamps and water-courses, over stony hills, and through thorny brakes. Finally, at three o'clock, we came to a field of cassava. Here we halted, made a fire, gathered some of the roots, and, having roasted them, ate of them plentifully. This food renewed our strength. We had been more than thirty-three hours without a particle of nourishment.

Then, after I had taken my meal, I thought it would be better to burn some of my clothes which were saturated with blood, so that the natives might not suspect that I had been wounded, for they all thought I was a spirit, and consequently invulnerable to the implements of war. So we lighted a larger fire, and the blood-stained clothes were burned. After this I laid down to rest a little, but not before I had offered a silent thanksgiving to that gracious Providence who had so marvellously preserved my little band of followers and myself.

We rested for the remainder of the night on the hard ground, and at daylight continued our march, but mistook the path, and finally came to a plantation belonging to an old man, the next in authority to the king of Niembouai-Olomba. By that time it was mid-day. He had heard of our fight a short time before. We were received kindly by the old man, and, after we had partaken of the food his people had cooked for us, my men gave him an account of our deadly encounter with the Ashangos.

Then the old man said, " What an Oguizi you have had with you! It is no wonder that none of you were killed, for I have heard by the messenger that brought the news that sometimes he would hide and change himself into an elephant, and charge the Ashangos, and throw fire from his trunk, and would then become a man again. At other times we hear that the Oguizi turned himself into a leopard, and as the sharpshooters came after you he pounced upon them from the branches of the trees, and that when tired of being a leopard he would transform himself into a gorilla, and roar till the trees of the forest shook and toppled down upon your enemies. The Mouaou-Kombo and Mobana people sent us word that we must fight you, but their quarrels are not ours. We are your friends."

But there was no time to be lost on the way, and after a little talk we bade good-bye to our kind host, and once more directed our steps toward the setting sun.

CHAPTER XXX.

I NEED not recount to you our journey back, only that there was no more fighting, and that we returned by exactly the same road we had taken going eastward, reached the same villages, and were received everywhere with great kindness by the different tribes and their chiefs, who seemed all so glad to see us. Kombila, Nchiengain, Mayolo, begged me to come back again. But when we reached the Ashira country, I did not go to see Olenda's people, nor did we stop at any village belonging to his clan, but went and tarried at Angouka's village, where we were hospitably welcomed, his people saying, " Why did not Quengueza bring you to us instead of taking you to Olenda?" Then we glided down the now placid waters of the Ovenga and the Rembo.

From the Ashira country to the sea-shore a picture of desolation everywhere met our eyes. The poor Bakalais seemed to have suffered heavily from the plague; many of their villages were silent, and as we entered them nothing but grim skeletons were presented to our view. Obindji, Malaouen, and my hunters were all dead; three men only were left of the Obindji village.

But when I reached Goumbi the havoc made by the plague seemed the most terrible of all. Every one of the nephews of the king who had gone to the Ashira country with us was dead; all my friends were dead. I felt the sincerest compassion for poor Quengueza: Goumbi had been abandoned, and all his warriors, his slaves, his wives, his family, his children, had been taken from him.

This plague had been a fearful visitation, and hundreds of thousands of people must have been carried off by it.

Finally I reached my settlement on the River Commi, and on my way there I missed many faces; but I was rejoiced that friend Ranpano's life had been spared. How glad the good old chief was to see me! He gave me back the shirt I had given him on my departure. " I knew you would not die," said the old chief.

We had all returned safely but one—Retonda. Many of those who had said of us when we started upon our journey, " We shall see them no more; they are going into the jaws of the leopards; they are courting death," were no more. The plague, which had spared us, had swept them away.

I had gone safely through pestilence, fire, famine, and war, and when I looked at the sea once more my heart rose in gratitude to that God who had so marvellously watched over me, the humble traveller in Equatorial Africa.

I found at the mouth of the river an English trading-vessel ready to start for London. The name of the vessel was the *Marance*, Captain Pitts, and six days after my arrival on the coast, at the close of the year 1866, I sailed for England.

And thus I left the shores of Equatorial Africa, followed to the beach with the blessings and good wishes of its inhabitants.

Since that time years have gone by, but I think often of the fierce encounters I have had with the wild beasts in that far-off country; of our camp-fires; of the Dwarfs; of dear, good Quengueza; of my hunters, Aboko, Niamkala, and Fasiko; of Malaouen, Querlaouen, Gambo; of friend Obindji, the Bakalai chief of Mayolo; of Ndiayai, the king of the Cannibals; of Remandji; of my brave boys, Igala, Rebouka, Mouitchi, Ngoma, Rapelina, Igalo, and dear Macondai, and of other friends, and I hope that I may meet them again in the Spirit Land.

And now, my dear young friends, let us bid for ever adieu to the regions of Equatorial Africa, whither I have taken you in imagination, and concerning which I have given you a faithful record of what I did, saw, and heard there.

I think we have had some pleasant hours together, and, at the same time, I hope that your knowledge of that unknown part of the world has been enlarged by the reading of the volumes I have specially written for your benefit.

Let us always be friends, and when I travel again in distant lands I shall not fail to tell you what I have seen in my journeyings.

Norway, Sweden, and Lapland are the countries where I am going to take you next. Meanwhile I say good-bye.

THE END.

VERY IMPORTANT NEW BOOKS.
Special List for 1872.

A Splendid New Gift-Book.

The uncertain and evanescent character of all books illustrated by Photography is so well known, that it was thought a Gathering of our finest Modern Paintings, engraved upon Steel in the highest style of art, would form an acceptable Gift-Book for the coming festive season.

BEAUTIFUL PICTURES BY BRITISH ARTISTS.

A Gathering of Favourites from our Picture Galleries. 1800—1870. Including examples by WILKIE, CONSTABLE, J. M. W. TURNER, MULREADY, Sir EDWIN LANDSEER, MACLISE, LESLIE, E. M. WARD, FRITH, JOHN GILBERT, ANSDELL, MARCUS STONE, Sir NOEL PATON, EYRE CROWE, O'NEIL, FAED, MADOX BROWN. All Engraved in the highest style of Art by the most Eminent English Engravers. Edited, with Notices of the Artists, by SYDNEY ARMYTAGE, M.A. The whole forming a Magnificent Volume, in imperial 4to, bound in Byzantine cloth gilt, 21s.

** The value of the Paintings here indelibly reflected by the engraver's art is estimated at £50,000. IT IS AN ART BOOK FOR ALL TIME.

AARON PENLEY'S SKETCHING IN WATER COLOURS. 21s.

By the Author of "The English School of Painting in Water-Colours," &c. ILLUSTRATED WITH TWENTY-ONE BEAUTIFUL CHROMO-LITHOGRAPHS, produced with the utmost care to resemble original WATER-COLOUR DRAWINGS. Small folio, the text tastefully printed, in handsome binding, gilt edges, suitable for the Drawing-room table, price 21s.

** It has long been felt that the magnificent work of the great English master of Painting in Water-colours, published at £4 4s., was too dear for general circulation. The above embodies all the instructions of the distinguished author, with Twenty-one beautiful Specimens of Water-colour Painting. IT IS A MOST CHARMING PRESENT FOR A YOUNG LADY.

The Famous "Fraser" Portraits.

THE "MACLISE GALLERY" OF ILLUSTRIOUS LITERARY

PORTRAITS, Drawn and Engraved by the late DANIEL MACLISE, R.A. With Letterpress Descriptions by the late WILLIAM MAGINN, "The Doctor." Now first issued in a complete form, from the Original Plates, &c. 4to, nearly 400 pages. An elegant and most interesting volume.

** "What a truly charming book of pictures and prose, the quintessence, as it were, of Maclise and Maginn, giving the very form and pressure of their literary time, would this century of illustrious characters make "—*Notes and Queries,* March 11, 1871.

JOHN CAMDEN HOTTEN, 74 AND 75, PICCADILLY, LONDON.

Very Important New Books.

CURIOSITIES OF LONDON. Exhibiting the most Rare and Remarkable Objects of Interest in the Metropolis; with nearly Sixty Years' Personal Recollections. By JOHN TIMBS, F.S.A. New Edition, Corrected and Enlarged, 21s.

** "A most valuable and interesting work, and a mine of information to all who desire any particulars about London, past and present. It contains nearly 1,000 closely printed pages."

BOW CHURCH AND CHEAPSIDE, 1750.

LONDON CHARACTERS: The Humour, Pathos, and *Peculiarities of London Life.* By HENRY MAYHEW (Author of " London Labour and the London Poor)," and other Writers. With upwards of 70 Characteristic Illustrations of London Life. Crown 8vo, 480 pages, 7s. 6d.

KNIGHT'S (Charles) PICTORIAL HISTORY OF LONDON, *Ancient and Modern.* With nearly 700 Engravings of Buildings, Antiquities, Costumes, Remarkable Characters, Curiosities, &c., &c. 6 vols. imp. 8vo, bound in 3, cloth neat, 35s.

** The most delightful book ever written about Old and Modern London. It is a perfect mine of information, and should be in every English Library. If looked at from the point of cheapness alone, the work is a perfect marvel, containing as it does more than 2,500 large and handsomely printed pages, crowded with pictures.

JOHN CAMDEN HOTTEN, 74 AND 75, PICCADILLY, LONDON.

THE HISTORY OF ADVERTISING, in all Ages and Countries. A Companion to the "HISTORY OF SIGNBOARDS." With many very amusing Anecdotes and Examples of Successful Advertisers. By Messrs. LARWOOD and HOTTEN.   [*In preparation.*

MARY HOLLIS: A Romance of the Days of Charles II. and *William Prince of Orange.* From the Dutch of H. J. SCHIMMEL, "the Sir Walter Scott of Holland." 3 vols. cr. 8vo, £1 11s. 6d.

*** *This novel relates to one of the most interesting periods of our history. It has created the greatest excitement on the Continent, where it quickly passed through several editions. It is now translated from the Dutch with the assistance of the author.*

New Series of Illustrated Humorous Novels.

1. THE STORY OF A HONEYMOON. By CHAS. H. ROSS and AMBROSE CLARKE. With numerous Illustrations, crown 8vo, cloth gilt, 6s.

*** *An inimitable story of the adventures and troubles of a newly-married couple. Not unlike Mr. Burnand's "Happy Thoughts."*

2. CENT. PER CENT: A Story written upon a Bill Stamp. By BLANCHARD JERROLD. With numerous Illustrations. Crown 8vo, cloth gilt, 6s.

*** *A capital novel, "intended not only for City readers, but for all interested in money matters."—Athenæum.*

MELCHIOR GORLES. By HENRY AITCHENBIE. 3 vols. 8vo, £1 11s. 6d.

*** *The New Novel, illustrative of "Mesmeric Influence," or whatever else we may choose to term that strange power which some persons exercise over others.*

YANKEE DROLLERIES. Edited by GEORGE AUGUSTUS SALA. Containing ARTEMUS WARD, BIGLOW PAPERS, ORPHEUS, C. KERR, MAJOR JACK DOWNING, and NASBY PAPERS. One of the Cheapest Books ever published. New Edition, on toned paper, cloth extra, 700 pages, 3s. 6d.

MORE YANKEE DROLLERIES. A Second Series of Celebrated Works by the best American Humorists. ARTEMUS WARD'S TRAVELS ; HANS BREITMANN ; PROFESSOR AT THE BREAKFAST-TABLE ; BIGLOW PAPERS, Part II.; JOSH BILLINGS. Introduction by G. A. SALA. Cr. 8vo, 700 pages, cloth extra, 3s. 6d.

Third Supply of YANKEE DROLLERIES. The best recent Works of American Humorists. A. WARD'S FENIANS, MARK TWAIN, AUTOCRAT OF THE BREAKFAST TABLE, BRET HARTE, INNOCENTS ABROAD. Introduction by G. A. SALA. Crown 8vo, 700 pages, cloth extra, 3s. 6d.

*** *An entirely new gathering of Transatlantic humour. Fourteen thousand copies have been sold of the first and second series.*

JOHN CAMDEN HOTTEN, 74 AND 75, PICCADILLY, LONDON.

Capital Shilling Books.

BISMARCK : *The Story of his Career, told for Popular* Reading. By Mr. GEO. BULLEN, of the British Museum. 1s.
  An admirable account of the " Man of Blood and Iron ;" giving numerous very characteristic anecdotes.

THE CONSCRIPT : *A Story of the French and German* War of 1813. By MM. ERCKMANN-CHATRIAN. 1s.
  The only unabridged English translation published.

WATERLOO. *A Story of the War of 1814.* By MM. ERCKMANN-CHATRIAN. The only unabridged translation. 1s.

KILLED AT SAARBRÜCK : *An Englishman's Adventures* during the War. By EDWARD LEGGE, Correspondent at the Seat of War. Cloth, 2s. 6d. ; paper, 1s.

NEVER CAUGHT : *The thrilling Narrative of a Blockade* Runner during the American War. 1s.

CHIPS FROM A ROUGH LOG. Amusing Account of a Voyage to the Antipodes. 1s.

THACKERAY, the Humourist and Man of Letters. A Story of his Life. By the Author of the " Life of Dickens." 1s.

HOWARD PAUL'S New Story Book, Lord BYRON in LOVE, &c. 1s.

MYSTERY OF MR. E. DROOD. A delightful Adaptation. By ORPHEUS C. KERR. 1s.

POLICEMAN Y : *His Opinions on War and the Millingtary.* With Illustrations by SODEN. Cloth, 2s. 6d.; paper, 1s.
  Readers of Thackeray's " Policeman X Ballads" will be much amused with the " Opinions" of his brother officer, " Policeman Y."

BIGLOW PAPERS. By J. R. LOWELL. The best and fullest edition of these Humorous and very Clever Verses. 1s.

ORPHEUS C. KERR [Office-Seeker] PAPERS. By R. S. NEWELL. A most mirth-provoking work. 1s.

JOSH BILLINGS : *His Book of Sayings.* Exceedingly droll, and of world-wide reputation. 1s.

VERE VEREKER'S VENGEANCE. By TOM HOOD. A delightful piece of humour. Idiotically illustrated by BRUNTON. 1s.

WIT AND HUMOUR. Verses by O. W. HOLMES, Author of the " Autocrat of the Breakfast Table." 1s.

JOHN CAMDEN HOTTEN, 74 AND 75, PICCADILLY, LONDON.

www.ingramcontent.com/pod-product-compliance
Lightning Source LLC
Chambersburg PA
CBHW020106030726
47498CB00006B/1968